WE'LL MEET AGAIN

Gosport, 1941. The Bluebird Girls — Rainey Bird, Bea Herron and Ivy Sparrow — are on their way to stardom. From working men's clubs to the glamour of the Savoy Hotel, fame and fortune beckon as the south coast's favourite singing trio work their way into the hearts of the nation.

But the war rages on, and reaching the top of their game will not be easy. Bea is still dealing with the fallout of a traumatic encounter last winter. Rainey is struggling with the whirlwind of life in show business. And Ivy, usually so self-possessed, is hopelessly in love . . .

As bombs rain down, can the girls keep their dream alive?

WE'LL MEET AGAIN

WE'LL MEET AGAIN

by

ROSIE ARCHER

Magna Large Print Books
Anstey,
Leicestershire

British Libarary Cataloguing in Publication Data.

A catalogue record of this book is available from the British Library

ISBN   978-0-7505-4782-6

First published in Great Britain by Quercus Editions Ltd, an Hachette UK company in 2019

Published in Large Print 2019 by arrangement with Quercus Editions Ltd.

Magna Large Print is an imprint of Library Magna Books Ltd.

Printed and bound in Great Britain by T. J. (International) Ltd., Padstow, Cornwall, PL28 8RW

For the Friday, Gosport,
Young at Heart Club.
Many thanks to Heather and Dawn,
who make it all worthwhile.

1

January 1941

'This war's spoiling everything!'

Jo looked around at scowling eighteen-year-old Bea perched on the edge of the car's rear seat. 'If the wind changes, your face'll stay like that.'

Bea's big blue eyes, fringed with long lashes, stared at her. It was inconceivable, thought Jo, that the girl could ever look anything less than beautiful, especially with her blonde hair tumbling about her shoulders as it was now.

Beside Bea, Jo's daughter Rainey, and Ivy, the third of the Bluebird Girls, were cuddled together among the gas masks, asleep. 'I don't see how you can say anything's spoiled,' Jo continued. 'You three received a standing ovation tonight at the King's Theatre.' Her thoughts returned to the whistles, stamping feet and shouts of 'Encore!' from the patrons.

'If it hadn't been for Moaning Minnie,' Bea persisted, 'we'd be in a restaurant now.'

Jo sighed. Sometimes Bea could be a pain in the neck, she thought. Through the windscreen, the January night's frost had created a fairyland, almost hiding the bomb damage.

Blackie Wilson, driving, slid his gaze briefly from the icy road to Jo. In desperation he raised his eyes heavenwards. 'I'm sorry, Bea. Jo and I

1

are trying to save your life by getting you away from the bombing in Portsmouth and home to Gosport.' His crumpled black suit, creased white shirt, tired face and clipped voice reflected the effort involved in leaving the flaming city behind them. 'I happen to think that you three have a great future ahead of you and I want you to be famous, not dead!'

'Humph!' was Bea's response.

Blackie took a hand from the steering wheel of the Ford Model Y and brushed his dark hair off his forehead. Not that that did any good, Jo noticed, because the glossy curls immediately bounced back to where they had been.

'We could have gone in the surface shelter the police and ARP wardens were directing us to,' insisted Bea.

She was like a dog with a bone when she wanted to prove a point, Jo thought.

'Not likely,' said Blackie. 'You wouldn't get me in one of those death traps. I've seen them being built. Brick walls and a concrete roof that's ready to crush the life out of you when it gets hit. I wanted you lot out of Portsmouth.'

'And I agreed because Blackie might be your manager but I'm your chaperone. It's my job to see you three girls are looked after.' Jo had promised Ivy and Bea's mothers that she would make sure no harm came to them while they were in her care.

She had hardly got the words out before she felt her daughter's knees push against the rear of her seat. She turned again to see Rainey smooth back her auburn hair and extricate herself from

2

Ivy, who was still asleep.

'Wassamatter?' Rainey asked groggily.

'You two fell asleep in this tin-can car,' said Bea. 'We're just about to cross over Portsdown Hill and I'm starving.'

'You're always hungry,' Rainey said. 'I think you've got worms.'

'I wish you two would stop bickering,' came Ivy's husky voice. 'Anyone would think today'd been the worst day of our lives instead of the best.' She gave Jo a dazzling smile that lit up her brown eyes.

'Wasn't it wonderful?' agreed Bea. 'Fancy us singing in front of that huge audience.'

Blackie shook his head helplessly.

Bea's moods were mercurial. There were times, Jo knew, when he and she could have strangled the girl. And now she needed to have a word with Bea.

Before going onstage the girl had been sick. That, combined with the weight she'd put on, meant Jo feared that the drunken episode with a sailor in the courtyard of the Fox public house three months ago had resulted in more than first-night nerves for Bea. But surely, she thought, Maud, Bea's mother, would have suspected something was amiss and said something. Perhaps Bea was unaware she might be pregnant. If she was, the neighbours' tongues would soon be wagging: unmarried mothers were the scum of the earth. And how would Bea cope when her stage career, just starting, was snatched away from her? A baby would complicate everything. As soon as she could, Jo

3

would get Bea on her own and talk to her.

Blackie wound down the window, letting in a freezing blast of cold air, and signalled with his hand, then turned onto the single-track road that would eventually lead them to Gosport. Jo marvelled that he could drive well in the blackout, with the car's headlights so dim they hardly lit the lonely road.

As if reading her mind Blackie said, 'I'm pulling over for a while.'

He stopped at a passing place on the summit of the chalk hill and turned off the engine. Jo shuddered at the panoramic view of burning Portsmouth set in the waters of the Solent. The acrid smell of cordite and dust drifted up to her.

She heard Blackie murmur, 'Bloody war.'

It was a different, quieter world up here, Jo thought. Deserted white fields and frosted trees. The girls were immersed in their thoughts now. Blackie was listening at the open window.

'My plane spotting's not as good as it might be,' he said. 'Listen.'

A sound familiar to Jo was filling the air. It was coming south again, towards the harbour and the Allied ships berthed in Portsmouth Dockyard, towards the munitions yards and the airfields.

She could make out the planes now, a swarm of aircraft, too many to count. The smaller ones were fighter planes, she supposed. They reminded her of the silverfish that inhabited her terraced house.

'I don't believe it,' Blackie said, staring at her. 'More German planes, and so many of them. How in God's name did they get through?'

4

In the dim light Jo looked into his odd-coloured eyes. She thought of them as his ghost eyes. Some people called them lucky. She moved closer to him. If she had been alone witnessing this enemy aircraft attack she would have been even more terrified than she was. Of course she was frightened, especially for the three girls in the back of the car, but Blackie had survived Dunkirk by good judgement and luck and she felt safer when he was at her side.

The low, pulsing drone grew ever louder. The first black dots began falling from the planes in the sky to the water and the earth below the hill. Then came the *whump* of explosions, smoke billowing afresh from the region of the dockyard. This raid seemed bigger than any of the others Jo had witnessed since the war had started sixteen months ago. She felt for Blackie's hand and was reassured by the squeeze of his fingers.

Rainey gave a cry as a deafening noise broke out from somewhere behind them.

'That's our anti-aircraft guns,' Blackie said. 'See the searchlights?'

Beams of light criss-crossed the sky and Jo could make out still more smoke rising from new fires burning orange and yellow. Oh, how she hated the sound of the screaming bombs. She was certain she could feel the hill shake as enemy missiles ripped apart the workplaces and living quarters of the city people below.

'You all right, girls?' she managed. She knew they were frightened: their silence confirmed that.

The roar of the planes began to recede, to be

replaced by the clanging of fire engines and police vehicles. The blessed all-clear had sounded.

'Thank Christ they're now on their way home,' said Blackie.

Bea was crying and Ivy was comforting her. You could always depend on Ivy to do the right thing at the right time, thought Jo, her heart thumping nineteen to the dozen. She smiled at the seventeen-year-old, who looked more like an Egyptian princess than a Gosport girl.

'I'm glad we weren't down there in that lot,' said Bea, the tears on her cheeks glistening. There was a momentary silence as Blackie's eyes caught Jo's.

'Can we leave now?' Rainey asked, in a small voice.

Blackie let go Jo's hand and started the engine. 'I think so,' he said.

2

'Jo, do you mind if we go straight to your house? I'd like to give Ivy and Bea's parents time to arrive home. That raid was particularly brutal and there might be transport delays, especially across the harbour,' said Blackie.

'Of course,' said Jo. Petrol was rationed, so most people used the ferry boats to get to and from Portsmouth.

The car had reached Gosport after skirting around fresh piles of smoking rubble that had once been shops and houses lining the main road. Normally on a Saturday night people would be in the streets, going in and out of the pubs, having a good time, but not tonight. Jo gasped as Blackie swerved to avoid a requisitioned taxi, hauling a water pump in a trailer.

Blackie swore. 'There's more accidents because of the blackout than casualties from bombs,' he said.

Jo didn't think that could be possible but she wasn't going to argue with him. The stink of soot and brick dust from the demolished buildings seeped into the car. She, too, thought it a good idea for them to stay together until they were certain the girls' parents and homes were safe, but she didn't say so.

Ivy said, 'I've got a key . . . '

'I'd rather you weren't above the café on your own,' Blackie said.

Bert, who owned the Central Café where Della, Ivy's mum, and Ivy lodged, had closed it tonight to see the Bluebird Girls at the King's Theatre.

Bea said, 'I could do with a cup of tea.'

'Couldn't we all,' agreed Jo. 'I'll put the kettle on as soon as we get home.'

'If we've got a home,' said Rainey.

Jo glared at her daughter, then tried to make light of the situation. 'O ye of little faith,' she said. Nevertheless she crossed her fingers.

Bea had naturally accepted she would stay with Jo. Maud would know where to find her daughter: the girls practically lived in each other's houses.

Bea, Rainey and Ivy had worked hard to create the singing group the Bluebird Girls, with the help of Alice Wilkes, who ran the school choir where the girls had first met. Blackie had introduced them to Madame Nellie Walker, the Portsmouth impresario, who now funded, advised and booked concerts for them. She wanted three Bluebird Girls, and if Bea was pregnant, everything they had worked for would be as nothing.

Blackie drove past the Criterion Picture House, mercifully undamaged, where *The Old Maid*, starring Bette Davis, was advertised. She wouldn't mind seeing that, Jo thought. Uppermost in her mind, though, was her home. Had it been hit by a bomb?

'Thank God!' Jo was relieved to discover her terraced house was still standing when Blackie pulled up outside it in Albert Street. She said a

8

little prayer of thanks beneath her breath before she carefully stepped from the car to the icy pavement. 'Blackie, please will you bring the costumes in from the boot?'

Her heart had practically split with pride as she'd watched the girls from the wings at the King's Theatre. She'd thought how grown-up they'd looked dressed in air-force uniforms, and when they'd changed into glittery blue evening dresses. They'd moved to small dance steps that Blackie had devised, and their voices were totally in harmony as they'd sung their last song, 'Over The Rainbow', to tumultuous applause. Afterwards they had expected to be taken to a restaurant to celebrate, but Moaning Minnie had decided otherwise.

After they'd thrown their coats at the pegs behind the front door, it wasn't long before the small kitchen, warmed by the black-leaded range, was filled with chattering voices.

Jo noted that the electricity still worked. Rainey had gone straight through to the scullery and she heard the pop of the gas, thank goodness, as her daughter put on the kettle.

'Glad to be home?' Blackie stood beside her and she could smell his cologne mixed with fresh sweat; it was both comforting and intoxicating to her. Without waiting for her answer he asked, 'Where do you want these?' In his arms were the stage costumes.

'Front room, I think.' Jo waved towards the passage. 'I'll look them over later for stains and tears before I put them away for next time . . . There will be a next time, won't there?'

9

'You think a Saturday matinee and a single evening show is the end of the Bluebird Girls?' Blackie leaned towards her. 'The *Portsmouth Evening News* and the daily papers will be singing their praises in next week's press.' He gave her one of his devastating smiles. 'And I've a few irons in the fire I gathered while we were at the theatre today.'

Jo hoped he might say more but he simply winked at her and set off along the passage to put away the costumes.

Ivy was kneeling on the clippie mat in front of the range, poking the fire. 'I've put a log on,' she said, 'I hope that's all right.'

'Course it is, love,' Jo replied. 'We need to be warm.' She made a mental note to pop upstairs and check the bedrooms for broken windows and bomb damage. Ivy's mother and Bert had no transport so Blackie would take Ivy home when he'd heard the café was still standing. Meanwhile she needed to feed them all. 'I expect you're all hungry. I'll see what I've got.'

In the larder there was a loaf with the crust taken off, margarine and some lard. A tin of corned beef sat on the shelf next to the condensed milk. There was a tiny piece of cheese that was looking very sorry for itself. Jo had been so busy with the girls she'd neglected shopping. Rationing had been introduced the previous year and she hated the queues: when it was her turn to be served the shop had invariably sold out of everything. Then she remembered the bag of potatoes in the scullery.

'Chips,' she said, picking up her apron from

the back of a kitchen chair and tying it around her waist. 'I can do you chip butties or condensed milk on bread.' She mentioned the corned beef but Rainey poked her head around the scullery door and grimaced.

'Chips and a condensed-milk butty,' sang out Bea.

Rainey put the tea tray on the kitchen table just as Blackie returned to the kitchen. 'Did I hear chip butties mentioned?' he asked.

'You did, and you can help with peeling the potatoes,' Jo said. 'And don't peel the skins too thick!'

It wasn't long before the small scullery was full of activity. Blackie, his white shirt sleeves rolled above his elbows, was peeling dirt-encrusted potatoes in the butler sink, helped by Ivy. Bea sliced the loaf and Jo stood at the stove with a frying pan containing lard and chips.

'Cut them thinner,' said Jo, using a flat wooden spatula to move them about.

Blackie said, 'I've never done this before.'

She glanced at him and then at the very oddly shaped chips. 'I can see that!' she said. His lovely eyes were sparkling and his smile was a mile wide. 'You were in the services, weren't you?' she teased.

'I didn't do any cooking,' he said.

The girls were laughing and chattering. Jo stepped back and opened the oven door to take out the dish piled high with chips keeping warm. 'Have you finished cutting the bread, Bea? These need eating.'

Later, Blackie sat in an armchair by the range,

11

his long legs out straight. 'The girls seem to have forgotten how tired they were earlier.'

Rainey sat at the table shaking more vinegar on her chips. Ivy was perched on the stool in front of the range, watching the flames behind the bars. Her empty plate was beside her.

'Looking at the fairies in the fire?' Jo asked her, though she guessed the girl was thinking about Eddie, Bea's elder brother. Ivy seemed to have developed a bit of a crush on the young builder.

'Just hoping everyone gets back safe,' Ivy whispered.

Eddie was a few years older than Bea. Broad-shouldered and blond, he was every bit as handsome as Bea was vivacious. More than his share of girls fancied him, and a few married women, too, by all accounts. Still, you couldn't help who you fell in love with, thought Jo, and once or twice she'd noticed Eddie's eyes linger on Ivy just a little longer than was necessary.

'Can I have a condensed-milk sandwich?' asked Bea.

'I don't know where you put it all,' moaned Ivy.

Jo remembered she wanted to talk to Bea. 'Will you come into the front room, Bea, just for a moment?' She turned to Rainey. 'Can you make her a sandwich? I think there's enough bread left.' She rose, leaving her greasy plate on the table, and turned towards the passage. Bea hoisted herself up from the armchair beneath the window, a questioning look on her face. Jo smiled, trying to put her at her ease.

12

'Have I done anything wrong, Jo?' Bea's big blue eyes sought hers.

Jo was at the front-room door, her hand on the brass knob.

'No, love, I just want a word — '

And that was as far as Jo got before her front-door knocker was practically banged off its hinge.

3

'It's Eddie! I can hear his voice!' Bea flicked up the latch on Jo's front door and there stood her brother with a small blonde girl Jo had never set eyes on before. Bea threw herself at him.

'Am I glad to see you back safely!' he said. He stepped away from Bea and gave Jo a hug, let her go, then gathered up his sister again. 'You were bloody terrific up there on that stage tonight!'

'Wasn't I just?' answered Bea, striking a pose with her hand on her hip. 'Who's this?' She stared at the girl.

Bea was excited and Jo could see she'd forgotten they'd been about to have a chat. Jo couldn't blame her. They'd all been worrying about whether their families had made it back to Gosport after the vicious bombing. 'Come on in out of the cold,' she said. Eddie's builder's van was hugging the pavement.

'This is Sunshine,' he said, throwing an arm about the girl's shoulders. She looked about twenty, thought Jo, with a smile that lit up her pixie face, like a field of daisies. Her clothes were colourful and obviously home-made. Around her neck and almost trailing on the icy pavement was a multicoloured patchwork scarf. Her name suited her.

'Hello,' said Jo, warmly, 'I'm Jo.' She ushered the pair of them and Bea into the kitchen. 'We've got visitors. This is Sunshine,' she announced.

Blackie was still sitting by the fire. His eyes were closed but he opened them, gave a sleepy smile and murmured a welcome to the newcomers. Jo could hear the sound of plates being washed in the scullery. Bless Ivy and Rainey, she thought. It was one chore she wouldn't have to do.

'Where's your mum?' Jo asked Eddie.

'I've taken her home and dropped off Della and Bert at the café. Plenty of room in the van, see? Thank God our homes are still standing.' His blue eyes grew dark. 'There's lots in the town that aren't.'

'Are you going to introduce us properly, then?' She was trying to take his mind off the damaged homes he'd seen.

Eddie gave the girl at his side a quick smile. 'Sunshine works in the place where Granddad lives at Bridgemary. She's a cleaner there.' He shook his head and his blond hair fell across his forehead. 'I didn't know her until we got talking during the interval at the King's. When the siren went I could see she was scared so I told her to come along with me and Mum.' He nodded at Blackie, then explained to Sunshine, 'Blackie's their manager.'

Rainey looked in from the scullery door, a tea-towel in her hand. 'I thought it was you,' she said to Eddie. 'I'm Rainey,' she added, for Sunshine's benefit.

'You were fantastic tonight,' Eddie told her.

Rainey grinned. 'Thank you,' she said.

'I suppose you're going to whisk your sister off now,' Blackie said. 'I was quite happy to deliver

15

her and Ivy home in my car.'

Ivy poked her head around the door. Immediately her gaze fell on Sunshine, with Eddie's arm still protectively slung round her shoulders. Her ready smile slipped and Jo noticed the warmth leave her eyes. Oh, my goodness, she thought. Ivy's jealous.

'Hello, Ivy,' said Eddie. 'This is Sunshine. You certainly had the audience in the palm of your hand tonight. Your sultry voice nearly knocked them off their seats!'

'Thank you,' Ivy said coolly.

'You were wonderful,' gushed Sunshine.

Ivy was silent for a moment, gazing at Eddie. Then she turned to the girl. 'That's a funny name — Sunshine?'

'I was left on a seat in the park when I was a few days old. A hospital nurse named me. She said it was a sunshiny day!'

Everyone smiled because she'd said it without any self-pity.

'I'm not ready to leave yet,' Ivy said brightly, turning towards Blackie. 'Perhaps Blackie can drop me off later.'

Ivy doesn't want to share a lift home with Sunshine, Jo thought. All eyes suddenly moved to Blackie, who was yawning. He'd worked hard today and it showed. Much as Jo sympathized with Ivy and her feelings, it would do Blackie good not to have to drive into town just to give Ivy a lift home.

'It's no problem,' insisted Eddie.

Ivy was too nice to argue, thought Jo. She was right.

'Well, if it's no trouble,' Ivy said very politely.

Eddie obviously hadn't picked up on her mood, thought Jo. Sunshine, however, was giving her a funny look.

Bea turned to Jo. 'Oh, we were going to have a talk, weren't we?'

Jo shook her head. 'It'll do for another time, love. You get off home to see your mum.'

When Ivy and Bea had dressed for the cold and left in the van with Sunshine and Eddie, Jo breathed a sigh of relief. Today had been a milestone. The Bluebird Girls were a success, but she was no nearer to finding out the truth about Bea. Was she or was she not pregnant?

'I'm going to bed, Mum.' Rainey gave her a hug. 'Today was the best day of my life.'

Jo pushed away a curl of Rainey's auburn hair that had fallen across her face. 'You deserve the success I hope you'll get,' she said. 'It's what your father would have wanted.' For a few seconds there was silence as they thought over what Jo had said. Then Rainey moved away and began climbing the stairs.

In the kitchen, Blackie slept. His dark curls were ruffled. He looks like a little boy, thought Jo, as she went through to the scullery. Ivy and Rainey had left everything tidy: the plates put away on the shelves and wet tea-towels draped over the oven door to dry. The girls had even wiped down the copper in the corner and left the stone sink clean and bright.

Jo thought back to 1939 when the war had just started. Her house hadn't looked as inviting as it did now when she'd first come to live here but it

17

had been her bolthole. She and Rainey had been running away from her husband Alfie, an army corporal who was a little too handy with his fists. Jo hadn't known then that Alfie would save Blackie's life in France. Blackie had survived Dunkirk but was injured. He had spent time in hospital, and afterwards walked the streets of Portsmouth looking for her and Rainey so he could tell her how bravely Alfie had died.

Alfie had pressed upon Blackie a photograph of Rainey, telling him the girl had a better voice than Vera Lynn.

Blackie, a protégé of Madame Walker, had pressured her husband Herbert to visit a local pantomime in which Rainey, Ivy and Bea were singing. Blackie had been instrumental in helping the girls achieve their dream of singing before an audience on the stage.

Jo filled the kettle ready for the morning and placed it back on the gas stove. She yawned. It had been a long day . . . a day that was likely to change all their lives for ever. A bubble of excitement rose inside her. Today was a new beginning, for Blackie, for her and for the Bluebirds.

Jo walked back into the kitchen. The range was burning low again but it gave off warmth and comfort. Blackie was fast asleep. She smiled fondly at him, her eyes travelling over his dark curls and down to his finely shaped lips that curved upwards at the corners with a hint of a smile. She took his suit jacket from the back of a kitchen chair where he had left it and carefully draped it over him.

Switching off the light, she went upstairs to her own room.

4

When Jo went downstairs the next morning, Blackie had gone. There was a pencilled note that read, 'Sorry, Jo, I overstepped the mark by falling asleep.' Jo smiled to herself. At least she hadn't had to face him in her dressing-gown. She hadn't heard his car start. She hoped he'd managed to leave very early without any of the neighbours seeing him or tongues would wag.

Swiftly she set about raking out the range and soon had a good fire going. The windows had iced over with a snowflake pattern she knew would thaw when the kitchen warmed up. As soon as the kettle boiled she made tea. She switched on the wireless, knowing it wouldn't wake Rainey, who slept like a log. Glenn Miller was playing 'In The Mood' and Jo hummed along, happy that at last things were going as she wanted for herself and Rainey.

She sat at the kitchen table and drank her tea. Once upon a time she'd taken at least two spoonfuls of sugar in each cup. Now, because of rationing, she went without happily.

She fingered the grey slacks and red puffed-sleeve woollen jumper on the table that she'd brought downstairs to put on when she'd had a strip wash in the scullery and wondered what she could give Rainey for breakfast. Last night the girls had practically eaten her out of house and home. But what fun they'd had, with

Blackie peeling the potatoes. Not many men would have stood at the sink doing a woman's job while four women teased him! But that was Blackie, always ready to surprise her.

She went over to the food cupboard and looked in the bread bin. A heel of a loaf sat there, almost as hard as iron. If she cut it in two she could toast it for Rainey. Spread with marge, it would taste fine. She herself wasn't particularly hungry. The opened tin of condensed milk sat on the shelf. Bea had had some, then. Jo sighed. She hadn't talked to Bea last night about the weight she was piling on, but she dared not leave it much longer.

She moved into the scullery and poured cold water into the washing-up bowl. While she washed herself with Imperial Leather soap, her mind was filled with the dilemma of what to do about Bea.

For the sake of Rainey and Ivy's dreams, she and Maud must think of something. Jo had been friends with Bea's mother for long enough to know a baby wouldn't fit in with her scheme of things either. Children take a lot of looking after and Maud was experiencing freedom: she was no longer nursing her shell-shocked father-in-law, Solomon, Bea and Eddie's granddad, now that he had moved to Bridgemary.

As Jo dressed, she was eaten up with worry about Bea. Miscarriages happened, didn't they?

It was then a thought struck her. She paused while brushing her hair in front of the foxed mirror, ashamed that such a hateful thing could enter her mind. Dare she suggest an abortion?

Abortion was illegal. What did she know of back-street abortionists?

Another thought ran through her mind. She might not know about such things but Della, Ivy's mother, would. Until recently she had worked in a Gosport massage parlour and must have come across such problems among the other girls who worked there.

Jo caught sight of herself in the mirror. Her blonde hair framed her face with curls but her green eyes, which auburn-haired Rainey had inherited, now looked cold and hard. Did her alien thoughts confirm she would do anything to make sure nothing stood in the way of the Bluebirds' success?

Jo shook herself. What kind of woman was she? She took a deep breath, then blew out the air slowly. Stop this at once! she chided herself. How do you even know if Bea, who has endured so much heartache during the past months, is pregnant?

A knock on the door brought her out of her thoughts.

A draught of bitterly cold air swept into the passage along with Syd Kennedy. He kicked the front door shut behind him then scooped her up in a hug. 'Brrr! It's freezing out there,' he said, setting her down again.

'Come through into the warm,' Jo said, leading the way back into the kitchen. 'What are you doing in Gosport on a Sunday?'

Syd pulled her back. 'I can't stop,' he said, feet planted firmly in the passage.

Syd owned a small garage and repair shop in

Alverstoke village near where Jo worked at the paper shop. She noticed he had on a stained but clean pair of blue overalls so had probably called in while on a job. He'd been a good friend, repairing the small car in which she and Rainey had driven to Gosport. He'd also made it possible for her to sell it at a good price so she had a little money put by for emergencies. She would always be grateful to Syd for encouraging her to regain the confidence that Alfie had knocked out of her.

'I'm not stopping,' Syd said again. 'It was a great evening at the theatre last night, crowned by the appearance of the girls. They were fantastic, Jo. I've got a job near Ann's Hill, customer's car won't start, so I thought I'd pop in to see you. When the air raid started last night I went backstage to find you but was told you'd already left. Can't say I blame you. That must have been one of the heaviest raids the south's had so far.' He smiled warmly. 'I'm hoping ol' Adolf will leave us alone tonight.' He took a deep breath and reddened. 'I'd like to take you and Rainey out for a bite to eat tonight, then on to the pictures. I know you like Bette Davis.'

Jo thought quickly. 'Syd, you're the answer to my prayers. I'd love that and I'm sure Rainey would as well.' Grocery shops were closed on Sundays so she had to leave any shopping until Monday when she finished work at the Alverstoke newsagent. She had promised to do the four-in-the-morning shift when the daily papers arrived. A thought struck her. 'It's possible Rainey might have other plans. Maybe she's arranged to see Bea or Ivy. If so, you'll have to make do with just my company.'

A smile lit Syd's honest, freckled face. 'I'll call at six, then.'

Despite the cold, Jo waited on the doorstep, the door pulled to, while she waved Syd off.

When she got back to the kitchen, Rainey was feeling the teapot to see if it was hot. The knitted cosy sat on the table, like a discarded bobble hat.

'You'll have to make another pot, love,' Jo said. 'I can do you toast for breakfast.'

'I'm not hungry, Mum,' Rainey said.

'Just as well! You lot ate everything in sight last night. Syd's offered to take us for a meal this evening, and then the pictures.'

Rainey wrinkled her nose. 'I said I'd go to Bea's this morning. They've got chicken for Sunday dinner. Apparently, Eddie had to take the bird as payment for replacing glass in a neighbour's window.'

'Lucky you, eating chicken,' said Jo. That's you fed today, she thought happily. Rainey, already dressed in a skirt and jumper, continued on her way out to the scullery. Jo heard the kettle being shaken and the pop of the gas.

Then, once again, someone banged the door knocker.

5

'It's like Euston station here today,' said Jo, staring at Blackie. 'Come on in.'

Blackie shrugged himself out of his overcoat and hung it on a peg. In the warmth of the kitchen, he said, 'Was that your friend Syd Kennedy's van I passed on the road just now?'

Rainey poked her head round the scullery door. 'It was, and he's taking Mum to see Bette Davis tonight. Do you want a cuppa?'

Blackie nodded at her. 'Well, that's put my nose out of joint because I was going to ask your mother out as well.' He laughed and his mouth crinkled at the corners in the way Jo liked. 'It was supposed to be an apology for falling asleep here last night.' He was suddenly thoughtful. 'Actually, there's something I've been meaning to suggest for a while.'

Jo was mystified.

'Spit it out,' said Rainey.

'I can't keep driving around from Portsmouth every time I need to talk to you — not enough petrol, for one thing. And it's just not convenient to travel backwards and forwards across the ferry. I'm going to need to be in contact with you more now, Jo, especially when, like today, I have news of other venues that want to take the Bluebird Girls — '

He had to stop because Rainey was clapping and shouting, 'Wow! Cor! When?'

'Stop it, Rainey! Let's hear what he's got to say.' Jo frowned at her and looked at Blackie.

'You need to have a telephone installed.'

Jo thought about it. Although she was working, as was Rainey, the extra costs of bus travel, sandwiches and food purchased in cafés when the girls were practising their act at the local David Bogue Hall were eating into her weekly income. 'I can't afford it,' she said.

He stared at her. 'It'll be paid for out of the earnings the girls will eventually make when we've paid back what we owe to Madame for the clothes, the rent of the practice hall and other sundries,' he said. 'I'll sort out the initial cost. I don't want you to worry about a thing. It may be a while before a telephone can be installed, what with the war and everything.'

'Right,' said Jo. 'I suppose that's settled, then.' She could see the advantages of having a phone line.

'Good-oh!' said Rainey. 'If we had a phone, you could have called and invited Mum out before Syd got round here.' She retreated into the scullery, only to reappear moments later with a tray containing the teapot, cups, saucers and a milk jug. Jo knew Rainey preferred Blackie to Syd. She said Syd was moody. Jo knew Syd was unhappy because he'd hoped to join the air force but failed the medical. He had a right to feel out of sorts at times.

Blackie was clearly baffled.

'Don't take any notice of her,' Jo said. During the last couple of weeks she had enjoyed spending time with him. He made her feel

26

secure. She kept her feelings to herself, though: to share anything like that with Rainey was courting disaster.

Rainey poured tea for her mother and Blackie, then sat down in an armchair. 'I'm off to Bea's in a moment,' she said. 'Can I tell her and Ivy that we've more shows to do?'

'If you like. I know how excited you all are about being onstage,' Blackie said. 'But, remember, nothing is definite yet.'

'Where are the shows to be held?'

'That's to be kept under wraps until I know more about the venues and have spoken to your mum about it,' Blackie said.

'Don't be late home,' warned Jo. 'You're working at the armaments factory tonight.'

'Oh, Mum, that's ages away!' Within moments she'd kissed Jo goodbye, said cheerio to Blackie, dressed herself warmly in coat, woollen scarf and gloves and had left the house.

Jo took a deep breath and said, 'Right. Where are the girls expected to go and when?'

Blackie took a notebook out of his inside jacket pocket. 'Two venues are working-men's clubs, one at Southampton and one at Portsmouth. The Rainbow Club at Birmingham wants them for a week. Another is a Burns Night supper.' He paused. 'If we accept that, it'll mean learning a few Scottish songs and maybe having the girls wearing some sort of token tartan, sashes maybe.'

'Where's it happening?' Jo wanted to know.

'Nice venue. An exclusive hotel in Stratford-upon-Avon.'

'I like the sound of that. Not so sure about the working-men's clubs.'

'Jo, don't knock the customers! Bums on seats are bums on seats! If the girls can win over audiences they're on their way. Every act treading the boards has had to work its way up. There are no overnight sensations. The stars who appear to have all the luck are those who've worked hardest.'

Jo stared at him. 'Sorry,' she said. 'I forgot for a moment that you know these things. You're also aware of what the girls are capable of.'

'I promise I won't push them too hard. These jobs have come in overnight and I wouldn't mind betting that during the week there'll be more offers.' He paused. 'Ivy, Bea and Rainey should start thinking about giving up working at the munitions factory and you need to hand in your notice at the paper shop.'

'We can't live on air.'

'It's a risk that has to be taken.'

'But we need to pay back Madame for her outlay and so far no money has changed hands.'

'Stop worrying. The ticket sales for last night will settle most of Madame's initial loan. It's always hard at the beginning, Jo, for everyone. Normally I'd say, 'Don't give up your jobs' but the Bluebird Girls can't be in two places at once. In any case, I can always be relied on to put my hand in my pocket.'

Jo thought about the savings she had. If necessary they could use them. 'You really think our three have what it takes to get to the top?'

'I know so. We work our socks off and take

whatever money we're offered from the venues, but I'm sure it won't be long before we're setting our own fees.'

Mollified, Jo said, 'So, I'd better start explaining to Bea and Ivy's mothers that their daughters will be sleeping away from home.'

'Yes, Jo. It's called 'living in digs'.'

Jo was perplexed. Blackie ran his finger through the curls that were forever falling across his forehead. 'It means living with a landlady, usually in one room. If you're lucky she'll cook you an evening meal. Digging in, or digs!'

'Well, I never!' said Jo.

Blackie smiled. 'And as you're already booked for tonight with Mr Syd Kennedy, I'd better leave you to it. Enjoy the picture — I know you like Bette Davis. I'll be on to the phone people first thing tomorrow.'

Jo waved him off at the door. Shivering anew with the sudden exposure to the cold, she went back into the warm kitchen. So, she thought, they'd be travelling together, would they, the girls, Blackie and her?

And he'd remembered she liked Bette Davis.

6

'So this is the Yellow Room, is it?' Ivy stood next to Bea and Rainey as Fat Malcolm, the manager at Priddy's Hard munitions factory, explained what was expected of them. All three had been taken off the line in the main workroom where they'd previously been filling shell cases and transferred to the dreaded Yellow Room. The noise from the machinery grated in Ivy's ears, practically shutting out Frank Sinatra's voice from the wireless.

'Yes. You'll need to protect your throats and noses. A scarf will do nicely otherwise the Lyddite will make you cough and sneeze. Get any on your tongue and you'll find out how bitter it is.' Fat Malcolm gave a grin that showed his blackened teeth.

Ivy saw that the women's heads were practically hidden by swathes of yellow-stained material wrapped around their turbans and faces.

'In case you're wondering why you're in here, it's because three new girls have taken your places while you've been absent and the boss decided to leave them where they are, being as you'll probably want even more time off sometime or other.' His sarcastic tone settled in Ivy's heart, like a stone.

She stared at the windows, ceiling and walls covered with yellow powder and the six workers already sitting at benches. Their hands and faces, from the little she could discern, varied in colour from pale yellow to mahogany. The women acknowledged them with hostile stares.

Malcolm pointed to a bench in the corner. 'Your workspaces,' he explained.

The three of them, along with all of the other workers, had been searched before they began their shifts. Objects that could cause sparks were removed — hair pins, jewellery. Wedding rings were taped over. Naturally, smoking was banned, with cigarettes and matches locked away. Work-boots were provided: leather shoes might cause fiery particles. In the changing room the women put on their dungarees and left their handbags and clothes in lockers.

Ivy watched as Fat Malcolm picked up an object from the table in his sausage-like fingers. 'This is a beeswax mould and needs to be inserted before the Lyddite liquid, which when melted looks like vinegar, can harden inside the shells.' He turned the empty mould in his hands, showing them in turn.

'Before the Lyddite solidifies completely, the mould is removed, leaving a space down the middle of the shell. Then the explosive goes in, and you screw on the cap. That's what you three will be doing.' He made a sucking noise with his teeth. 'The cap must not be screwed into the detonator, else you'll be blown to bits and take the whole bleedin' factory with you.'

One of Ivy's strengths was the ability to look life in the face and get on with it. It wasn't her way to shirk unpleasant jobs but she could tell

31

Malcolm, short, squat and swarthy, was more than happy to instil the fear of death into the three of them.

'What is Lyddite?'

Malcolm looked at Rainey as though she shouldn't have dared to ask. 'It's a bright yellow powder, comes from Lydd in Kent. It arrives here in wooden tubs and has to be boiled after it's sifted to get the lumps out. When it's melted down . . . ' Malcolm pointed with his discoloured fingers to a bench at the side of the large room where women were carefully pouring liquid into shell cases, then setting them aside, 'you pour it in,' he said.

Then left it to harden, Ivy supposed.

'C'mon, girls, we've got a war to win,' he said. Ivy thought he was in a hurry because he didn't want to answer any more questions. 'Marge!' he called, to one of the women. 'Sort these three out.' With a sickening grin, he left them to it.

The heavy-set woman pulled aside her scarf, heaved herself up from her seat and sauntered towards them. 'I'm Marge,' she said, as though they might have already forgotten her name. She was as brown as a hazelnut and had no teeth at all.

Just as Ivy was about to smile and greet her, Marge said, 'You'll find working here a bit different from prancing about on the stage like you was last Saturday afternoon.' She looked for confirmation from two of the other women she been sitting near, both of whom were nodding in agreement. Ivy felt herself freeze. Marge added,

'Me and my sister Lottie saw the Bluebird Girls was advertised on the poster in the canteen, before Max Miller at the King's. You could have knocked us down with a feather when we saw you three tarts all dolled up and squawking. What you doing working here, taking jobs away from decent women what needs 'em when you got a glamorous job like that?'

Ivy was just about to tell the woman they hadn't been paid anything yet for singing, when Rainey put out a hand to still her and said, 'What we do when we're not working here is none of your business! Are you going to show us our jobs or not?'

Marge laughed. 'You got red hair — you the fiery one, then?'

Bea said quietly, 'We can all be fiery when we wants. Stop trying to do us down. We're only the same as you, doing a job to help stop Hitler taking over this country.'

'Ooh! Hark at Blondie! You lot was all dolled up in blue glitter last Saturday. Well, you're all dressed in blue again now, navy overalls and white turbans, so how about giving us a little song?' Marge stood with her boots planted wide apart and her hands on her ample hips, daring them to defy her.

'How about you doing as Malcolm told you, Marge?' Ivy had found her voice again.

The fat woman's eyes narrowed to slits and her mouth pressed to a thin line. She took a step towards Ivy.

'All right, Marge. That's quite enough!'

Six words that made Marge turn quickly and

stare at the thin, elderly woman sitting at the far end of the room.

Ivy breathed a big sigh of relief.

A sudden silence seemed to fill the room, an intake of breath that practically swallowed the noise of the machinery and the wireless.

'I was only having a bit of a game with them, Florrie,' Marge said apologetically. 'I didn't mean no harm.' She picked up the same mould that Malcolm had handled.

'There's a time for games and a time for work.' The elderly woman had removed her scarf to speak. 'Get some of those old scarves out the drawer for them.' She covered her nose and mouth once more and continued removing a mould from a shell case.

Marge lumbered to a large cupboard. As she opened the bottom drawer, yellow dust danced about. She pulled out several dirty cotton scarves and handed one each to Bea, Ivy and Rainey.

'Thanks,' said Ivy. It was clear the other women in the room respected Florrie. Ivy wondered about her.

It was a quieter, sullen Marge who helped them tie the scarves and who showed them how to set the moulds into the cooling Lyddite.

The wireless was now playing dance music. Because of the dust, or maybe the scarves hampering their speech, the women worked in silence.

Ivy soon got into a sort of rhythm handling the moulds but it wasn't long before her fingers were stained yellow and her eyes began to itch and water. She didn't dare wipe them for fear of the

34

powder getting into her eyes. Her throat felt parched. She wondered who had used the scarf before her. Her mum, Della, had brought her up to be fanatical about cleanliness. She stole a glance at Bea and Rainey: both were practically unrecognizable, wrapped like Egyptian mummies. She missed the camaraderie and jokes they'd shared when they'd handled shells in the big assembly workshop.

Finally, the bell rang for the night break. The machinery ground to a halt. Ivy's eyes went to Florrie, who was pulling aside her scarf.

'Canteen time, girls. Don't be late back.' There was severity in Florrie's voice, no smile on her thin face.

Ivy couldn't wait to get out of the Yellow Room. As soon as she was in the corridor she ripped off her turban, shook her head and said, after a short but severe coughing fit, 'I could kill for a cup of tea!'

In the cold stone passageway, workers from other sections pushed noisily past them.

'Let's get to the canteen,' said Bea. After shoving their scarves into the pockets of their dungarees she and Rainey each grabbed one of Ivy's arms and marched her along to the lavatory so they could join the queue of women waiting to relieve themselves, wash their hands and stare at themselves in the cracked mirror.

The first thing Ivy did when a cubicle became vacant was hawk up globules of yellow phlegm that she spat into the pan. 'I can't face eating anything after all that,' she said, wiping her mouth and red eyes with a clean handkerchief.

'My throat feels like sandpaper.'

'Don't suppose there's much choice in the canteen anyway, this time of night,' said Rainey, who had money to buy food that evening, though usually she took in sandwiches.

The noisy canteen smelled of onions and cigarettes. 'At least we can breathe in here,' said Ivy, sliding onto a spare seat after making sure there was room for the three of them around the table. 'Anyone want a bacon sandwich?' She clutched her Oxo tin to her chest. 'Bert made them.'

Bert's bacon sandwiches were famous in Gosport. He had friends who dabbled in the black market and the local coppers turned a blind eye, in return for free breakfasts. He was like a father to Ivy, who'd never known her real dad, and it was Bert's mission in life to make sure Ivy, as well as his customers, was well fed.

'Please,' said Bea. She took a bite of the doorstep with crisp bacon hanging from its edges. 'Heaven,' she added. A piece of rind caught on her bottom lip and she licked it up and swallowed it. Rainey and Ivy laughed.

'What?' said Bea. 'Bacon's too good to waste! Anyway, you have one of my sarnies. Mum stripped that chicken!' She had finished the bacon sandwich. 'Now I want something sweet to take away the taste in that horrible room,' she said. Her deep blue eyes twinkled.

'Take this.' Rainey emptied her purse into Bea's hands. 'There should be enough there for teas all round and scones or rock cakes. See what you can get.'

Ivy watched Bea jump to her feet and, hips swaying, saunter towards the queue waiting to be served. She'd left her turban on the back of the chair and her blonde hair rippled in waves across her shoulders. As soon as she reached the line one of the storemen said something to her that made her toss her head and laugh loudly.

Ivy nudged Rainey. 'She's a man magnet!' They both laughed. Then Ivy said, 'Actually, I was wrong. It's all a show with Bea, isn't it?' She looked at the queue moving slowly and Bea, still laughing, with the lad from the stores. 'Have you noticed that she only larks about with men she knows? She shies away from anyone new, like she's afraid.'

Rainey said, 'Just as well. We're here to look after her. It's a pity we weren't there that night down the Fox when — '

'Let's not talk about that now,' warned Ivy. She ran her fingers through her dark hair and shook her fringe. 'Bea hasn't got over what that sailor did and I don't think she ever will.' She chewed a piece of chicken. 'What do you think about the Yellow Room?'

'Yes, what do you think of the Yellow Room?' The new speaker's voice was low and husky.

Ivy looked up at the dark shape hovering over her. Florrie was smiling, her face transformed to faded prettiness. She had removed her turban to reveal long hair that still held a touch of blonde and was piled on her head in an untidy bun.

Ivy, quickly gathering her senses, for the woman's sudden appearance had unnerved her, said, 'Thank you for speaking up for us. I thought we were in trouble back there.' She waved a hand in the direction of the canteen's open door. Before she could say any more, Florrie sat down on Bea's chair and carried on talking without waiting for an answer to her previous question.

'I'm off home now but you'll be all right for the rest of your shift tonight. Don't think too badly of Marge. Like most of us, she's under a lot of strain. During the past month she's lost her husband and a son.'

Rainey found her voice. 'That doesn't give her the right to be nasty to us.'

'Marge isn't thinking straight. You three have your lives ahead of you. She's bitter.'

A silence followed while Ivy stared at Rainey. It was like she could read Rainey's mind. 'So you're saying we should cut Marge some slack?'

'If you can. Her bitterness has to run its course. Better still, you should pack this job in.'

Rainey opened her mouth to speak but Ivy got in first. 'There's a war on and we're doing our bit, same as you. What gives you the right to tell us what we should do?'

'None at all but I've worked here as long as the factory's been running. I've done my time in all the departments. Some people think that gives me a bit of status.' She paused. Ivy found she was staring into brown eyes that had tiny golden flecks, like a sunburst, around her dark pupils. They were remarkably kind eyes.

'And?' asked Ivy.

'I, too, saw and heard you sing last Saturday. My daughter was on the bill.'

At this revelation she turned away, but Ivy was sure she'd seen the glisten of tears in those wonderful eyes. She was about to ask Florrie more when the woman said, 'If you go on taking the Lyddite into your lungs, scarves or no scarves, you won't be able to breathe, let alone sing.'

'We need to work.' Rainey was adamant.

'Not in the Yellow Room,' Florrie said. 'You three could do more good cheering up our lads than making shells to kill people.'

'We need bookings to do that,' said Rainey.

'Then do what my girl did. Take anything and everything that comes along. Work for free if it gets you another job.'

Ivy could see Bea coming towards the table with a tray. She was walking carefully, trying not to spill the tea. She was also happily oblivious to their conversation and eating a jam scone. The remainder of it sat with a pile of rock cakes on a plate.

Florrie rose from the chair. 'You're very talented, the three of you,' she said. 'My girl,' she spoke softly, with sadness, 'never knows I'm in the audience.'

The girls waited for her to continue. 'Her father died of influenza after the Great War. She said she wanted to stay with me. But I knew her heart was in the theatre so I as good as told her to clear out of the house. She thought I didn't want her.' She shook her head. 'That wasn't true. I just wanted a better life for her away from Gosport. We don't speak now . . . ' She sighed.

'Just a minute,' said Ivy. 'Your daughter,

what's her stage name?'

Florrie ignored Ivy's question, and said instead, 'I'm telling you three to follow your hearts, not to kill yourselves in this stinking place, war or no war.'

She turned towards the exit.

'Your daughter's name?' implored Ivy.

Florrie turned. 'Little Annette,' she said.

Ivy was still staring, dumbfounded, into Rainey's eyes when Bea put the tray down. They had met Little Annette, a faded but talented actress who, despite her age, clung to her 'child' act. She had been brutally critical of them. Each thought they had made an enemy for life with very little effort.

The cups and saucers overflowed with tea and the tray was swimming with it. A couple of the rock cakes looked decidedly soggy.

'Sorry, I spilled it. That assistant always fills the cups to the brim. I've eaten two jam scones. I knew you wouldn't really mind.' She looked at Ivy, then at Rainey, her eyes the colour of the sky on a fine day. 'You don't, do you?'

7

Blackie's heart was heavy at the sight of the destruction along Forton Road. Gosport had been subjected to heavy bombing over the last couple of nights. He let an oath slip out as he skirted rubble and felt something scrape the underside of his car. It was such a bother having to drive round from Portsmouth every time he needed to talk to Jo. Luckily Herbert Peters, his friend and Madame Nellie Walker's husband, knew a bloke in the motor trade who provided him with extra gallons of agricultural petrol. It was dyed pink, of course, and illegal to use, but after he'd strained it through a few loaves of bread, the colour was indistinguishable from that of ordinary petrol. Normally law-abiding, Blackie wasn't averse to a little law-stretching during wartime. Herbert had also had a word with someone who had promised to do what they could to speed the waiting time for Jo's telephone installation.

The last time he'd seen Jo she'd been about to swan off to the pictures with Syd Kennedy. On his way home to Portsmouth he'd tried to analyse why he minded so much. After all, the garage-owner had known Jo far longer than Blackie had and, by all accounts, had been a good friend to her. It was funny to think of Jo without the confidence she exuded now but, apparently, she'd been cowed by her now dead husband, Alfie. Syd had proved to her that she could begin to trust men again. So he should be grateful to Syd for that — otherwise she certainly wouldn't be the rock she was now. She was invaluable to him in helping to make the Bluebird Girls the success they would no doubt become.

He wondered how Jo would take the news about the shows he had secured for the trio. That the work was pouring in was a good thing. That their appearances were requested up and down the country was an obstacle to overcome. After that first show at the King's Theatre the newspaper critics had loved them. Madame Walker's telephone had hardly stopped ringing.

As he turned into Albert Street he was aware of a new bomb crater on the corner where the greengrocer's had been. Kiddies were playing among the rubble, jumping up and down on bedsprings. He was filled anew with fear for Jo and her daughter's safety. A telephone wouldn't save them from Hitler's bombs but it would enable him to reassure himself they were safe.

He knocked at Jo's door and was rewarded by the sound of footsteps coming down the passage. She looked pleased to see him. 'If you want to talk to Rainey, she's still asleep, I'm afraid,' she told him. 'She's worn out. Priddy's munitions factory has the girls working under such awful conditions.'

'That's one of the things we need to discuss,' he said.

Jo now stood in the scullery doorway waving the kettle at him.

'Yes, please,' he said. 'A cuppa would be nice.'

He heard the pop of the gas in the scullery and Jo came into the kitchen. 'Won't be long,' she said.

Settled at the table he came straight to the point 'Can you ask for a couple of weeks off work, Jo?' Before she had time to answer, he went on, 'Same goes for the girls, of course.'

'You've got definite bookings for them?' Her face broke into a smile, which quickly became a frown. He knew she was thinking about the expense. While they all had jobs to fall back on, money was coming in to pay bills. She disappeared as the kettle whistled.

'They're wanted for a week in Birmingham at the Rainbow Club. Good venue and they'll pay promptly. I've got bookings for those working-men's clubs I told you about and I've confirmed Stratford-upon-Avon. The Sailors' Hospitality Club in Queen Street, Portsmouth, have also booked them.' He looked at her as she came back into the kitchen with the teapot on a tray. She sat at the table opposite him and he could see she was thinking about what he'd said. Her fingers were working at the bobble on top of the tea cosy. 'Don't snap that off,' he said. 'They'll make more money than they'd get from the bomb factory . . . '

'Then what?' He saw the worry on her face. 'What happens when the two weeks are up?'

'Things are moving fast. I didn't want to tell you yet as it's not confirmed but Madame Walker is negotiating a week-long engagement at the Coliseum in Portsmouth for around Easter.

43

They'll come on before the headliners. And she's after a record deal in London.' He sighed. 'I shouldn't have opened my big mouth as nothing's confirmed about that yet. But what Madame is angling for is to send the girls to entertain the troops. Have you heard of ENSA?'

Jo shook her head.

'Madame's friends Basil Dean and Leslie Henson have been instrumental in setting up the Entertainments National Service Association. It's to mobilize the theatre to entertain our lads here and abroad. She thinks it's a bit early to include the Bluebirds, as they need experience . . . '

Jo was staring at him, her beautiful green eyes almost boring into his soul. If he expected her to scream and shout with joy it didn't happen. He knew she was worrying about money.

'If I ask for time off from the newsagent's, I've no doubt Mr and Mrs Harrington will give it gladly, but it will put them in an awkward position. They might have to think about getting in a replacement for me.'

'And you're thinking that the replacement might become permanent?'

She sighed. 'Yes. I've already cycled to Alverstoke early this morning to cover the daily papers but this part-time business is really not good for them. You can't guarantee further bookings, can you?'

'There's no guarantees in show business, Jo. It's a leap of faith.'

'Faith doesn't pay the rent.'

Blackie stood up, went towards her and put his

44

hands on her shoulders. Beneath his fingers her body felt warm, pliant. He said, 'I have money. If this goes wrong, which it won't, I will personally bankroll the Bluebird Girls and make good any monies payable to Madame Walker.'

He saw her eyes fill with tears. 'You'd do that?' she asked, in a very small voice.

'I believe in them.' He pulled her close and allowed his lips to graze the top of her head. He could smell the fragrance of freshly shampooed hair mixed with her body heat. He wanted to tilt her face back and kiss her properly, but the timing wasn't right.

'I have a little money put by from the sale of my car, remember?' she said.

Blackie nodded.

'If I have to I'll use that. Are you telling me to believe that the harder the girls work, the luckier they'll get?'

'I am, Jo. I am.'

She pulled away from him and he felt the sudden loss of her. He looked at the table, at the tea going cold. As he moved to pick up a cup, she said, 'Come with me to Maud's house so we can discuss this with her and Bea.'

'Of course,' he said.

Jo went out of the warm kitchen and he heard her light footsteps on the stairs, the murmur of voices as she spoke to Rainey, then Rainey squealing excitedly. After a short while Jo came downstairs, smiling. 'Rainey said she'll talk to the manager of the munitions factory tonight about taking more time off. Of course, she's thrilled about the extra concerts. She says they need to practise, though.'

He put the cup back on the tray and followed Jo into the hall where she was pulling on her coat. 'It's going to be all hard work from now on, Jo,' he said. 'But they've got the talent and the looks to get themselves noticed. We can do this together, you and I, and as the money comes rolling in we can repay Madame Walker for her faith in Rainey, Bea and Ivy. The Bluebirds are going to top the bill in every theatre, Jo. We'll make them stars!'

8

Jo left Blackie talking to Eddie and Maud in the kitchen and went upstairs to Bea's room. She gave a polite knock on the white-painted door but went in without waiting for a reply. Bea was snuggled up in her feather quilt but struggled to a sitting position. Straight away she noticed that the girl's curly blonde fringe had taken on a dirty hue. 'I wish you'd tuck your lovely hair well out of the way beneath your work turban.'

'And hello to you too, Jo!' returned Bea.

They giggled together.

'I don't look nice with it scraped back under that itchy thing,' said Bea. 'It's bad enough wearing that awful scarf. I'm a bit vain, you know!'

Jo looked around the room, which smelled of perfume and face powder, then back at Bea before she sat on the edge of the bed. Bea was the untidiest person she had ever come across, but the girl wouldn't leave the house unless she looked perfect. 'I know you are, love. Look, I'll come straight to the point because there's a couple of things we need to discuss. Blackie's got more work for the three of you, but it means staying away from home for a couple of weeks.'

She was going to ask Bea how she felt about that, but the girl flung herself at her. 'I *love* singing up there on the stage. It's the most wonderful feeling . . . ' She pulled away from Jo,

47

suddenly serious. 'Is it all right with Mum? What about Priddy's?'

Jo looked into her bright eyes. 'Blackie's downstairs now talking to her and Eddie. We'll have to ask for more time off from the munitions factory, and we must go into town and see Della to get her permission for Ivy to come.'

Bea was jiggling in the bed with excitement. Jo caught at her waving hands and took a deep breath before she spoke. 'Calm down. I need to ask you a personal question and I don't want you to start screaming at me.' Bea could be volatile. She tightened her grip on the girl's fingers. 'I promise you this is just between me and you.' The questioning look in Bea's eyes almost made her falter as she asked, 'After what happened in the yard at the Fox, is everything all right?'

You could have cut the silence with a knife.

Bea looked bewildered.

Jo tried again. 'Your stage clothes? I had to keep getting them let out. Then, before you went onstage at the King's, you were sick.'

Jo could hear the seconds ticking past on the bedside clock before Bea said quietly, 'You think I'm pregnant?'

Jo let go of her hands, but she didn't look away from those brilliant blue eyes. 'I'm asking if your weight gain has anything to do with that night?'

Bea said, very precisely, 'Of course it does.'

Jo drew a deep breath. In a flash she saw the hopes and dreams of the three Bluebird Girls fluttering away, like pieces of torn paper in a gale. There was no way Bea could perform onstage, unmarried and pregnant. Jo also saw before her a girl who needed help, desperately.

Bea picked up Jo's hands and squeezed them. 'But not in the way you're thinking, Jo.' Bea shook her head. Her blonde hair cascaded about her shoulders. 'I'm not having a baby. In fact, I'm sure I'll never want to be alone with a man again for as long as I live.'

Once her words had sunk in, Jo gave a huge sigh of relief. The Bluebird Girls had their future ahead of them. Then she thought about what Bea had said. 'Right. I can't say I'm not relieved but . . . '

'But why don't my clothes fit me?' Bea smiled at her.

Jo nodded. Bea was calm and talking openly with her. In fact, it was almost as if she wanted someone to confide in. Jo was more than pleased it could be her. From her experience with Rainey, she knew a daughter couldn't always say what she wanted to her mother. She had to hold on to Bea's trust. Silent tears now streamed down Bea's face as the words came swiftly.

'Rainey and Ivy stuck by me when everyone else was gossiping. I promised them I wouldn't let what had happened hold me back. I got into that mess through drinking. I liked gin and orange and how it made me feel, relaxed — too relaxed. I'll never forget that awful sailor. It was hard giving up what had become a crutch for me to lean on but I couldn't break my promise to the girls.' Bea wiped her nose with a hand. 'So I've found another support. Food. Especially sweet things, when I can get them . . . '

Jo folded Bea into her arms, the girl's tears

49

dampening her neck. Her heart went out to the child, trying to cope with emotions she couldn't come to terms with. After a while Jo looked into Bea's tear-streaked face. 'Oh, my love,' she said, then held her close once more.

Bea sniffed and this time it was she who pulled away. 'I haven't talked to Mum but I think she knows what's going on.' A tiny smile lifted the corners of her lips. 'She's been marking the condensed milk tin, so she's guessed someone's eating it with a spoon.'

'How about I keep an eye on you and what you eat while we're away?'

'You'd do that for me?' Bea was incredulous.

'Of course I will. Actually, love, now we're going 'on the road', so to speak, I'd imagine that, with all the rushing around, we'll all lose weight. Wartime rations won't allow for much sweet stuff to come our way, and rehearsals will soon take off any extra ounces you might have put on.' Jo stood up.

Bea looked much happier. 'Thanks, Jo,' she said. 'I'm glad it's all out in the open. I feel better now I've told you everything.'

'Jo!' Maud called up the stairs.

Bea grabbed at Jo's arm, pulling her back. 'Suppose I was pregnant, would you have helped me?'

Jo stared into the girl's eyes. 'You know I would, Bea. You know I would.' Then she shouted downstairs, 'Coming, Maud.' She looked back at Bea. 'Your mum will tell you what Blackie's decided about travelling.' A sudden thought struck her. 'Will you go with Rainey tonight to ask the manager at Priddy's for time off?'

Bea nodded. 'It's best all three of us go together.'

'We're going down to Gosport town now to talk to Della and Ivy,' Jo said, 'but I can't see any problems there.' She stood in the doorway looking at Bea. 'It's going to be all right,' she said. 'I think stage work is exactly the crutch you need from now on.'

Downstairs, Maud, in her wrap-around pinafore, snapped, 'Your tea's going cold. Is everything all right?'

Jo nodded and looked at Blackie. 'She's thrilled to bits,' she said. She felt as though a ton weight had been lifted from her shoulders.

Eddie was sprawled in a chair. He'd been reading a book before Jo and Blackie had arrived. Such a handsome lad, thought Jo. It was unusual for him to be at home on a weekday, especially wearing a suit and his waistcoat. He had his own building firm and was the main breadwinner for the family so Jo was used to seeing him in his work clothes.

'You look smart,' she said. 'Been somewhere special?'

'I've just negotiated for some German prisoners of war from St Vincent Barracks to work with the few blokes I've got left now most of them have gone to fight,' he said.

'Surely there are no new houses being built.' There was difficulty in obtaining building materials. 'Not while Hitler's bombing us?'

'No, but I need help with repairing damaged

51

homes. Salvage materials take care of that. So many homeless people.'

'Where are you working, then?' she asked.

'Bridgemary, near where Granddad's living.' He grinned at her. 'I thought I'd catch up on a few jobs around the house today.'

'Not dressed in those clothes,' said Maud. 'He's more likely sitting by the fire and catching up on his reading.' Maud still had rag curlers in the front of her hair.

Eddie rolled his eyes. 'Nothing escapes my mother,' he said.

He was blond and strong with a sense of humour, the dependable type. No wonder Ivy had a crush on him, Jo thought. 'Are you all right with what Blackie's got planned for the girls, Maud?'

'As long as you're with them, Jo, I know they'll be looked after.'

Blackie winked at Jo. 'I'd like to leave soon to see Ivy, Della and Bert. I don't want to be out if we have another air raid, do you?' He passed a piece of paper to Maud. 'These are the dates for the concerts. The girls need to ask the manager for nearly three weeks off, including all the travelling.'

As Blackie outlined the tour details to Maud, Jo turned to Eddie. 'These German prisoners, are they happy to be working outside in the cold, repairing buildings?'

'I don't think they have much of a say in it, but with our own men away fighting, the labour has to come from somewhere to patch up the houses the buggers have bombed.'

'I suppose so,' she said. 'Aren't you worried some might try to escape?'

'They'll have guards with them. They'd need passports, identity cards, ration books, money and good spoken English to get far. Remember, this is an island so they'd find it difficult to escape without papers.'

'And are you still seeing Sunshine?'

Eddie threw back his head and laughed. 'What's this, the Spanish Inquisition? I don't change my girlfriends as quick as that, Jo!'

Jo remembered Ivy's hungry eyes following Eddie. How like a bloke not to notice what was right in front of him.

'I've been in to see Granddad a few times. We're working right opposite Lavinia House. He likes Sunshine, says she's a good little worker. He's a different man now he has that woman friend of his, Gertie, popping in and forever taking him off to the spiritualist church.'

Maud sniffed, as if she didn't agree with any of it.

Jo tried to imagine the frail old man with a new lease of life. 'I never thought he believed in life after death.'

'It's that Gertie's fault,' said Maud. 'Putting daft ideas in his head!'

9

'Can I tempt you two to something to eat?'

Jo would have loved to have accepted Bert's offer. The smell of fried food in the warmth of the café was making her mouth water but Blackie was eager to drive back to Portsmouth so when he declined so did she. Fat sausages were browning in a large frying pan, grease splattering onto Bert's striped apron. Four men in work clothes and heavy boots sat smoking at a table, and at another in a corner two men in suits and ties sat with their trilbies and raincoats on a nearby chair, all waiting for food. Bing Crosby was crooning from the wireless high on a shelf. Della, sitting on a high stool, had been thumbing through a dog-eared copy of *Woman's Weekly*, drumming the fingers of one hand on the Formica counter. Her long, shiny red nails made a rat-tat-tat sound. Next to her Ivy had been idly watching her mother until Blackie and Jo came in. She and Della had swung towards them, smiling.

Jo listened as Blackie outlined his proposals for the next few weeks to Ivy and her mother. Condensation ran down the windows to be soaked up by the grubby net curtains. It was early afternoon but already dusk was settling in.

When Ivy clapped her hands and Della laughed in delight as she heard the news, Jo knew she would allow Ivy to go with the others on tour.

'We'll ask the manager for time off before we start our shifts tonight.' Ivy pushed her long brown hair behind her ears, and again Jo was struck by her loveliness. With her hypnotic dark eyes and a voice more sultry than Billie Holiday's, Ivy was the perfect foil for Rainey and Bea.

'That's settled, then,' said Blackie.

'If you don't want anything to eat I know you'll not refuse a cuppa.' Bert set down two mugs of dark tea.

'He never takes no for an answer.' Ivy beamed.

Jo certainly didn't mind sitting awhile in the warmth of the café even though the possibility of another night-time raid filled her with fear.

'Better pull down the black-out curtains,' said Della, slipping from the stool. 'Ivy, don't leave it too late before you get yourself ready for work.'

'Yes, Mum.' To Jo, Ivy said, 'Was Eddie at home today? Or haven't you been to Bea's yet?'

'Oh, he was there. He's negotiated for some German prisoners to work for him,' Jo said. Ivy would be eager for any morsel of news about Eddie.

'Did he say anything about that girl, Sunshine?'

Jo gave a small sigh. 'Not really. Anyway, you know it won't last — he likes to play the field, does Eddie.'

'It hurts that he forgets I exist,' said Ivy, quietly.

Jo glanced at Blackie, who was talking

animatedly to Bert as he set sausages on a plate with bacon, eggs and fried bread. The smell wafting over was heavenly.

'He might think he's too old for you.' Jo thought there was probably about nine years between them. It would seem as nothing later but now Eddie possibly thought of Ivy as a kid sister, like Bea. 'But,' she added, in an attempt to mollify Ivy, 'I'm sure he'd appreciate it if you write or telephone sometimes while we're away. You're friends, after all. I shall keep in touch with Syd.'

Ivy smiled so Jo knew she'd said the right thing.

'Della!' Bert called. She came tripping back in her high heels. 'These two plates are for the detectives taking time out,' he said quietly to her, and winked. Della picked up the hot plates with a tea-towel. Jo knew the police closed their eyes to Bert's black-market activities, especially when it meant a meal for them. They were always in the café. The food was good and they ate for free.

'If it's meant to be,' Jo added quietly, 'you and Eddie, it will be. Maybe going away will make him miss you.'

'Do you really think so?'

Jo shrugged. 'It happens.'

'I'm glad you understand,' Ivy said.

Jo pushed back a strand of Ivy's hair that had strayed across her fringe. She heard Blackie laugh at something Bert said. She looked at Blackie — he and Bert were in a world of their own making. 'Oh, I understand,' she said.

56

'Do you want to come back to my house? I can make cocoa,' Bea asked. 'Cocoa made with condensed milk is yummy.' She peered through the gloom and ice-laden trees lining Weevil Lane. 'It'll make us feel better,' she added.

'I think I'll go back to the café. The sooner I tell my mum and Bert we've been sacked, the better.' Ivy pulled her scarf tighter.

Rainey started to laugh. 'I thought when I asked for time off so soon after last time that vein in his greasy forehead was going to burst! His eyes practically popped out of his red face!'

''What d'you think this is — a bloody 'oliday camp? You've only just come back!'' Bea mimicked the manager's loud, irate voice. She was very good. Ivy joined Rainey with a hearty laugh.

'You didn't have to tell him it was more like a prison than a 'oliday camp!' Ivy was nearly choking with laughter.

'Let him put some other poor devils in the Yellow Room,' said Rainey. 'I don't mind telling you now I hated working in there.'

Ivy stepped over the white lines painted on the pavement to stop people falling off the kerb.

Bea gave a sigh of relief when they got to the corner near St George's Barracks. From here Ivy would walk along North Cross Street to the café. She and Rainey would go in the opposite direction towards Forton Road.

'We might have hated working in that place but we'd never have stopped working there if the tour hadn't come up,' said Ivy. 'We need to do something to help win the war against the Germans.'

'Well, we didn't give up that filthy job, we only asked for a break. We got the sack!' Rainey was adamant.

Bea nodded. 'Do you really think, as Blackie says, the stage work will come rolling in?' she asked.

'It had better, else we'll be looking for other jobs,' said Rainey.

Bea narrowed her eyes, as if she'd just remembered something. 'Priddy's wasn't like a holiday camp,' she said. 'I saw pictures in the *Evening News* before the war of Billy Butlin's holiday camp at Skegness. It looked lovely — a dance hall, a swimming pool, a funfair, people laughing and having a good time. That's nothing like Priddy's munitions factory, is it?'

10

'Tell them, Max! Tell them what you did before you got caught by these English dogs.' Hans, young and impressionable, was like an excited puppy. The pot-bellied stove didn't give out sufficient heat to warm the Nissen hut, but with a blanket around his shoulders, Hans hopped up and down in front of his idol as though he was dancing on hot coals.

Maximilian Müller lifted his eyes from the book he was reading and gave a slow, lazy smile. He stretched out his long, muscular legs and allowed the book to drop on to the blanket of his bunk bed. As usual, a small gathering of men waited patiently for him to talk.

'Why? Is it because you like to hear of their stupidity?' His glacial blue eyes settled on the young German's eager face. 'Remember, Hans, they are not the idiots we were led to believe.' He shrugged. 'We, after all, are the prisoners.'

He had told the story many times in the St Vincent Barracks, the holding place for prisoners of war, on the backwaters of Forton Creek, which eventually wormed its way to the Solent. With every new influx of captured Germans he was asked to repeat the tale. The men watching him were weary, scared and worried about the future for themselves and their families back home. No, he didn't mind retelling his story, not at all. It made him look a hero.

'As a Luftwaffe fighter pilot I flew as an escort to the bombers. My job was to stop the British shooting down our planes. Mostly we attacked the River Thames as far as London.' He was satisfied to see he had the men's full attention. 'It was not good weather, and the Spitfires simply waited high and unseen in the clouds for us. They came at us at high speeds, then disappeared. We lost many planes. I got hit. I had the fortitude to remember instructions that in such a situation I should turn off the engine and switch the propellers to gliding mode. Smoke made it difficult to navigate. My plane crash-landed in a field.'

There were murmurs from the men. Hans broke in, 'He is not finished yet. There's more.'

A smile played about Max's mouth. He used his fingers to push back his blond hair. 'I soon realized luck was with me. There was no explosion and I was unhurt, apart from a few grazes. When I had sufficiently gathered myself together after extricating myself from the wreckage I discovered that in the darkness no one had watched my plane come down. I divested myself of my leather flying gear and began walking along a narrow road. It was as black as Hell. I saw a signpost that had the name painted out, but I thought there was a village nearby for I could smell cooking and beer. Then I heard music.

'It was a country inn. There was a car in the driveway with messages daubed on it, ribbons tied across the bonnet. I deduced a wedding was in progress. I was in great need of a glass of beer.'

Some of the men laughed. One said, 'Who wouldn't be, after that?'

'Let him finish,' said Hans.

Max began again: 'A man came out and I heard him take a piss in the lavatory, little more than a lean-to by the side of the inn. I waited until he reappeared and went back into the inn. I went into the lean-to where there was a sink. I managed to clean the soot and oil from my face and hands. Then I entered the noisy bar.' A couple of gasps came from the men about him.

'I was hardly more than a child when I was taught English by an upper-class prisoner of war forced to work on my father's farm as a labourer during the Great War, and I'm quite familiar with quaint English customs and the language. No one in that room full of people took any notice of me. I saw there was a tapped barrel of beer to which fellows were helping themselves so I followed suit. There were plenty of glasses on a nearby table. No one stopped me so I sat on a bench and enjoyed my drink.'

More gasps came from the men about him, not just because he had had luck on his side but at his audacity. He had known that if he strode into the pub with a sense of purpose he would look as if he belonged there.

'Weren't you worried you would be discovered?'

Max looked at the young German, who had a heavy scar running along his chin. His skin was still inflamed so the wound was recent. It would stay with him for life. 'You are new here?' The young man nodded. 'You will be treated well. We get the same rations as British servicemen. There are girls who work in the kitchens and offices. Sometimes they smile and sometimes they talk to us.'

'What happened to you next?' Hans persisted.

Max laughed, showing even white teeth. 'Patience, Hans. Of course, I was not worried. But I was angry for allowing myself to be shot down without the necessary papers and English money. Oh, my English was faultless but what good was that if I couldn't escape from this island?' He became thoughtful. 'I will not make that mistake again.'

'Now finish the story,' said Hans.

'I sat watching the bride, a country girl, very young, very pretty, dancing with her new husband. They were very much in love and only had eyes for each other. A man in uniform came and sat down beside me. He asked me if I was a relative and I couldn't lie so I shook my head. Then he asked if I was Polish because he thought my uniform irregular.'

' 'No,' I said. 'I am a German pilot and I have been shot down. My aircraft is in a field along the lane.' I didn't get much further for he jumped to his feet and said, 'I arrest you in the name of King George.'

' 'That's quite all right,' I said to him. 'I have no intention of trying to escape without papers.' ' Max paused. 'I say to you now, I will escape. I will get home to Germany before this war ends and I will have money and identification.' He looked around at the group of men enthralled with his story. 'I don't intend to spend the rest of the war in this backwater called Gosport. I need to get home and continue to fight for the Fatherland.'

A cheer went up from the men.

Max knew he held them all in the palm of his hand.

* * *

Alice Wilkes replaced the telephone and turned to the man sitting in the armchair.

'Not only is Jo Bird the proud owner of a telephone now, Graham, but she's said my three little songbirds are on their way to see me.' She broke a Garibaldi biscuit in two and gave half to her little dog, Toto, and the other piece to Graham's Labrador, Bess.

'Do you want me to leave?' Graham raised unseeing eyes in her direction. She realized that although he was used to his blindness and the scars that peppered his face, the dear man was forever trying to save the feelings of people who might be shocked by his appearance.

Bess, having swallowed her biscuit, sat down at his feet again. Toto, not so well behaved, wagged his tail hopefully for more and looked up at Alice with moist eyes.

'Of course not,' said Alice. 'I'd like you to meet them properly. You were part of the judging team at Fareham's music festival when they were awarded second place, so they'll remember you. But they'll not stay long, something about having to get up early tomorrow. My Bluebirds are ready to fly far and wide, my love.' Alice walked

63

towards Graham and rested her hand upon his shoulder. 'I want them to see how happy you've made me . . . ' She trailed off as if her thoughts were elsewhere. Then she said, 'Now we've set a date for the wedding it's about time we let friends in on our little secret. What do you think?'

Graham raised a hand and gently covered her fingers. 'Are you sure it's what you want, my dear? To give up this house and your teaching post and settle in Fareham with me? Disbanding your evening choir at St John's School will be a wrench, especially after all the hard work you've put into coaching the Bluebirds.'

Alice bent and kissed his forehead. 'Everything I've accomplished has been but a prop to raise my spirits and fill my time, since losing you all those years ago. You've come back into my life and I don't intend to spend one unnecessary moment away from you.'

The doorbell rang and Toto was already in the hall barking excitedly.

'Hush, you silly dog! It's friends, not foes.'

Alice ushered the three girls into the warmth, her dog jumping and giving little barks of joy as they petted him in turn. 'Take off your coats or you won't feel the warmth of them when you leave.' Alice gathered Bea, Ivy and Rainey's outerwear, draping it over the newel post at the bottom of the stairs. She could feel the bite of the January cold on the air that had swept in with them. 'Go through to the living room.' She urged them along the wide hallway. 'Your mother's had a telephone installed, Rainey! She's given me her number. I must tell you how proud of you I was, seeing you at the King's Theatre.'

'The telephone is cos people need to get in touch with us now ... ' Bea faltered as she reached the living room. 'Oh!' She had come upon Graham, sitting near the fire with Bess at his feet. He began to rise to greet the callers.

'Girls, this is Graham Letterman, the man I'm going to marry!'

Stocky Alice Wilkes stood, feet planted apart, knowing she looked extremely proud of herself.

After a pause, there were gasps. Alice let out a trill of laughter. She had surprised them with her news. Each girl ventured forward either to shake Graham's welcoming hand or to put her arms about Alice.

'How ripping!' said Bea, with a huge grin.

'I remember you!' said Ivy. 'You were one of the judges at — '

'May I say I loved your performance?'

'You can say that as often as you like!' said Bea.

'Quite so, quite so,' said Alice. 'We'd like it if you would sing at the wedding reception.'

'Of course! We'd be honoured,' said Rainey, speaking for everyone.

Alice, happy, pointed towards the sofa. 'Oh, well done! Sit down, girls, and tell me why you needed to see me.'

'We *wanted* to see you, not needed,' said Ivy. 'And congratulations to you both. A wedding? That's a surprise.'

'Thank you, dear. Graham and I have known each other for many years.' She wanted to tell

65

them how her happiness had come about. 'We lost touch, but everything has turned out wonderfully now. Of course, I shall have to wind down my duties at St John's School, but it's about time I thought about retiring.'

'The choir?' Ivy asked quickly, a frown furrowing her forehead.

'The choir will be disbanded,' Alice confirmed. She'd made her decisions and she would stand by them. 'But that's enough of me, of us,' she said, going to Graham's chair and perching her ample body on its wide arm. Graham looked as happy as a dog with two tails that she was sitting so close to him.

Bess rose from the carpet and lolloped towards the kitchen, Toto following dutifully. Alice heard the sound of lapping tongues and the water-bowls moving along the lino floor. 'Can I ask why you're here?'

She saw both girls look towards Rainey — obviously they'd made her their spokeswoman.

'We've come to say thank you. If it hadn't been for you and 'The Bluebird Song' we wouldn't be embarking on a small tour. It's due to you that we were on the stage last Saturday. Thank goodness the public liked us. Blackie, our manager . . . ' Rainey stumbled ' . . . he thinks we have a future.' The last words came out in a rush.

'Oh, you do, my dears, you do.' Alice couldn't help interjecting.

Graham added, 'There were several on the judging podium at Fareham who thought you deserved first place in the competition. Little Annette, however, knows her business, and to take a chance on three unknown singers, no matter how good they are, is just not done. But you will go far, I know it.'

Alice looked at him, an adoring smile lifting her lips. Then she said, 'When and where are these performances to take place?'

'Tomorrow morning we leave for Stratford-upon-Avon. The twenty-fifth is Burns Night and we've been asked to sing at a hotel. Goodness knows what we'll wear. A couple of working-men's clubs want us. So does the Rainbow Club in Birmingham . . . '

'Burns Night?' Alice couldn't help herself. 'You'll need Scottish songs!'

She moved quickly from the arm of the chair and disappeared through an open door to where her piano stood. Lifting the top of the padded stool she riffled through the sheet music stored there. Then she went to a nearby cupboard and sorted through a box, lifting out bright materials. For a moment Alice stared at the cupboard's other contents. When she'd searched and found what she wanted, she returned to the living room.

She pressed her offerings into Ivy's hands. 'Your Blackie might need these — he can read music. I'm aware you three can't. Not that that matters. Neither can Vera Lynn nor Billie Holiday. These are popular Scottish songs written by Robert Burns. The sashes are Royal Stewart. By rights you're not entitled to wear a tartan that doesn't belong to you but I'm sure your audience will be pleased you've entered into the spirit of the evening.'

Alice smiled at the three expectant faces before her. 'I made the sashes for when the choir entertained at a hospital one Burns Night.' She gave a hearty laugh. 'Don't look at the finish on the stitching. I'm no seamstress!'

The remaining object was a piece of parchment. Alice turned it in her long fingers. 'This last is a copy of 'The Bluebird Song'. As you know, it's what brought you to people's notice. Perhaps it's not the kind of music audiences will want or expect you to sing on a stage, but maybe one day . . . ' Tears had risen in her eyes and Alice blinked them away ' . . . I'll hear you sing it again.' She sighed. 'Good luck to the three of you. There's no doubt you're on your way to fame and fortune.'

'Thank you! Thank you for everything,' Bea said, throwing her arms around Alice and nearly knocking her off her feet. 'Perhaps we could sing 'Bluebird' at your wedding reception.'

She let go long enough for Rainey to ask, 'You haven't told us when you're getting married.'

'We'll send you invitations!' One day, she thought, she would share with them the story of when, as a girl, she had first met Graham: their innocent walks to the bandstand on Stokes Bay and their shared love of music. Before he had left to fight in the Great War he had told her he was married. They hadn't exchanged surnames and, because of his family obligations, she had never expected to see him again. Her life was filled with music, teaching and tending her parents until their deaths. Memories of her lost love sustained her.

She'd thought Graham dead until she'd heard the blind judge's voice at the Fareham Music Festival. Later he told her that his wife had died, so they were at last free to enjoy the love that had previously been denied them. Alice smiled fondly at him. The girls were chattering away with him as though they'd been friends for years. Alice was so proud of Rainey, Bea and Ivy. I am an extremely fortunate woman, she thought.

Toto, obviously feeling left out, gave a small bark and jumped up onto Graham's lap where he was promptly treated to a pat and a tickle behind his ears.

Yes, extremely fortunate, Alice thought.

11

'You *are* good!' Blackie sat back on the piano stool and smiled at the girls. 'You've certainly learnt those Scottish songs quickly.' He looked towards Jo, who was watching the proceedings.

'Shall we tell him?' Jo nudged Rainey. They were standing on the small stage inside the ballroom at the White Horse Hotel in Stratford's Bridge Street.

Rainey grinned at Bea. 'We already knew them. Alice Wilkes introduced them to us before Christmas last year when the whole choir sang them for Hogmanay.'

'Well, it was decent of her to pass on the music to me,' he said. 'I had a terrible fear I was going to have to play by ear. The audience really wouldn't appreciate that. I'll have to make sure I know well in advance what they might like you to sing.'

'What is Burns Night anyway?'

Blackie smiled at Bea. 'On the twenty-fifth of January, the Scots honour Robert Burns's birthday by reading his poetry, singing, eating haggis, potatoes and mashed swede and drinking whisky. To celebrate a Scottish poet in a town dedicated to William Shakespeare, the English bard, is a great honour.'

'So we sing his Scottish songs? I like 'A Red, Red Rose' and 'The Rigs o' Barley'.' Bea gazed into space. Blackie reckoned she was probably thinking about the evening ahead. Bea was an enigma. Her looks belied her true nature. He often found her withdrawn and taking a back seat when the other two were discussing men, film stars and the new singing sensation, Frank Sinatra. He had an idea she'd had a worrying experience with a member of the opposite sex. Maybe sometime he'd ask Jo about Bea's background.

'I don't think I've eaten haggis. What is it?' Bea's blue eyes flashed towards him. 'We didn't get anything to eat at the hospital where we sang.'

'That's because Hogmanay and Burns Night are two different celebrations,' said Rainey.

'I believe it's sheep's liver, lungs and heart, minced up and mixed with suet, oats, onions and pepper. It tastes delicious.' He laughed at the horrified look on Bea's face.

'It's no worse than not knowing what goes in our sausages,' Ivy said. 'I'll try it.' Rainey was pulling a comical face.

'You'd all better have a taste because the first part of the evening is dedicated to addressing the haggis, talking about it — '

'Really?'

Blackie could see Bea didn't quite believe him. He laughed. 'Wait and see. It'll be a good evening.'

'How come we've been invited to sing?' Rainey asked.

'One of the organizers of tonight's do was in the audience at the King's Theatre. He thought you'd be a breath of fresh air, especially as

71

Robert Burns was very fond of the lasses, as he called them.'

Jo said, 'There's nowhere to change into your glittery dresses so I think it might be better if you wear the air-force uniforms with the Royal Stewart sashes pinned across your shoulders for the whole programme. It must have taken Mrs Wilkes ages to make them. It's so kind of her to think of you. Have you all noticed each sash has a pin in the shape of a Scottish emblem to attach it to your shoulders and stop it slipping? There's a silver thistle, a tiny spray of heather and a bluebell flower — '

'What do you think about her getting married?' Ivy interrupted.

'It's so romantic,' said Rainey. 'Just goes to show that true love lasts for ever.'

Bea pouted. 'I was looking forward to putting on that lovely blue dress tonight.'

'You'll get to wear it again,' said Jo, 'but I need to make sure you wear what's appropriate to different venues.'

Blackie said, 'I forgot to tell you. Madame's having some more clothes made up for you. Her dressmaker has all your measure — '

He didn't get time to finish the sentence because the girls were clapping. He had to shout to make himself heard above the racket: 'One more run-through, then I'll let you have the rest of the day off.' He began playing 'Comin' Thro' The Rye' and the girls enthusiastically joined in.

★　★　★

'Just do what you have to and don't draw attention to yourself,' Max said.

'I don't want to work outside in the cold,' replied Hans, hauling himself up into the open-top lorry parked by the Nissen hut near the creek. The prisoners, four of them, Max counted, were being shepherded into the vehicle ready for the drive to Bridgemary where they were to work as labourers. Two guards accompanied them.

'It doesn't matter what you want. Look at it as the next step forward in breaking out of this place,' said Max. The conversation ended as the guards climbed up into the vehicle.

Max looked at the frost clinging to the grass and the bushes on the banks of the creek. Even he knew you shouldn't use cement in this temperature. It wouldn't harden, so any bricklaying they might have to do would be useless. He smiled. The English needed new homes to replace the ones his countrymen were bombing. Since new materials were difficult to get hold of, scavenged second-hand building parts had to suffice. If the enemy wanted sub-standard housing, who was he to argue with that? At least getting out of the prison was a bonus. His next objective would be to find a girl. He'd already disregarded the ones working at St Vincent. None was worthy of his advances.

*　*　*

'I'm having such a lovely time in this hotel that I don't want to go home,' said Bea. The pudding she'd just finished had been heavenly, but Jo had shaken her head when the waitress asked if Bea wanted more.

'We're not going home. We're performing at a working-men's club tomorrow night,' said Rainey, 'and we're singing popular London songs. We've done those before so it shouldn't be hard as long as we get a practice in beforehand.'

'Which we will if we leave early enough,' said Blackie. He spooned the remainder of his apple crumble into his mouth, sighed and sat back on his chair in the dining room at the White Horse Hotel. He patted his stomach. 'Good meal, that,' he added. 'One of the perks of appearing at hotels is full board, and you get paid as well.'

Apparently the waitress must have misheard Bea's refusal. Another dish of apple crumble covered with cream was set on the table in front of her. She pushed it aside as soon as the waitress had departed. 'I should have asked her to take it away again,' Bea said.

'Are you not eating that, Bea?' Blackie asked.

'She's giving her stomach a rest from sweet things, aren't you, love?' said Jo.

Bea nodded. A conspiratorial look passed between them. Bea pushed her untouched plate towards him. 'You can eat it if you want. I know you won't see good food go to waste.' She smiled. 'Aren't we having haggis and tatties tonight?'

'So we are, but that won't happen until later and it's now I'm hungry.'

Ivy laughed and Rainey raised her eyes heavenwards.

'Oh dear! There's a familiar face we've not

74

seen since Fareham Music Festival, and one I hoped I'd never set eyes on again.' Ivy frowned.

'Who is it?' Bea asked, turning in her seat to stare around the dining room.

'Turn back! I don't want her to see us.'

'It's Little Annette,' Rainey said. 'What's she doing here?'

Blackie mumbled, through a mouthful of crumble, 'The woman has a remarkable speaking voice so is reading some of Robert Burns's poetry at the dinner.' A few tables away Bea saw the petite figure of indeterminate age sitting alone, pushing food around on her plate. Her thoughts went back to the Fareham Music Festival when they'd come upon her in the Ladies, her face caked with make-up to disguise her true age. Bea, Ivy and Rainey had been flushed with happiness at singing 'The Bluebird Song' before an audience, who had been generous with their praise. Annette had launched into a vitriolic diatribe. It was spiteful and unnecessary, and the girls had been surprised and hurt. They'd come away from the contest in second place. The first had gone to Little Annette.

There was no doubt the woman was a professional artist. At a distance she looked like the young girl she purported to be but close up the charade ended. She was still clinging to the child prodigy she'd once been.

'She looks lonely,' said Bea. 'I'll go and say hello.'

'She won't thank you for that,' said Blackie. 'She has a very sharp tongue. She has no manager now and has to make her own bookings. I'm sure she finds that hard. Years ago she made a huge impact on audiences. She knows her craft but for how long can an artist pretend to be young? She's scared to change her image.'

'She was on the bill with us at the King's Theatre. We were lucky we didn't run into her then,' said Rainey.

'Stop staring,' said Ivy. All that could be heard across the table was the scrape of Blackie's spoon across Bea's pudding dish.

'Her mother's such a lovely lady,' said Bea, suddenly, remembering when Florrie had stuck up for them in the Yellow Room.

'How do you know her?' Jo asked.

'She worked at the munitions factory,' Ivy said. 'She was very kind to us.'

Blackie patted his full stomach.

'You'll get fat,' Bea warned.

★　★　★

Later in the ballroom there were gleaming white cloths set on long tables and the cutlery glinted in the light. Jo watched the three girls, beautifully turned out in their stage air-force uniforms, each with a folded red tartan sash over their shoulders. She thought she had never seen them so happy or so beautiful, sitting at the top table sandwiched between her and Blackie. They outshone the other women dressed in their finery. Bea's blonde head was bent forward whispering to Ivy whose silky dark locks shone like polished ebony. Rainey smiled at Jo then flicked back her auburn curls. Jo was so proud of her, of all three.

Various tartans showed the different clans attending the dinner but not all the men were dressed in the traditional kilt and sporran. Some wore dinner suits.

Jo spotted Little Annette enter the room. She was shown to her place at the other end of the long table and immediately began a conversation with a smartly dressed woman. Curiously, she was dressed as a ragged urchin child. The bewhiskered man on her right acknowledged her, but then went back to talking to the man opposite him. Jo looked along the table and smiled at Blackie. She thought he looked very handsome in his dinner suit. He caught her eye and winked at her. Jo felt her neck grow hot, and warmth rise from the pit of her stomach.

'I feel so lucky to be here,' said Ivy. 'Now we've sat down what happens next?' The room smelled of spice, cigars and heavy perfumes.

'Speeches,' said Jo. 'When everyone's arrived.'

Getting ready in her hotel room, she had wondered if her one and only black dress would be smart enough for this evening. With little money and good materials hard to find in the shops, she didn't feel a new dress was a necessity. The government was talking about bringing in rationing for clothing later in the year. Now as she looked around her she saw the women guests were mainly elderly. They looked moneyed. Jo felt the Bluebirds gave a certain freshness to the occasion.

Grace was said. Eventually the haggis was piped in, as a special guest might be announced. It was steaming and fragrant. Bea was clearly enthralled by the spectacle. After the address to the haggis and the main course, toasts were made. Jo waved away the wine waiter as he came to refill the girls' glasses.

They were to sing at the end of the programme, after Little Annette had read two poems by Robert Burns.

Eventually it was time for her to rise from her chair and walk to the stage. All eyes were upon her. She had kicked off her shoes and her thin arms and legs gave her the appearance of a twelve-year-old. Her dishevelled urchin look had been chosen with great care.

'To a Mouse' went down to high acclaim. Jo had heard her sing in her pretend child's tone but was amazed at the clarity of Annette's voice and the emphasis she put on certain words to give the poem its well-deserved merit. She actually held the audience spellbound. There was no doubt about it: Little Annette was a professional. Jo had no reason to disbelieve her girls' story of what had occurred at Fareham but she wondered what had happened to the woman to make her so angry and bitter.

Annette ended her recitation with 'Whistle and I'll Come to You, My Lad'. When she'd finished she bowed her head and, to tumultuous applause, walked back to her seat.

'She's good but you're better,' said Blackie. 'Get up on that stage and sing your hearts out.' He rose, waited for Ivy, Bea and Rainey to move, then walked towards the piano. When the three girls stood centre stage, Blackie began playing the first of the six songs.

'Sweet Afton' went down well, followed by 'A Red, Red Rose'. Then he struck up with 'Ae Fond Kiss', 'The Rigs o' Barley' came next, and the audience was totally as one with the three saucy girls. When 'Comin' Thro' the Rye' began, Rainey urged the audience to sing along, and they did! They loved it! Feet were tapping and hands were clapping, but it was the last song of all that showed the audience's appreciation: 'What Can a Young Lassie Do Wi' an Auld Man?'

Bea sang on her own, with Rainey and Ivy backing her. But this was Bea at her best, every bit as cheeky and saucy as the beloved Marie Lloyd, suggestive and yet sweetly innocent. When the song finished, there was whistling amid the clapping. Some of the men stood up in appreciation and every woman was smiling. Jo felt as though her heart was about to burst with pride. More so for Bea, who seemed to come alive when she sang. It was as though she had another person inside her, a bubbly extrovert who existed only on the stage when the music began.

If Jo had ever had any doubts that the Bluebirds could make it, they were swept away by that thunderous applause.

Only one person, politely clapping, didn't look appreciative of the girls' efforts. Jo saw Annette's eyes were hard and fiery. If a spark could have ignited them, they would have burned down the entire hotel with the Bluebirds in it!

12

Max put down his trowel, stood up and rubbed his back. The hard work had warmed him on that cold, clear morning: he was unused to manual labour. He didn't think much of the dungarees he'd been given to wear, especially not with the huge white P for 'Prisoner' sewn on the leg. He needed to visit the lavatory. There was no latrine on site. The blond chap named Eddie had come to some arrangement with the owner of the lodging house across the street, a Mrs Manners. As yet no electricity or water had been reconnected to the crescent of bomb-damaged houses that Eddie was trying to make habitable.

Max had already endured ribald remarks from the English workers. 'What's the matter with your German bomber pilots? They need glasses? Can't they see the airfield's a couple of miles away?' He'd thought it best to laugh along with the fools.

Max had his eye on the cleaner. She was young, a tiny little thing, with blonde hair. She smiled a great deal, which he liked in a woman. When she'd been outside cleaning the guest-house windows he'd heard Eddie call her Sunshine, a strange name, he thought, for an English girl from a country that was grey, cold and damp. He also noticed an easy familiarity between the pair.

He walked over to Eddie, who was helping a

couple of elderly English workers hoist a wooden window frame into position. Eddie was soft like that, always willing to get his hands dirty even though he had men working for him. The guards looked on.

'I need the lavatory, guv'nor,' Max said. Most people called Eddie 'guv'nor'.

The frame was now leaning on the sill ready to be fitted into place. The men were taking a breather before lifting the heavy object again. Eddie wiped his hands on his dirty work clothes and stared at him. 'Do you know where to go?'

Max nodded. 'I'm not so desperate I can't give you a hand with that.' The two elderly men smiled warmly: neither had the strength they used to have. He and Eddie, with the two older men steadying the weighty object, set it in place.

Eddie stepped back. 'Thanks,' he said gruffly. Max nodded and set off across the road to Lavinia House. One of the guards followed him.

'Five minutes. I've got my eyes on you,' called Eddie. Max turned, grinned and nodded. Eddie was wise enough to know there would be no escapees because the guards from St Vincent kept an eye on the German prisoners. Besides, where could anyone go without money or papers? Max looked to the front door ahead where Sunshine had reappeared and was rubbing at the small stained-glass window in the top of the door.

'You are fighting a lost cause against dirt,' Max said to the girl. Now he was closer, he could see she was younger than he had thought. He stood a respectful few feet away from her, allowing her to look at him. 'There will be much more dust before the rebuilding across the road is finished.'

He saw her gaze towards the building site, most probably looking at Eddie for confirmation that Max could use the lavatory. Eddie must have nodded an affirmative for she smiled at him. 'Probably,' she said.

For a moment Max held her eyes. He could feel her warming to him. This always happened when he put his mind to it. He had a knack for charming women. Young and old, they fell for it every time. Of course, his Aryan looks helped.

'You need the lavatory? It's through there. I'm sorry, I must wait and see you off the premises.' She pulled open the door. He saw the blush appear on her neck. The guard began his wait. 'Go through,' she said. 'It's the second door along.'

'Thank you.' He made a big show of wiping his feet on the coir mat. He knew she'd appreciate that.

When he left the lavatory she was still polishing.

'Thank you,' he said, with a grin. Her lips lifted in a return smile and he stood for a few seconds doing nothing more than taking in her youth and freshness. The guard outside coughed. Max said, 'I must get back to work.' Another smile and he was walking across the frozen ground followed by the guard.

He knew without looking back that she was still watching him.

He had never failed to catch a woman's interest and it wasn't going to happen now.

His next step would be to convince her to help him.

That shouldn't be too hard, he thought.

Max's thoughts were disturbed by the sound of the air-raid siren. Moaning Minnie was warning everyone to take cover.

Through the high-pitched screech he heard Eddie swear and say, 'Here they come again.'

The Germans had downed tools and were waiting for their boss to tell them what to do. Max could feel the thread of fear sewing itself into the prisoners' thoughts. German pilots didn't differentiate between nationalities when bombing English soil.

Eddie seemed to have things under control. He called to the men, had them line up and, with the guards on either side, began marching them towards Lavinia House.

At the door the girl made them wait. It wasn't long before a rounded motherly woman dressed in a blue and white uniform came to the door. 'The public shelter was hit last week so you're welcome to come inside as soon as we've made sure our lodgers are safe. Several need help to get into the Anderson at the back of the premises. It shouldn't take long. We can offer tea, and Mrs Ford, our cook, might be persuaded to rustle up sandwiches later.'

There was a murmur of appreciation among the men.

After a short while they were shepherded along the corridor to a large room. Now deserted, it was obviously intended for leisure. There were several sofas and easy chairs mostly grouped around a fire burning in the grate. Thick curtains were draped at the windows and a wireless sat on the table near where playing cards were scattered.

A feeling of warmth, peace and tranquillity swept over Max.

'This is the best we can do to keep you safe,' Eddie said, 'until the council sort out a new shelter, but we could be working on another site by then. I'm afraid there's no guarantee that a stray bomb from one of your countrymen's planes won't land here.' He pointed to the chairs. 'Make yourselves comfortable. You'll not leave this room without permission.' Already the guards were standing at the door.

Some of the men hunkered down, trying to make themselves as small as possible, even though there was as yet no sound of enemy planes. Max moved away from the windows — flying glass could maim.

He was trying to lose young Hans, who was like a shadow. Sometimes the impressionable lad got on his nerves.

The girl stood close to Eddie. There was definitely something going on between them. The man's feelings showed in the effortless way he touched her hair, tucking the long blonde escaped strand back beneath her bright turban. Beneath her shapeless white apron, she wore a skirt made of the same coloured material. So, Max deduced, she was also a seamstress, a little homemaker. Oh, well, may the best man win her affection, he thought. No doubt it would be himself.

Max could now hear the rumble of aircraft and bombs whistling down. His countrymen were taking a chance as it was barely dark enough to hide the planes. Some of the men in the room ducked each time a blast was heard; through the windows clouds of dust and smoke began rising from the landed missiles.

Searchlights were now sweeping the heavy skies and Max could hear the ack-ack guns returning fire. It seemed airless in the big room. He could smell the sweaty stench of frightened men.

He heard Eddie ask about 'Solomon', then 'grandfather'.

'Gertie'll take good care of him,' came Sunshine's reply before she left the room. Max guessed Eddie had a relative, a grandfather, living in Lavinia House.

Max couldn't see the bombers but he could hear them, the steady drone of their engines with the intermittent thunder of explosions as bombs were released. His attention was taken by one of his fellow prisoners who had crawled beneath a table. The man was trembling, sweating, rocking from side to side. A prisoner bent low, trying to comfort the now crying man. Max heard Eddie say the nurse would soon return.

After a while the girl came back into the room holding a tray, which Eddie took from her. She left again and Eddie proceeded to move among the men offering them tea. He left the tray near the door.

As those around him drank, Max saw a way to remind the girl of his presence. He moved among the prisoners, collecting empty cups and putting them on the tray. When Sunshine returned with a plate of sandwiches Max was close by, an empty cup in one hand. All was going exactly as he'd hoped, especially as Eddie had moved across the room to close the curtains and shut out the sight of warfare.

'Thank you. You didn't have to do that,' she said to Max.

'You are kind enough to supply the tea. Why shouldn't I collect cups?'

Her knowing smile told him she was interested in him after their earlier conversation. He mentally congratulated himself. 'My name is Max. I expect to be working here for the foreseeable future. Dare I ask your name?' He already knew who she was, but politeness was necessary. He looked across to where Eddie had begun a conversation with one of the labourers.

'Sunshine,' she said, moving the crockery to make the tray easier to carry.

'Do you like working with elderly people?'

It was clear she hadn't expected him to begin a conversation with her but at that moment a loud explosion outside caused her to cower against him. He caught the smell of her hair. It reminded him of apples.

She looked up at him. 'Sorry,' she said, and moved back a pace, then added, 'I'm only part-time. I don't earn much but I can live in. What I need is another part-time job.'

'St Vincent Barracks need catering staff . . .' He trailed off. 'But perhaps you do not like to work where there are . . .'

'Men such as yourself? Prisoners, who require to be fed?'

She was teasing him. He liked her quick-thinking reply to his question. There was much to be said and so little time for him to speak. He looked down at her. She barely reached his chest. He gave a little laugh. His plan was unfolding.

It was fully dark when the bombing stopped and the sound of aircraft drifted away. Some labourers, replete with tea and sandwiches, were asleep, and woke when the all-clear sounded. Men began to stretch stiffened limbs and to talk to each other once more. The tension in the room lessened and Max heard the clanging of ambulance bells from the nearby main road. It was too dark to be working outside now. The air raid had stolen the working hours.

Mrs Manners stood at the door with a dustpan and brush in her hands talking to Eddie. 'I'd like to help our lodgers back to their rooms now,' Max heard her say. 'Can you move your men outside again? You're welcome to use our amenities in the future. It could be some time before another public shelter's built nearby. Direct hit, it was.'

Max heard Eddie say, 'Won't be long before we've finished the repairs to make those houses across the street habitable again. But thank you for your generosity.'

'I'd like to think the ordinary German families treat our boys with the respect they deserve,' she said. 'I've a son missing near Cologne.'

At Eddie's command, lines formed and the

Germans stood by to be ushered to a waiting lorry. The sobbing man who had been tended by Mrs Manners now listed against a friend. Poor bugger, thought Max. The girl, Sunshine, had been sent about her duties by Mrs Manners. But now she'd returned to stand just inside the door as the men left. The air outside stank of brick dust and Max could see the darkness of the sky tinged with yellow and orange where his countrymen had hit targets. As he walked past Sunshine he mouthed, 'Goodbye.' As their eyes met, he felt the pull of her desire, and was satisfied that he had sought her out. He hoped Eddie wouldn't move him to another job too soon. In just a little while he could have her right where he wanted her.

13

'Cor, what couldn't I do for you, darlin'!' The loud words from the fat bloke with sweat stains beneath the arms of his shirt and his sparse grey hair combed over his balding head were directed at Bea. They made her feel sick.

The hall was stuffy with cigarette smoke. The Bluebird Girls, dressed in their air-force stage clothes, were trying vainly to sing above the heckling. The audience composed of eighty or so men, some accompanied by their wives or girlfriends and most gripping pint pots of beer, didn't seem at all interested in listening to popular songs. Even Blackie winced at some of the ribald comments. Bea saw the miserable look on his face as he battled away at the piano.

'C'mon, girls,' he was mouthing, urging them to stick it out, even though the audience seemed to want to hear nothing but the quality of their own insults hurled at the trio.

The trouble was, Bea guessed, that the audience had been drinking solidly for several hours before the girls were due onstage. Blackie had told them they were filling in for a saucy comic, who had let the club down and was known for telling near-the-knuckle blue jokes.

Bea glanced at Ivy, whose large dark eyes were filled with tears. Her husky voice was cracking with the strain of trying to carry on, to give of her best even though the audience clearly didn't deserve it. Bea's heart went out to her — she was usually the strong one.

Rainey's green eyes were almost slits and her forehead a crease of worry. She loved to sing, no matter what distractions were presented, but Bea could see that even she was finding it difficult to concentrate on the music's tempo with the result that she, though she was the lead singer, was allowing Bea and Ivy to carry the tune.

'Show us your legs!' This came from a red-haired man, who hadn't bothered to remove his fag from his mouth.

For the first time ever, onstage, Bea hated being up there. She felt like a piece of meat on sale in a butcher's window with a crowd of ration-booked women peering in. The girls were not being given a chance to show the audience what they could do. The angrier she became, the more she was reminded of the sailor, with no thought to her feelings, in the dingy backyard of the Fox pub.

She wanted to walk off the lino-covered stage and retreat into the manager's office, where they'd been allowed to change, grab her clothes and run, anywhere, away from this horrible working-men's club near the docks in Southampton.

But then they wouldn't get paid.

When the gossip-mongers had finished with them, after telling people the Bluebird Girls had walked off the stage, it was possible they'd never get another local booking. If there was a journalist in the audience this farce might even reach the newspapers. Who would want to book a singing group that didn't fulfil its commitments?

She stared at Jo standing near the busy bar.

Jo was mouthing, 'Stick it out!' but Bea could feel her temper rising.

Blackie started the introduction to 'I Didn't Know What Time It Was'.

A pot-bellied man at the back shouted, 'It's half past nine, my lovelies!' He was elbowed by the woman at his side who cackled raucously. Bea couldn't help herself. As even more laughter from the crowd rose she shouted back at him, 'Oh, you can tell the time, then?'

The look on the man's ruddy, veined face was a picture. He was silent for a moment, then burst out laughing. His woman stared at him, then scratched her blonde head, frowning. Rainey and Ivy continued singing.

'You can meet me anytime, ducks,' shouted another wag, a middle-aged man in a paint-splashed white shirt and navy overalls, with the arms tied around his huge middle.

'Not until you buy another shirt!' Bea yelled, breaking away from the song. There was a fresh burst of laughter. This time, though, Bea felt the laughter was with her, not at her.

'In The Mood' was their next offering.

'I'm in the mood!' yelled the red-faced man.

'I bet you are!' shouted Bea. She laughed as his woman glared at him. 'Why don't you shut up and give us a chance to sing?'

The crowd had now quietened, waiting to see what would happen next.

Blackie played a wrong note from laughing.

The red-faced man looked amazed, but slowly a smile crept across his face and he grinned. He waved a hand, admonishing the audience to further silence.

Rainey and Ivy continued, putting their hearts and voices into the jazzy music. Bea began singing again and clapping her hands in time to the beat. She was urging the audience to join in, and they did! Bea saw Jo smiling at her.

When the music came to an end, the crowd cheered.

'We'll Meet Again', more Bea's solo than a song for all three voices, was next. The crowd, subdued, began singing along with her when she encouraged them. Bea was surprised when Blackie played the chorus again but she sang out and waved her arms, begging the entire hall to join in the well-loved song. The last note faded and the crowd was cheering her, waving pint glasses, spilling precious beer and yelling, 'Well done, Blondie!'

Even Jo had been singing. Bea smiled down at Blackie, who gave her a huge wink. Bea was in her element. The relief on Ivy and Rainey's faces was evident.

The piano morphed into 'There'll Always Be An England'. The girls always saluted during this final song. Bea spotted a movement behind the bar and the manager handed a box of small flags to Jo, who began handing them out to customers. As the flags were issued around the hall the men and women stood up and began singing about 'their' England and waving the flags patriotically. Bea smiled down at Blackie.

She knew he'd not waste a moment of the heightened feelings running through the club, and he didn't: he played the last song again.

When the final note rang out, for a moment there was silence. The flags had stopped waving.

Then the cheering and stamping began.

In the office, getting changed into their ordinary clothes, Rainey said, 'I don't know how you managed to answer that crowd back and get them on our side, but you did. Well done, Bea.' She threw her arms around her.

'I don't know what happened,' said Bea. 'I just wanted them to stop spoiling our music. They were being unfair to us.'

'I think you're marvellous,' said Jo, packing shoes and hats into a large holdall.

'And me,' Ivy said. 'Weren't you scared?' She folded her stage skirt neatly.

'That's the funny thing,' said Bea. 'Because I was with you I wasn't scared. A lot of those blokes were drunk, and if I'd been alone I couldn't have answered them back for fear of what they'd do, but I wasn't alone, was I?' She buttoned her blouse.

Just then there was a knock on the door, and as the girls were dressed, Jo opened it. Blackie stood there with an envelope in his hand. His face was wreathed in smiles. 'We've been paid for tonight but the best part is that Big Alf, the bloke who was heckling you most, sent round a couple of pint pots for tips for you girls — and they're full of cash!' He showed them a bulky brown carrier bag with string handles that was obviously heavy.

Behind him, the heckler in the paint-splodged shirt, Big Alf, said, 'I'm really sorry I gave you girls a hard time. We don't suffer fools gladly and thank God you had the guts to stand up to me. You're lovely girls all of you.' He paused. 'The manager will be along soon to apologize for the members' bad behaviour and has begged me to ask if you'll consider a return visit?'

'Of course we will,' laughed Bea, 'but only if some of your blokes get on the stage first, roll up their trousers to their knees and sing, so we can heckle them!'

14

Sunshine patted a cushion into place. The prisoners had been smoking and she'd opened the windows to let in the cold air to dispel the stink of tobacco. 'Most of our residents smoke but there's one or two make a fuss if they come in here and find the smell hanging about.'

Eddie stood in the centre of the room with a tin can he'd been emptying dog ends into from dirty ashtrays. He looked ill at ease, like a small boy who'd been told by his mother to help clear up, Sunshine thought. She looked around the large room, with its easy chairs lining the walls and the occasional tables replaced in their usual spots. Even the playing cards were back on the table. 'All back to normal, now. The men were pretty well behaved, I thought,' she said.

'Couldn't be anything else with their guards watching, could they?' He'd put the tin on a table and come up behind her, snaking his arms around her waist. 'Give us a kiss, Sunshine.'

'So that's what you came back for after you'd seen the Germans loaded on their lorry back to St Vincent! A bit of slap and tickle, not to help me clean up.'

He twisted her around so that she faced him, bent his head and kissed her. Usually she longed for him to touch her but this time she wriggled away. She was curious about the blond pilot and wanted to ask Eddie about him. She couldn't do

95

that if she was in a clinch, could she?

'What if someone comes in?' she said. 'I'll lose my job, cuddling with you when I should be working.'

'No one will see,' Eddie said, with a boyish grin.

'Oh, won't they?'

Sunshine laughed. 'See,' she said, stepping neatly away from Eddie and turning to the grey-haired elderly man with the sea-blue eyes. 'Caught in the act by your own grandfather, eh, Solomon?'

'I was young once, though you wouldn't think so to look at me now,' Solomon said. 'I only want to know if you're coming in to see me before you leave, Eddie.'

The smell of violet perfume was in the air. A small wiry woman, dressed smartly in a dark two-piece costume and black court shoes, stood at Solomon's side. A black coat hung over her arm. Gold and jet earrings dangled, and bright red lipstick gave her once-pretty face colour.

'Course I am,' said Eddie. To the woman he said, 'I don't know what you're doing to my granddad, Gertie, but every time I see him he looks younger.'

Gertie blushed, which added yet more colour to her face.

Sunshine knew that was true. The old man suffered infrequently from bouts of shell shock but being constantly in the company of Gertie, who seemed to have taken a shine to the old man, had done marvels for his confidence. She wondered if they'd been in the shelter or had just returned from one of Gertie's 'jaunts', as Solomon called them. She frequently carted him off to the spiritualist church or to visiting clairvoyants she read about in the *Evening News*. Gertie confirmed this: 'There was a séance at the church.'

'Any luck with finding out what happened to Oliver?'

Gertie shook her head. She had had her son late in life and idolized him. 'All the time my Oliver doesn't get through to me there's every chance he's still alive. If he'd passed over he'd get in touch, I know he would.' She pulled at Solomon's sleeve. 'C'mon, let's go and put the kettle on. Leave these youngsters to what they want to get up to.'

When they'd gone Eddie said, 'Do you think her son's still alive?'

Sunshine stared at him. 'There were sixty-five survivors of the *Jervis Bay* rescued by that Swedish vessel. Her boy wasn't one of them. The rest of the ship's crew didn't stand a chance in that icy Atlantic water off Iceland, so what do you think?'

'I think she's a mother who believes her son is out there somewhere,' he said. 'A mother's love for her child is powerfully strong.'

Sunshine wanted children, blond babies she could love and cherish. She'd make sure their growing up would be full of joyful memories, not at all like her own childhood. She swept away the unhappiness her thoughts had brought. 'Tell me about your prisoners. Are they good workers?'

'I think so,' he said. 'That blond one seems to

97

know what he's doing. Bit on the cheeky side but a willing worker.'

'What about the others?' She didn't want Eddie to know she was interested only in Max.

'Seem all right,' Eddie said. 'At least I can get some repair work done now I've got help.' He bent forward and kissed her forehead. 'I'll go home and get washed and changed. Otherwise there won't be enough of the evening left to take you out for a drink,' he said. 'I can be back here by seven.'

She'd done her quota of work for the day. It would be nice sitting in the Green Dragon. Tonight there was a darts match and they always put on a good spread for the visiting players. There would be music. She might even get Eddie on his feet for a dance. Eddie gave her a lingering kiss before she waved him off at the front door. If only he would ask her to marry him!

She liked living here. Mrs Manners treated her like a daughter. Or, at least, like a daughter might be treated, Sunshine thought. She was happy among the people who lived in Lavinia House. The only fly in the ointment was that her part-time wages didn't allow her to save for what she wanted most: a home of her own. She remembered the German's talk of workers needed in the kitchens at St Vincent. She might make enquiries — she could easily do two jobs if Mrs Manners agreed, couldn't she?

Sunshine unlocked her room and went inside.

Clean and bright, she'd thought it Heaven when she moved in. She switched the wireless on. Bing Crosby was singing. Her friend, her sewing machine, sat on a small table in the corner. Over it was folded a colourful dress that only needed hemming. She'd scoured jumble sales for good materials so she could make her own clothes, and in the chest of drawers there were several pieces of washed fabric she hoped one day to make into children's things. Of course, she needed a husband first.

In the short time she'd known him she'd thought she'd fallen head over heels in love with Eddie Herron. The rheumatic fever he'd had as a child meant he couldn't join the services but he had his own business, a van, he was kind and considerate and extremely good-looking: perfect husband material. When he kissed her he made her tingle. But allowing him kisses was as far as she was prepared to go. If he wanted more, Eddie had to put a ring on her finger, an engagement ring, at least.

A knock on the door announced Mrs Manners, and Sunshine ushered her into the room and closed the door. 'Everything all right, love? You off out with Eddie?' Mabel Manners sat herself down on the edge of Sunshine's bed.

'Yes,' said Sunshine, as she pulled a pair of light grey slacks and a fluffy strawberry pink jumper from the hangers in the single wardrobe.

'He's a nice steady bloke, that one.'

Sunshine nodded. She sat down in front of the dressing-table mirror and began to pull a brush through her hair.

'Any nearer to him popping the question?'

Sunshine sighed.

'Ah, well, you got plenty of time,' Mabel said.

'I just want a place of my own,' said Sunshine. 'And a family.'

'That's natural, you being brought up by a foster mother. Especially one who wasn't kind to you.'

Sunshine thought of the conversations she'd had with Mabel, when she'd finally felt able to pour out her heart to her.

An enormous bulk of a woman, Mrs Pennyfeather had filled her large house with fostered children for which she was well paid. She kept them short of food and skimped on blankets and decent clothing. Sunshine had been in constant fear of the cold and the bigger children, Mrs Pennyfeather's satellites, who bullied her and the younger ones. For a time she'd resorted to sleeping in a wardrobe in the babies' room because one of the boys had tried to get into the bed she'd shared with another girl. School was a hit-and-miss affair because often the older girls, for fun, stole Sunshine's shoes and clothing. Bread and dripping was a regular meal, well before the war and rationing. Mrs Pennyfeather's practices went ignored by the authorities because the woman 'always had room for one more'.

Eventually Fate caught up with her. A missing child's body was discovered buried in the large back garden. A court case followed and Mrs Pennyfeather went to prison, the children scattered to better homes. Sunshine had then been old enough to work. Her love of children and experience in looking after them had led her to a nanny's job. Her two adored charges, the boy and the baby girl of a naval couple in Alverstoke, had filled her heart with joy. When the war started, the husband had been posted abroad and his wife and children went with him. Sunshine had been bereft until last year when the cleaning job in Lavinia House became available.

'I popped in to ask if you'd like to share a meal with me but I won't tempt you if you're off with your young man.'

'Sorry,' said Sunshine. 'It'd be a shame to leave it when Eddie comes. He's looking forward to the food at the Green Dragon.'

Sunshine walked down the passageway with her towards the bathroom. Mabel left her to go into her own quarters.

Later Sunshine foraged in her dressing-table drawer for her powder and lipstick. She'd hardly finished coating her lashes with mascara when there was another knock on her door and Eddie called, 'It's me.'

'Just coming.' She grabbed her coat from the back of the chair and switched off the wireless. She was well aware that visitors in her room were frowned upon.

As soon as she opened the door, Eddie kissed her forehead. He smelled of carbolic soap. His coat collar was turned up against the cold. 'You look lovely,' he said.

'Thank you.' Sunshine tied a silky scarf around her head and knotted it beneath her chin. Hand in hand they left the building.

15

Jo ran up the white marble steps to the entrance of Birmingham's Rainbow Club. She clutched the Beecham's Powders she hoped would dispel Blackie's massive headache, a relic of the long drive from Southampton with three bickering girls in the back of his car.

Emotions flowed freely after the excitement onstage and being stuck in a car didn't give the girls space to let off steam.

Blackie was supposed to be practising with the bass player and the saxophonist before tonight's show but Jo had persuaded him to rest for an hour or so.

'Mrs Bird, this package arrived the moment you stepped out of the door.'

Jo made a detour to the highly polished desk and took the parcel handed to her. The return address said it was from Madame Walker. The new dresses had arrived!

'Thank you,' she said to the smiling receptionist, a pretty little girl in a dark red costume. Antique gold-painted furniture, maroon velvet furnishings and a huge glass chandelier made the reception area look very glamorous, she thought. Clutching the parcel and the Beecham's Powders, Jo walked to the newly installed electric lift where the attendant requested the floor number.

As the lift rose, Jo's stomach plummeted. She

wished now she'd attempted the wide stairs to their rooms. The girls, of course, had been in awe of the contraption. Blackie had taken it in his stride, as he did with everything, but he was so much more worldly wise than her. What if it broke down and she was stuck in it alone with the young man? She took solace from the thought that using the lift was his job and he'd know what to do in an emergency.

She thought about their entrance earlier when the porter had shown them to their opulent suite on the top floor, and Blackie's first words as the door was opened: 'I hope we don't have to pay for this out of our wages!'

Bea had run around the suite opening doors and peering into the rooms. There were four en-suite bedrooms, an enormous lounge and a kitchen area, all beautifully decorated in gold and red. Every time Bea saw something she liked she clapped her hands with joy. Rainey and Ivy showed a little more decorum but Jo knew they were just as excited and impressed.

'Look at those roses!' Jo had been amazed. 'Where did they get scented red roses in wartime? Are we in the wrong rooms?'

Blackie had tipped the waiting porter after the luggage had been brought in, then said, 'No. This is what I love about being on the road.' His beautiful odd-coloured eyes held hers. 'We never know where we're going to end up sleeping and this time we've struck lucky! We're here for seven nights so let's hope the food is as good as the accommodation.' Then he'd held his hand to his forehead and she could see, from the dark circles round his eyes, that his headache was getting the better of him.

'We've already decided on the sleeping arrangements,' called Ivy. 'Rainey and I are going to share. You two have a room each. Bea gets the smallest. Neither of us likes sleeping with her because she snuggles closer and closer. Eventually you're left on the edge of the bed, ready to fall out. If you move and go round the other side, she turns over and does it all again.'

'I don't know what I do when I'm asleep.' Bea was indignant. 'Jo, tell her I'm not responsible!'

'I wish you lot would stop bickering,' snapped Blackie.

It was at that point Jo had decided to find a chemist.

Now, with the powders for Blackie and the new costumes for the girls clutched beneath her arm, all she wanted was a cup of tea and five minutes' peace and quiet. Maybe she could answer the latest letter she'd had from Syd.

She hadn't brought a room key with her so she knocked and Blackie let her in.

'Thank God you're back,' he said. 'Did you get any tablets?'

She pressed the folded packets of powder into his hand. 'I thought you'd be in bed. How do you feel?'

He grimaced. She shook the parcel at him. 'New costumes from Madame Walker,' she said. 'Has someone put the kettle on?'

He nodded. Jo sighed with relief and handed him the brown paper parcel. She could hear the soft hum of voices. 'At least they aren't arguing,' she said, with a smile, making her way to the kitchen area where cups and saucers had been set out next to a teapot, with a red cosy. She put her purse on the table and threw her coat over the back of a chair.

'Shall I call them in here to see what she's sent?'

'Let's have five minutes' peace first.' Her heart fluttered as Blackie gave her a long, lazy smile that told her he knew exactly how she was feeling. She spied a large box of chocolates on the table. 'They weren't there before.'

'A maid brought them in just as you left. Tom Marks, the owner of the club, will be along to see us in a short while.'

Jo took off her jacket and folded it over her outdoor coat. 'Nice and warm in here,' she said, watching as he mixed Beecham's Powders with water and drank the concoction. 'I hope they do the trick for your headache,' she added.

He shook his head resignedly. 'I never thought travelling with four beautiful women would drive me to drink!' He picked up the teapot and began pouring two cups of tea.

'Smooth talker,' Jo said, and put a hand over a third cup to stop him pouring more. 'Let's have ours first. All hell will be let loose when they find out the new costumes have arrived.' She watched as he added milk for both of them and ignored the sugar bowl. Because of the shortages Blackie, too, had become used to drinking tea without sugar.

Blackie moved her cup and saucer towards her and Jo draped herself over a tall stool. She slipped off her high heels with a contented sigh and watched as Blackie loosened his tie, pulled it from his neck, then removed his suit jacket, taking his wallet from its inside pocket and throwing it at the chair that held her clothing.

'It's nice to be quiet for a moment,' he said. Then he fumbled in his wallet. 'How much do I owe for the Beecham Powders?'

Jo put down her cup. 'Come into some money, have we?'

'I hope when we get paid after this week we'll show profit enough to have professional photographs taken of the Bluebirds. The cost can be phenomenal, but Ivy told me Bert knows a man who takes wonderful pictures. We'll need to provide publicity shots for the venues. I'll ask Bert when we get back to Gosport. First I must start repaying Madame and Herbert their contribution. The Bluebird Girls have to look terrific in these austere times, but it all comes at a price.'

'They're worth it and are pulling their weight,' said Jo. 'Look how Bea turned that working-men's venue around with her cheek. They had a whip round as well as paying our fee. And don't forget I've got savings.' She had two hundred pounds in the post office from the sale of her car.

'We can manage without that,' Blackie snapped.

'All right, all right. I only offered.' About to finish her tea, she was startled by his sharp tone.

A door opened and out trooped the girls. Rainey was the first to spot the parcel. 'Is that what I think it is?'

Jo nodded. 'Take it into the bedroom and come out and surprise us when you've put them on.'

Rainey picked up the parcel and the trio disappeared.

'If the new dresses fit, it might be nice for them to do two changes tonight,' Jo said. She could hear giggles and chatter. She was hoping that Bea hadn't put on any more weight. The dressmaker had all three girls' measurements but found it difficult to keep up with Bea's fluctuating inches.

Blackie laughed at the noise coming from the bedroom. 'I reckon they like the frocks.' Then, more seriously, 'We'd better go down and look at the stage area to see if you can actually do a quick change. At the last few places it's not been possible.'

Jo remembered with a shudder the grubby working-men's clubs. The one in Southampton had been a palace compared to the one in Portsmouth.

A knock on the door cut short her thoughts. Blackie was laughing at her scrabbling to put her shoes back on.

She heard him say, 'Welcome, come in.' She turned to see a maid carrying a large basket of fruit. The man accompanying her bade her place it on the table, then leave. Jo gasped. Oranges! Apples and oranges! She couldn't remember the last time she'd seen an orange, let alone tasted one. The words came without her realizing she'd spoken: 'How did you find oranges?'

The man stepped forward, grasping Blackie's

outstretched hand. 'I'm Tom Marks, the owner of the Rainbow, and I hope you and your entourage will have a pleasant stay.' He let Blackie's hand drop. 'I'm sorry the fruit and chocolates weren't already in this suite to welcome you. A small delivery delay.'

He turned to Jo and gave her a smile that didn't reach his hazel eyes. 'I know you're Jo, if I may call you that?' She nodded. The man dazzled her. His suit looked very expensive and there was a faint smell of bergamot. 'If there is anything you or your girls need, just ask. I can obtain most things.'

Jo was aware immediately of his magnetism. This was someone who was used to getting his own way. He was every bit as tall as Blackie but there the resemblance ended. His hair was a deep auburn, lightly oiled so it looked almost black and was swept back from his forehead. Her eyes took in his even features and lingered on what she guessed was a tattoo on his neck. Part of a snake's head peeped above the expensive silk shirt collar. Jo associated tattoos with rough, seafaring men; it gave him an air of mystery. If he was aware she stared too long he wasn't bothered by it.

There was a moment of silence, then Blackie said, 'I'm sure I speak for everyone when I thank you for your hospitable welcome. There is one more thing I would ask.'

'Anything,' said Tom. He was answering Blackie but still looking at Jo, who felt she was about to melt beneath his stare. She was very aware that she was dishevelled from travelling.

'Can you show us where the girls are to perform? I also need to meet the bass player and saxophonist I'll be working with tonight.'

'Certainly,' Tom said. 'If you're ready now?'

The bedroom door burst open and Rainey stepped into the living area holding the metallic gold bodice of a dress close to her upper body. The sheath-like skirt fitted tightly to her hips and fishtailed out at her ankles. 'We can't get the backs done up . . . ' She trailed off as she became aware of the man's presence.

Jo saw her face redden and her fingers tighten at the dress top, holding it closer to her.

'Oh! I'm sorry! I didn't know anyone was here . . . ' Her daughter was staring at Tom Marks.

A smile broke across the man's face. 'Don't be sorry on my account. May I say how lovely you look in that dress you're very nearly wearing?'

'Turn around, young lady,' Jo snapped. She sprang to her feet and zipped up the back of the dress. A sudden feeling of protectiveness came over her as she stepped in front of her daughter, blocking the men's view.

She moved back a pace and looked Rainey up and down. 'It doesn't leave much to the imagination,' she said. 'Are the other dresses as revealing?'

Rainey nodded and her magnificent auburn hair settled around her bare shoulders, like a red-gold cape. 'Similar, but different,' she added.

'Just like those beautiful blue dresses?' The voice belonged to Tom Marks.

'Yes,' said Rainey, turning to face him. 'You've

obviously seen us onstage before.'

'Of course,' he drawled. 'That's why I asked you to perform here. At my other clubs too, I hope.'

Jo could feel the air in the room prickle with electricity. Tom Marks had witnessed the Bluebirds' act and wanted them to perform at his clubs. That was all it was, wasn't it? So why did she feel something wasn't quite right?

'Good acts encourage patrons to enter the Rainbow Club to eat, to drink and to gamble.' He stepped forward and took Rainey's hand. 'I'm very pleased to make your acquaintance at last,' he said. He kissed the back of her fingers in an old-fashioned gesture, then turned to Blackie. 'If you and Jo would like to follow me, I'll give you a guided tour of the club and introduce you, Blackie, to the other musicians.'

Jo, her head reeling, saw Rainey was at a loss to respond to Tom's behaviour. Blushing, her daughter turned towards the bedroom.

She and Blackie followed him out of the suite.

16

Max listened to the night sounds around him. It was amazing just how much noise there was while men slept. Someone was crying softly. Not that he blamed the man for showing his feelings. After all, who wouldn't rather be free in their own country than cooped up in a Nissen hut next to a creek in Gosport in the bleakness of early February?

There were eighty men to a hut. The wooden bunks took up most of the space, with a couple of tables, a few benches and a pot-bellied stove to keep the place barely warm. He sighed. They were treated well enough by the army guards and ate three meals a day, the same rations as British servicemen, not that the general public agreed with that. They were often spat at while marching in the town to and from their workplaces and told they should starve. The favoured few workers were taken to Bridgemary by lorry. Only good-conduct prisoners were allowed to work outside. He'd made sure he was among them.

When he'd first been captured, he had been interrogated about German military matters and his loyalty towards the Nazis. The result was that he wore a grey patch on his dark, scratchy British clothing. Black meant hard-core feelings. White was no particular feelings either way against the regime. He'd lied successfully about all he was asked, for it was his greatest desire to return to Germany and push the British off the face of the earth. He disliked intensely having the large white P painted on his trouser leg. That was a gross indignity.

He didn't think for a minute that his plan to escape might fail. Why should it? He'd carefully considered all options and the silly blonde trollop was behaving just as he'd thought she would. German or English, there really wasn't any difference between susceptible women who wanted to believe what they were led to believe.

He smiled to himself. After his first assault on her feelings that afternoon of the air raid, she would expect him to be looking out for her, trying to make eye contact with her. He was also aware he must make his seduction quickly because any day he could be moved on from the barracks at St Vincent. There had been whispers about prisoners being sent to Warsash to work on farms. Hampshire was renowned for its strawberry fields; pickers would be needed before the June harvest.

For two days he'd ignored her completely.

He'd watched her looking for him. A good sign she was interested, and why shouldn't she be? Wasn't he everything a woman could possibly want in a man? He didn't have his freedom but that would change. Sunshine would make that possible.

And already it had begun.

Breakfast at St Vincent began at seven for the prisoners working on the outside. Who should have been there that morning, ladling out

112

porridge in the big hall, but Sunshine.

'Thanks for telling me kitchen staff were needed,' she'd said. He was aware his ladleful was generous. The white overall she wore practically swamped her small figure. He had feigned surprise at her presence.

The prisoners in the queue were not supposed to linger.

'Have you moved here to Gosport?'

She shook her head. 'I'm doing both jobs.' He was touched by her childish joy at seeing him. 'I'll be here for tonight's meal,' she'd said, putting two thick slices of heavy bread on his plate.

'Move along there!' The guard was insistent. Max had given her a smile and watched the colour rise to her face. His step was jaunty as he found a space at a table, sat and began to eat in the noisy, smelly room. Once or twice he looked up from his bowl and caught her eyes on him. He had allowed his gaze to linger.

That evening he'd explained his behaviour to her.

'I'm sorry.' He'd stared into her trusting eyes. 'I didn't realize you are the girlfriend of my boss. There is no way I could possibly hurt his feelings. I must put you out of my mind.' Then he had walked quickly to the table and begun eating the mutton stew that was more vegetables than meat. He'd sent wistful glances her way.

He had come to the conclusion that the English were very much like his own countrymen. Good and bad, gangsters and philanthropists. He had realized then that every area of British society included people who could be of use to him. Since his capture he had made it his business to find out from various sources, both inside and outside the prison, that in Gosport's town centre there was a man who could provide false papers and a passport for him. But it would require money. Money he didn't have. But he did have good looks and a silver tongue, and he intended to make the best use of those assets.

Max slept.

★ ★ ★

'I went to see Granddad this afternoon,' said Maud. She was toasting bread in front of the grate in the kitchen.

Eddie heard his mother's voice and turned down the page on *Sad Cypress*. He was partial to Agatha Christie. 'Was he all right?' he asked. 'I'm working right in front of his place but don't find the time to pop in as much as I'd like.'

'You don't need to worry yourself. That Gertie keeps her beady eyes on him.'

'Who'd have thought he'd find a fancy woman at his age?' He watched his mother turn the piece of bread so it could brown on the other side, then hold it towards the hot coals. The smell of toast was lovely, he thought.

'She's not his fancy woman, she's a very nice person,' said Maud. She looked up and he caught her eye and smiled. 'I never saw Sunshine,' she said. 'Day off?'

'Not really,' he said. 'She's got herself another

part-time job.' He saw the piece of toast join its twin on the plate and his mother dig the prongs of the long fork into another slice of bread. 'You want me to marge those?' he asked.

'Can if you like. They're for you. Where's this job, then?' Maud asked. 'Eat it before it gets cold.'

Eddie smiled at his mother again. Sometimes she treated him like he was still a kid. Not that he minded — he supposed to most parents their offspring, however grown-up, would always be children. Not that Sunshine had known much about parents, being brought up in that terrible place, he thought. That was probably why she was eager to be settled with a home of her own. Was that what he wanted, though?

'St Vincent. In the kitchens,' he muttered, through a mouthful of toast.

'Ain't you worried with all those men?'

'I can't chain her to me, can I? If she wants me she'll stay. It cuts both ways, Mum.'

''Bout time you thought about settling down. I'd like some grandchildren about the place.'

He took another bite, chewed, then sighed deeply.

They were happy enough together, and there was no doubt Sunshine'd make someone a lovely wife. She'd be a caring mum and all. For him? He wasn't sure. But they'd hardly been going out long enough for him to make up his mind.

A picture of Ivy rose unbidden in his head.

He shook it away. She was just a kid. And yet she wasn't, was she? Ivy was just a few months younger than Bea, and after all his sister had been through, he didn't think of her as a kid, did he? He didn't want to dwell on what had happened to Bea in the backyard at the Fox: it made him so angry. He was angry with himself for being unable to do anything about it. He was older than Bea: he should have been looking after her that night. But he hadn't been there, hadn't witnessed the sailor running away. Since then, Ivy and Rainey had shown his family what good friends they were to Bea and he would be eternally grateful to them for that.

Thinking about Ivy made him feel all warm inside. Once when their fingers had touched he could have sworn he felt something like an electric charge. He'd believed she'd felt it too, that indefinable something. But that was a while ago, long before Sunshine. He'd have been a fine bloke to take liberties with Ivy then, wouldn't he?

Not that he'd take liberties with any woman unless she wanted him to. And there'd been a few who hadn't minded. Not Sunshine, though.

'Ain't you going to finish it?'

His mother's words broke into his thoughts. He picked up the last slice of toast.

★   ★   ★

Blackie sipped his Scotch. If he wasn't careful he'd have the granddaddy of all hangovers tomorrow.

He'd have liked to ignore the blackout, stand on the balcony with the curtains blowing in the wind and look out over Birmingham. Maybe,

116

just maybe, the fresh air would help him sleep. But he daren't turn the bedroom lamp off: the darkness would swallow him. Just like the inky blackness had got to him after Alfie Bird had blown himself up, back in France, saving Blackie's life.

He finished the Scotch and, with an unsteady hand, poured himself more. In the night's silence the bottle chinked loudly against the glass. He began pacing his bedroom again.

What a bloody fool he'd been earlier.

In the gaming room tonight he'd been more than ready to squander all the results of the hard work the three girls, Jo and he had put into creating the Bluebird Girls. How could he have been so damned stupid?

A light knock on his door caused him to pause in his travels across the carpet.

A second, firmer knock and he opened his door to find Jo standing in her dressing-gown, her tousled hair adding to the worry in her eyes. Without speaking, she slipped inside and closed the door behind her.

He stared at her, raised his glass and asked, 'Can I interest you in a Scotch?'

'Why can't you sleep?'

It was obvious he'd woken her. She smelled of talcum powder.

'Is it your headache?'

A day's driving with three girls bickering because they were tired had caused that. He shook his head. 'Your Beecham's Powders solved that problem.' He took a mouthful of whisky, saw with surprise it was the last in the glass and moved towards the small table that held the tray of spirits.

'You don't need any more,' Jo said. She insinuated herself in front of the low table. If he wanted another drink, he'd have to ask her to move aside. He stared at her. She held out her hand for his glass and he relinquished it, like a naughty child handing over something he shouldn't have. Jo put the glass on the tray. He watched her every movement before he sighed, then moved wearily and unsteadily towards the bed and sat down.

'You can't keep me awake with your floor pacing and not tell me what's wrong,' she said. 'I'm going nowhere until I know what's worrying you.'

He knew when she used that tone she meant what she'd said.

'I'm ashamed.' He patted the bedspread by the side of him, a signal for her to join him. She pulled her flowered dressing-gown around herself and sat. He could smell her freshly shampooed hair. He wanted to give in to his emotions and cry but what good would that do? He'd only lose more of his self-respect.

In the time he'd known Jo, she'd proved her strength over and over again and looked up to him for advancing the girls' careers. How would she feel about him when he told her he had almost ruined everything?

'I'm waiting,' she said. She was so close he could breathe her in. 'Whatever it is, it happened after the girls and I went to bed. It couldn't be anything to do with their act tonight. They were dead on their feet with all the travelling and no rest, yet they went on that stage and gave their all. The audience was eating out of their hands. Tom Marks had a smile a mile wide, and that double change from the blue glittery dresses to the gold ones went like a dream.' She paused. 'If you're cross with me because I wouldn't allow them to stay up any longer after the show but packed them off to bed . . . ' She paused again. 'I'm sorry, but I felt Rainey had had enough attention paid to her by that Tom Marks and sleep would do them more good than drinks in smoke-filled rooms.'

He reached up and put his fingers gently to her mouth to stem the flow of words. Jo, obviously surprised by the intimate gesture, faltered but didn't move away.

'It's not that. You did right — we were all tired. It was me.' He pressed his lips together into a thin line, then stared into her lovely green eyes. After a while he said, 'We moved into the casino. I played poker. Lost money.' He gave a bitter laugh.

The silence that followed seemed ominous. She allowed him to continue, her eyes betraying nothing.

'Nothing new there. I used to play in the barracks and lose my army pay before I'd got it.'

She was staring at him, eyes like unfathomable pools.

'The trouble is, you always believe the cards will turn and be on your side. Of course they don't, but there's always that belief, the excitement that whispers, 'The next card . . . ''

'How much?'

'It's not the money,' he said, his voice rising. 'I had enough personal cash in the bank to pay the promissory note — just. It's what Tom Marks suggested and the fact I considered it before I walked away from that table.'

'What was that?' Her voice was a whisper.

'He suggested a version of double or quits.'

Jo was frowning. 'What did he want?'

'The Bluebird Girls.'

'I don't understand.' Jo's face was now a white mask.

'If I won, he'd hand over double the winnings, a very large sum, I must admit. If I lost, he'd cancel my debt but take over the girls' management.'

He heard Jo's intake of breath. Saw the horror in her eyes. 'I've already told you I walked away. But I considered his offer, Jo. I considered it.'

Outside, the dawn chorus had begun. For a while Blackie listened to the birds, and then he began to cry, allowing the tears to roll down his cheeks. So what if Jo thought he was a weakling for crying? It had been one of the most strenuous things he had ever done in his life, to get up and walk away from that table, from Tom Marks. And now he felt like a wrung-out dishcloth. Glad he had told Jo because he didn't want secrets between them, not the kind of secrets that really mattered between a man and a woman. She and the girls felt he was some kind of saviour, a man to make things happen for them. He was and he wasn't. He was just a man.

Jo pulled him into her warm body. 'The main

thing is you walked away,' she said. 'Not that you wanted to gamble. It took guts to do that, real guts.'

He put his arms around her. 'Do you really think that?' he asked.

She disengaged herself and gazed into his eyes. Her fingers brushed his curls back from his forehead and she gave a sudden smile as he felt them fall back into their usual places. 'Get into bed,' she said. 'None of us is perfect. We make mistakes, do things we shouldn't and push people away. There's still time before we need to get up. Sleep.'

'Stay with me, Jo,' he said. 'Just hold me awhile.'

She pulled back the rumpled bedclothes and slipped between the sheets.

'You'll do that, Jo?' He was so tired. 'You'll do this for me?'

She smiled at him. 'Willingly. The only way is to forgive and then we can move forward,' she said.

17

Bea paused, the strawberry cream touching her lips. It took all her strength of will to lift her hand away and gaze at the thick coating of chocolate. She could practically taste it. She tore her eyes away from Tom Marks's present, which she had crept out of her bedroom and stolen while the others slept. The guilt she was feeling looking at the purloined box of chocolates was twofold.

Tom Marks had meant the gift to be enjoyed by all of them. Not just her. Her longing for sweetness had forced her to tiptoe, after she had ascertained that Blackie, Jo, Rainey and Ivy were asleep, into the living area and carry the box into her own room. Its contents mesmerized her. Coconut cream from tropical palms, exotic Turkish delight and her favourite, strawberry cream, soft, pink and fruity.

Stealing was alien to her. If her mother, Maud, ever found out she'd become a thief it would break her heart.

And what about Jo? She had told Jo that she would cut down on eating sweet things before she became the size of a house and could no longer find clothes to fit her. With Jo's help, she now slipped easily into the gorgeous stage frocks that Madame provided. Bea gazed at the golden creation lying across the chair. She knew she looked the cat's whiskers in it, the shimmering cloth clinging to all her curves. The weight she had put on had disappeared.

The smell of chocolate on her fingers drew her eyes back to the strawberry cream. Surely just one wouldn't hurt.

Bea sighed. She couldn't stop at one. She would greedily eat a second, a third, a fourth and gorge until the box was empty.

How would she feel then? She would be guilty of stealing. She would have let Jo down by breaking her promise to her. She wouldn't have the courage to face Ivy and Rainey, who were her friends. The best kind of friends. Hadn't they stuck by her after she had drunk too much and the sailor had assaulted her? What kind of monster was she if she couldn't keep her promises to the people who loved her?

With the force of a demon she dislodged the sticky sweet and threw it as far as she could. The chocolate at first stuck to the painted wall, then slid slowly downwards, leaving a brown splodge that narrowed and finally disappeared when it reached the carpet. Power ran through Bea's body. She retrieved her handkerchief from under her pillow and wiped the wall clean, then wrapped the remains of the chocolate in it. Tomorrow she would throw it away. She marvelled that all desire to taste the sweetness had disappeared.

Bea picked up the box, checked that the rest of the chocolates sat nicely in their brown frilly papers, closed the cardboard lid and took it with her to her bedroom door. She listened carefully in case any of the others were about, turned the door handle and crept out, happy that her eyes had become accustomed to the dark. She replaced the chocolates next to the roses.

Before she reached her own room again, she froze. She could hear voices. They seemed to be coming from Blackie's room. Perhaps he was having a bad dream. He sometimes had nightmares. She knew serving in war-torn France did that to men. Her grandfather suffered from shell shock.

Bea went back into her bedroom. Peace enveloped her, and she smiled to herself.

★   ★   ★

Jo had thought it would be difficult to talk to Blackie at breakfast. Not so: he was affable, charming, thoughtful, all the things he usually was but with a certain softness in his attitude towards her.

Last night she'd held him, breathing in his masculine scent. When she judged his breathing was regular, she carefully disentangled herself from his warm body and left him sleeping. She'd considered staying with him until morning but decided there might be too many questions to answer if one of her charges went into her bedroom early and discovered her missing.

She didn't despise Blackie for losing his money. Rather, she admired him for beating his demons. For standing up to Tom Marks.

Something about the club-owner reminded her of Alfie. The cocksure walk. The smiles that never reached his eyes. And she didn't like the way he stared at Rainey, as though he was undressing her with a look.

Alfie had controlled Jo, stolen her confidence, made her feel she was worthless. It had taken Syd Kennedy, with his kindness, to give her back the personality Alfie had erased. Dear Syd, dependable Syd, had made her whole again, made her see that all men weren't fists and lies.

One day he might ask her to marry him. It's possible it would have happened already had she not taken on the job of chaperoning the girls. But you couldn't marry a man because he was kind. Syd would have preferred her to continue working for the Harringtons in the paper shop, but Jo was determined to help her daughter follow her dream. If it meant becoming the glue that held the Bluebird Girls, herself and Blackie together, then so be it. And what of the enigma that was Blackie? Last night he'd needed her, which she'd liked. He'd proved his masculinity, his bravery at Dunkirk, and now he'd allowed her to see a side of him no man ever had ever shown her before: his vulnerability.

She couldn't tell him, certainly not yet, maybe never, that she loved him.

⋆   ⋆   ⋆

'I feel as though I've been on holiday,' said Rainey, making herself comfortable in the back of Blackie's car. 'Being treated like royalty at the Rainbow Club . . . Well, most of the time.' A shadow passed across her face.

125

'Move over, Princess. There's three of us needs to fit in there,' said Ivy, elbowing herself against Rainey.

'Do not, I repeat, do not start arguing,' said Blackie. 'It's a long drive to Portsmouth from here, and if we're to be onstage tonight at the Royal Sailors' Club, I don't want to be worn out when we arrive. I want us to give a good show.'

Jo broke in before an argument flared: 'Eventually, we'll be sleeping in our own beds,' she said. 'Won't that be nice?' She received a few noncommittal mumbles in reply. As Blackie sat down in the driver's seat she whispered, hoping none of the girls would hear, 'Did Tom Marks pay you?'

'He promised to put a cheque in the post.' Blackie let his gaze linger on Jo for a while. 'Don't worry, it'll be all right. I didn't want to press him too hard about the payment as he was most insistent this morning on filling the car with petrol.' He paused. 'And I wasn't going to look a gift horse in the mouth by asking him where the petrol had come from.' He changed the subject. 'You know who's on the bill tonight at the Rainbow?'

Last night the Bluebirds had had to sing above the sound of bombs whistling down, returning fire from ack-ack guns and the drone of planes. The audience, bless them, had stayed at their fancy tables, pretending everything was normal and a war wasn't happening outside.

Jo didn't answer, so Blackie told her, 'It's Little Annette. She's on before Tommy Trinder.'

'Is he the comic who says, 'You lucky people'?' chimed in Bea.

'That's right,' said Blackie. 'He's a very funny bloke.'

'I don't know how Little Annette gets so many jobs,' said Bea. 'It's not as if she's glamorous.'

'Don't be mean,' Jo threw in quickly. 'She was top of the bill everywhere until age caught up with her.'

'She's still up there with the top-liners,' said Blackie. 'People remember her when she was a child.'

'She's not any more,' said Bea. 'She's old.'

'Doesn't mean she's lost her talent!' Blackie was indignant. 'Everyone thought she'd be even more successful if she changed her act, but she wouldn't.'

'Her mother works at Priddy's,' said Rainey. 'She's a lovely lady, well respected.'

'Does Little Annette keep in touch with her?' Blackie sounded interested.

'Don't know. Her mother was in the audience the night we appeared at the King's.'

'Rainey, just because her mother goes to see her doesn't mean they get on. I seem to remember something about a row, a long time ago . . . ' Blackie had been in the variety business all his life and had met many famous people. He absorbed gossip like a sponge.

They were driving through built-up areas past factories. So far Jo, happily, hadn't seen much evidence of last night's bombing. In the distance she could see a canal with a boat going peacefully through a lock. Fields came into view

127

with winter's desolation imprinted on them, a few houses with smoke drifting from their chimneys.

'You're not going to knit in here!' Rainey exclaimed crossly.

Jo turned around. Ivy, sitting in the middle of the cramped back seat, had produced a huge bag of multi-coloured balls of wool. On two very long needles sat a square of plain knitting and she was attempting to cast off.

'Mum, tell her there's not enough room — she'll poke our eyes out!'

'I'm making blankets for the Women's Voluntary Service to give to people who've got bombed out of their homes.' Ivy put down her needles and took from the hessian bag a large number of different-coloured knitted squares. She spread them over her lap. 'All from unravelled jumpers,' she said proudly. 'I got them off stalls in the Bull Ring market. When I've made enough squares I can sew them together.'

'Very worthy, Ivy love, but perhaps not to be knitted in such close proximity to the others on a long drive,' said Jo. Ivy looked mutinous. 'Was the market still running? I heard the Bull Ring was hit by incendiary bombs last year.'

'It was, Jo,' put in Blackie. 'They wrecked the roof. Used to be six hundred stalls there. Traders are hardy people, though. They came back.'

'But I've been working all week on this.' Ivy's mouth set in a hard line.

Jo had wondered where she disappeared to each night as soon as the club's show was over. She'd thought she'd gone to the bedroom she'd shared with Rainey to read. Ivy was never without a book. Now she realized soft-hearted Ivy had been doing her bit for the war. She had to think quickly. 'When Blackie stops for a break, I'll change places with you. There's more room in the front and you can knit here. How do you feel about that?' Before she looked back at Ivy, she glanced at Blackie, who took his eyes briefly from the road and nodded agreement.

Ivy began reluctantly putting her knitting back into the bag. 'Thanks,' she said. 'I'm glad someone understands that not everyone is as fortunate as us.' She glared at Rainey.

Jo thought that was a peculiar thing for Ivy to say and decided to try to lighten the chilly atmosphere. 'I wonder if we've had any engagements come in while we've been away.'

'That wouldn't worry Princess Rainey,' Ivy snapped. 'She's had the offer of a permanent job at Tom Marks's place.'

'I told you to keep that to yourself,' Rainey hissed. 'Anyway, I have no intention of taking him up on it.' An icy chill ran down Jo's spine as Rainey added, 'You promised you wouldn't say anything.'

'Shouldn't have been so mean about my knitting, then! And your mother should know.'

'For God's sake,' said Blackie.

'What's this about?' Jo knew she had to keep calm but she needed to find out the reason for Ivy's outburst.

There was a moment of silence. Then Rainey spoke. 'It was that first morning, before breakfast.' She gave a huge sigh, almost, Jo thought, like she was relieved to speak. 'I went down to the dining room. It wasn't open, too early. There were a few other people about so I decided to wait. Tom Marks was behind the desk in the foyer talking to the cashier. He called me over. Said he'd seen us at the King's Theatre. That's how come we got the week's work. Then he said he thought I was especially good the previous evening and he was disappointed I'd gone to bed so early.' She paused. 'He said he liked my gold dress.' Jo stared at her and could see the brightness of tears in her green eyes. Rainey carried on, her voice brittle: 'Tom sent the assistant out to the back, then he said, 'If ever you want to sing on your own, I'll book you.''

'He's a dirty ol' man,' said Ivy, 'and that horrible tattoo on his neck . . . '

'Ssh!' urged Bea. 'What happened next?'

'He grabbed my hand that was on the counter and started squeezing it.'

Jo could feel her temper rising.

Rainey pulled a face. 'I thought about the day before when he was leering at me.' She looked straight at Jo. 'I didn't know he was in the room when I came through in that gold dress to ask you to do it up for me, Mum.'

'It's all right, Rainey.'

'No, it's not, Mum. He made me feel sick. I mean, he's good-looking . . . for an old bloke.'

Blackie coughed. Jo thought he and Tom Marks were around the same age. No wonder he'd coughed.

'What happened then?' Bea was fascinated.

130

'Yes, what happened then?' asked Jo.

'The cashier came back with a bag of money. Tom Marks let go of my hand but he was whispering. He said I could appear at the club permanently, earn good money and . . . '

'And what, Rainey?' Jo was berating herself for letting this happen. A fine mother she was. She was supposed to chaperone the girls and she wasn't even looking after her own daughter properly.

'He said I could make it big with him looking after me. He said I could make a lot of money with my looks and figure. He asked me to meet him in the gardens later, after breakfast . . . '

Jo's heart was beating fast. 'And?'

Ivy's knitting bag slipped to the floor.

'I didn't say anything to that. He reminded me of my dad, all that red hair and that stupid tattoo.' A faraway look came into her eyes. 'I remembered seeing Dad cuddling that woman. They were at the pictures, didn't know I was there. It made me feel sick! Tom Marks made me feel sick. But I didn't want to say anything that would spoil the booking we had for the week at the club. Just then I saw people were being allowed in to breakfast so I smiled at him and went to the dining room. I sat at a table and drank a cup of tea. I was angry that he thought he had the right to suggest anything like that. I didn't have anything to eat — I felt too sick.'

'Did you go into the garden?' Bea asked.

'Of course not!' Rainey gave her a withering look. 'I spent the rest of the week keeping out of his way.' She stared hard at her mother. 'He's married. Did you know that?'

Jo shook her head. Ivy gasped. 'The rotter,' she muttered.

'The maid told me his wife stays in the country outside Birmingham. He's got a couple of kiddies as well. I hate men like that. He's just like my dad was.' Jo held Rainey's gaze. An unspoken moment passed between them. Jo saw the legacy her married life had left on her daughter and felt her shame rise.

'I know what you're thinking, Mum,' said Rainey. 'I'm not naïve. I do know there are good men in the world.' She smiled, and it seemed to Jo that a rainbow had lit up the car. 'You only have to look at Bert and our Blackie to see decent men. I'm glad we're on our way home now.'

'I wish you'd told me,' said Blackie.

Aware that he'd had his own problems with Tom Marks, Jo felt relieved he hadn't known. The result would have been an argument, maybe a fight. And what would that have accomplished? No, thought Jo. Rainey, despite her youth, had handled the situation in an adult way and she was proud of her. 'Perhaps it's just as well you didn't know,' said Jo. Then, to Rainey, 'You know you did the right thing in keeping away from him, don't you?'

'Of course I do. I'm sorry I didn't say anything to you, Mum.'

'I'm sorry you had to go through that on your own,' Jo said. She didn't think there was anything else to be gained by going over and over Rainey's experience now. They'd talk more when they were alone. She must keep a closer eye on all her charges in future.

'Some men are like that, aren't they?' said Bea, in a small voice. 'Out for what they can get?'

'Oh, Bea, I shouldn't have said anything,' wailed Ivy.

Rainey broke in, 'I didn't mean to remind you.'

'Remind me? It's with me all the time.' Jo saw Bea's pretty face screw up with sadness.

'What are you on about?' Blackie asked. 'Sounds very mysterious.'

He knew nothing of Bea's ordeal in the yard at the Fox and Jo was at a loss as to what to say. She was about to speak when Rainey and Ivy said swiftly in unison, 'Oh, nothing!'

Blackie glanced at Jo. 'I don't know, women and their secrets. You four are tighter than a hangman's knot.' He put out his hand and covered Jo's fingers, squeezing them. His warmth instantly revived her. 'I won't let this go with Tom Marks, Jo. You know that, don't you?'

Jo felt her spirits rise further when Blackie wound down the car's window and indicated he was about to pull off the road. 'There's a smashing café along here,' he said brightly. 'I think we could all do with a cuppa.'

18

He'd held her in his arms, just briefly, and then it had happened. He'd kissed Sunshine! Of course he'd had every intention of doing so but never in his wildest dreams had he realized the opportunity would present itself today. She'd been surprised, but she didn't push him away. If it hadn't been for the damned army guard, who knew what else might have occurred?

Max was too excited to sleep, even though the lights had been extinguished some time ago. The cacophony of noises and different smells in the Nissen hut added to his arousal. What was it she'd said: 'I'd like to make it clear, Max, that there's no understanding between me and Eddie. We're only friends.'

Max had walked to the line of wooden outhouses to collect tools. Crocuses had begun blooming in the garden square just inside the main gate of St Vincent. He'd volunteered to dig out weeds in the grass so that the initial V planted in bulbs would be shown to best effect when the flowers were fully open. Saturdays were lazy days, without work for the labouring prisoners, but Max preferred to keep busy. Especially as he'd discovered Sunshine worked a few hours at weekends in the nearby kitchens.

The shacks near the creek were used for storage. Most were padlocked but, like the shacks themselves, the locks were easily accessible.

It was by chance that Sunshine had been sent to collect vegetables. Max had followed her, keeping an eye on the guard who'd stopped to share a cigarette with a prisoner.

Once she was inside, Max entered and pulled the door to. The hut smelled of damp sacking. He was careful not to alarm her and she'd spoken first, telling him about Eddie.

He'd said in reply, 'Come here.' She'd stepped towards him, closing the space between them, and he'd put his arms around her. Oh, he was careful not to make a grab for her — that wouldn't have done at all.

She felt small against him. He could almost hear her heart beating. He put his hand beneath her chin and lifted her face towards him so that he could press his lips to hers. Then he had released her, swiftly, so she could see he hadn't meant to harm or worry her. He had stared into her eyes and whispered, 'I think of you all the time.'

Then, with the garden tools in his hand and the imprint of his kiss on her lips, he'd marched swiftly out into the cold of the late afternoon, saying to the guard as he passed, 'Not long now before spring takes a proper hold.'

The guard had merely nodded at him. Max had known in that moment that he and Sunshine would meet again. He'd begun whistling. He decided then that he would take responsibility for tending that piece of garden.

Of course the British Army men guarded exits and entrances to St Vincent Barracks. They also patrolled the perimeter fences, but security was sometimes lax. After all, where could a German disappear to without papers or passport? Britain was an island, after all, wasn't it? To be fed well, allowed the privilege of working outside was fine for most of the inmates, for now. Anyway, Germany would soon conquer the small island. Max knew he had the intelligence and charisma to get back to his beloved homeland before the war ended.

⋆   ⋆   ⋆

Jo wasn't yet used to the telephone. It made her jump whenever it rang and now was no exception. She climbed out of bed, yawned as she grabbed her flowered dressing-gown and ran, slipper-less, downstairs.

''Lo, Blackie, you woke me,' she said accusingly, when she heard his voice. The black Bakelite object was cold in her hand.

'Have you heard the news on the wireless?'

'How could I when I've just woken up?'

'Sorry, Jo, but there's some bad news. Birmingham got hit last night. The Rainbow copped it.'

For a moment she couldn't speak.

'Jo? Are you there?'

'How do you know this?' she asked. The wireless never gave out exact locations.

'Piers Road district, it said. I made enquiries.' Blackie paused. 'Many casualties, few survivors. Tom Marks isn't one of them.'

After taking in what he'd said she asked, 'Tommy Trinder?'

'He'd left early for the studios to make a Ministry of Information film.' He was breathless as he continued, 'I need you to do something for me. Little Annette's been hurt. The girls said they knew how to contact her mother. Could they get her to phone the hospital, or me? Annette's in a bad way.'

Blackie was still talking but Jo wasn't listening. She would wake Rainey as soon as he got off the phone. It could have been them caught in last night's bomb blast. One more day spent at the club and they might all have died. She pushed away the awful thoughts as she heard his voice again: 'You know what the authorities are like about taking time to do things. We must get Annette's mother to her as soon as possible.'

'All right,' she said. 'I'll see to it.' Without saying goodbye she replaced the telephone in its cradle.

And then she was upstairs, shaking Rainey awake.

'Aw, Mum, the all-clear didn't sound until this morning and you made us stay in that beastly Anderson shelter.'

Jo stopped her falling asleep again by shaking her shoulder much more fiercely.

'I'm tired,' Rainey complained.

'So am I,' said Jo. She thought about the previous evening when, just as Blackie's car disappeared around the corner and he was on his way back to Portsmouth, the siren had begun wailing. Jo wasn't taking any chances: she'd bundled Rainey down to the bottom of the garden and into the shelter. Aeroplanes were already overhead with their uneven drone of engines. Jo guessed the coast was in for another sleepless night.

Rainey had slept almost as soon as her head touched the bunk-bed pillow.

Jo had lain on the narrow bed below her daughter, listening to the cacophony of sound outside and smelling the cordite that seemed determined to seep inside the shelter. She'd thought about the show they'd put on that evening to stop herself worrying about the noise outside.

The Royal Sailors' Club had loved the Bluebirds. The girls had been on top form. And they'd been paid for their performance immediately they were ready to leave. Three sleepy girls had been driven to their homes but Moaning Minnie had let it be known there was still a war on. The all-clear had sounded at four this morning when Jo and Rainey had swapped damp bedding for their own soft beds.

Another shake now and Rainey said crossly, 'All right, all right! I'm awake.'

Half an hour later Jo saw Rainey pedalling off on her bicycle down Albert Street to catch the night shift as they left Priddy's munitions factory.

Jo shouted, 'I'll keep my fingers crossed you find Annette's mum.'

Rainey yelled back, 'I'll have more luck doing that than Blackie has of getting Tom Marks's cheque in the post!'

19

Madame Nellie Walker's voice was firm. 'I've made arrangements with Lloyd's to allow you money when you need it. You'll reimburse Charlie Smith, the photographer, at the Central Café on the following Wednesday after he has shown you the proofs of the Bluebirds. I'll trust you and Charlie to pick the best. Cash you receive from pubs and clubs during the next week or so should hopefully pay your immediate needs while Blackie's absent. He has assured me he'll keep in touch with you.' She was detailing proposed venues for the girls while Blackie was away. 'Maud's son, Eddie, has been engaged to drive you to venues.'

'But we won't have a pianist,' Jo said. Blackie played for them, and the girls wouldn't be at their best without accompaniment.

'Quite so, but I've booked a three-piece ensemble that will fit the bill admirably. At each venue they should be set up when you arrive.'

Jo breathed a sigh of relief. She would cope on her own while Blackie was in Birmingham, with Little Annette's mother, Florrie, because, obviously, Nellie Walker had complete faith in her!

'Everything should be back on track before Easter when the Coliseum in Portsmouth will receive the girls for a week's engagement. I've also negotiated with Geraldo at the Savoy for the Bluebirds to take over the vocalist's spot while his resident female singer is occupied elsewhere. This is not a long engagement, but it will be broadcast.'

'On the wireless?' Jo's voice had risen to a squeak of surprise.

'Of course the wireless, my dear.' Nellie Walker gave a soft laugh. 'I would advise that you all keep on the right side of Geraldo while in London. He's a *tour de force* with ENSA.'

Jo said goodbye to Madame, replaced the receiver and sat down on the chair nearest the range while she took in all that Nellie Walker's phone call had imparted. Before she'd had time to think everything through, Rainey clattered downstairs.

'Who was that, Mum?'

'Nellie Walker,' muttered Jo, her head still reeling.

'Did she say how Little Annette was?'

Jo shook her head. 'I don't think there's any change there. Blackie's on his way back to Birmingham with her mother. It seems that theatrical folk all pull together in an emergency. Apparently, Annette was dug out from the rubble unconscious after being trapped with an employee from the club. She begged the woman, who was not as seriously hurt, to contact Madame Walker. Annette's in a bad way.'

'You haven't heard when Blackie will be back?'

'No. I'm to take charge.'

'Good.' Rainey's mouth widened to a smile. 'When's our first date?'

'Tomorrow night at the Black Bear in town.'

Rainey's smile dropped. 'Oh! That's not a

140

joke, is it? We really are singing tomorrow?'

Jo nodded. 'Put the kettle on, love. You'll need a cuppa when I tell you you're going on the wireless as well!'

★ ★ ★

The ruin that had once been the Rainbow Club reminded Blackie of a marble mountain. The rain glancing off the white stone was bringing with it dirt and brick dust from the air. The once palatial Arabian-style building was now no more than a huge pile of discoloured rubble.

It was difficult to imagine anyone had come out of that alive, Blackie thought, but a few lucky people had survived. He doubted very much that Annette thought herself lucky. What good was a dancer who had lost a leg?

He'd left Florrie, her mother, at the hospital bedside. The doctors said there was a good chance Annette would survive her injuries. Physically, it was possible; mentally was another thing. Annette was driven to succeed in her career. The only good to have come from all this was that mother and daughter were reunited.

'Blackie!'

He turned.

'Thought I'd find you here now the salvage workers have gone.' Florrie's faded hair was plastered wetly to her head but her bun still sported the glittery decorative pins she favoured.

'I thought you'd be at the hospital?'

'She's in and out of consciousness. I was told it would be a good time to go back to the

141

boarding-house to eat and sleep for a while.'

Blackie put his arm around Florrie's thin shoulders. She reminded him of a newly hatched bird, scrawny, pale and almost fleshless.

'I can't thank you enough for all you've done,' she said.

'Who else are you going to turn to but your best friend's son?' he said. He remembered her as a fashionable, pretty blonde in a fringed flapper dress holding a glass of bubbly as his own mother, Dandi, stepped down the wide stairs at the Alhambra Theatre on the arm of his father to greet Florrie. Dandi had practically jumped into Florrie's arms. He remembered his mother saying, 'When you've been to infants' school with a friend, you know them inside out.'

Back then Dandi and William Wilson were the darlings of Portsmouth's variety shows. Later, Little Annette was making a name for herself but was sadly estranged from Florrie. Blackie was a very small boy, who thought all the world lived at parties, dressed in pretty clothes and laughed. That had ended when the car accident killed his parents.

'Let's get inside out of this damned rain,' he said now, pulling Florrie towards the open door of a pub.

A port and lemon for her and a pint of ale for himself helped him to think more clearly. Steam rose from their wet clothes as the fire warmed them. He took off his hat and put it on the table.

He'd asked her if she wanted something to eat but the curled-up sandwiches behind the glass counter tempted neither of them.

Florrie put down her glass, opened her handbag, took out a handkerchief and wiped her face. He wasn't sure if the dampness came from tears or rain. Her skin had been yellowed by the dangerous powder she worked with at the munitions factory. 'I'm going to stop up here until I know what's happening with my girl,' she said. 'She won't thank me for it but we need each other now. One thing I do know, she'll be vile to me.' They managed a grim smile. Annette's temper was legendary.

Florrie's face also told of the life she'd led. Every line could probably tell a story, he thought. He wondered how his mother would have looked at Florrie's age and tried to dispel the sadness the thought provoked.

'Are you listening to me?' She prodded his knee.

He nodded.

'There's no need for you to babysit me,' she said, tucking the handkerchief up her sleeve. 'I'll be all right. She's not coming out any time soon.'

'How will you manage?'

'I've got a bit put by, Blackie. And Madame's made me promise to ask.' Then she said brightly, 'You need to get back to those three pretty girls. They're going to be big, aren't they?'

'I hope so,' Blackie said.

'Any luck with the wages you're owed?'

'I'll not see Tom Marks's money,' he replied, 'and I despise myself for begging handouts from Madame.'

Florrie shook her head. 'She's only too glad to help. She and Herbert think the world of you.

They're behind you all the way.'

He wanted to confide in her, tell her he'd gambled again and lost personal money, but he didn't. She had her own problems and they were more than he could ever bear. He stood up, bent forward and kissed the top of her head. 'You know where I am,' he said, tipping his hat back onto his curls.

Outside, the rain hadn't let up. More than anything he wanted to be sitting in Jo's kitchen in the threadbare chair near the range, listening to her sing as she cooked in the spotless scullery. To him, Jo was like an oasis in the desert.

20

Sunshine wiped the sweat from her forehead with the back of her hand. The windows were running with condensation from the pots bubbling on the huge range. Every so often another cloud of steam would burst forth as a kitchen hand lifted a lid. Why on earth had she decided to take on a job that she hated?

At the tap above the sink, she cupped her hands and drank. As the water cooled her face and throat, she reminded herself she knew very well why she'd decided to work part-time in the St Vincent kitchens, preparing and serving food. It wasn't for the officers in the training establishment of the Fleet Air Arm or the torpedo training section or even for the German prisoners sectioned off in the Nissen huts down near the creek. She'd taken this job to be near Max.

She rubbed at the window. Now she could see the V of colour that was crocuses in full bloom in the garden square he tended so carefully. Around the edges in the brown earth, daffodils, their petals closely furled, were waiting to burst into glorious yellow. Just looking at something Max loved made her feel better. She glanced at the wooden wall clock. Another few minutes and she would see him walk past the garden plot. Later she could take the wicker basket she used for collecting perishable food and make her way to the sheds. She hoped he'd be alone today. Hans dogged his footsteps. If the young German was there she would stay in the hot kitchens and hope tomorrow would be different.

When she and Max were alone in the shed they would often make gentle fun of Hans's obsession with him. Max couldn't forbid the impressionable boy to follow him during his gardening duties, but no one could know of Sunshine and Max's meetings.

A pan clattered to the stone floor, dropped by one of the other workers. Sometimes the noise and smell in the kitchen was almost more than she could bear. Rats prowled the store cupboards; mice left faeces in dishes. The discomfort was worth the precious time Sunshine spent with Max because she longed to be with him. He was unlike any man she'd known before.

She liked to watch his beautiful lips move as he whispered to her of his parents' farm, his country and his hopes for their future together. 'They will treat you like a goddess,' he had said, 'because you are the choice of their first-born son.' He would inherit the farm, he had told her, and their children would follow in his footsteps. She listened, hypnotized. No man had ever talked of such things before, of the love he had for her. Of how beautiful she would look on her wedding day in Germany. Of how their love would grow with each passing year. He was going to give her the life she'd dreamt of, which no man had ever offered her before. Her belief in him was unshakeable so she gave him in return the one thing she valued most: her virginity.

Their lovemaking was often hurried but afterwards Max would murmur in her ear of his desire for her, and when he kissed her, she trembled at the electricity in his fingers as they roved over her skin.

'It's unbearable to have to wait until the war is over before I can take you back to Pulheim,' he moaned. His lips moved over her, kissing, sucking, pressing.

At night, alone in her bedroom at Lavinia House, Sunshine wept silent tears for Max and their forbidden love. She had seen little of Eddie because working at two jobs left her too tired for much else. And now Eddie's days were spent working in Gosport and his nights driving the Bluebirds to their various venues.

'I can't afford to turn down the extra money,' he'd told her. Oh, she knew he still cared for her but the intensity of those first meetings they'd shared had burned itself out and only the glow of friendship remained.

Sunshine couldn't believe that in such a short while the answer to her dreams had appeared in the form of England's enemy. But Max wasn't her enemy: he was simply a man far from home, who had been captured fighting for his country. That she had fallen for him in such a short time only proved to her that he was indeed the man she had been waiting for her whole life.

The kitchens at St Vincent were a hive of industry. The sinks were full of clattering crockery, laughter and ribald comments batted back and forth, and all the while Sunshine watched and waited.

And then she saw him, walking past the cookhouse windows. His legs were strong, his back was broad and in the brightness of the day his blondness was as a lure to her. He was alone. She breathed a sigh of anticipation. She turned quickly from the window lest anyone catch her watching. She gave him time to disappear around the side buildings, then collected her basket and went outside where the spring sun was vainly trying to warm the cobbles.

When Sunshine reached the shed it looked deserted, except for the missing padlock. She pushed open the door and went inside. As her eyes became accustomed to the dark she made out Max lying on the used potato sacks. He had made a nest for them. She put the basket to one side and sank to the floor to be with him. Moments passed when neither spoke but she heard his breathing, steady, rhythmic. Then his hand came reassuringly to the small of her back. Suddenly he pulled it away. She felt somehow cheated. It was as if he had stopped wanting her.

'What's the matter?' Her voice was low.

'I don't know that I dare go on meeting you like this.' He looked away from her. This was not the welcome she'd expected.

Her heart felt as if it had been flattened by a stone.

Then, though she had barely digested his words, his arms snaked around her and he pulled her tightly to his body. She could hardly breathe.

'If you knew how much I long to be with you . . . ' He groaned.

And then he was kissing her, his tongue exploring her mouth as though he was healing the damage his words had caused. He pulled away again and stared into her eyes.

'I want you to run away with me,' he said.

Sunshine allowed the words to settle in her brain. Finally, 'How is that possible?' she asked.

'I have heard of a man who lives in Gosport who will provide papers.'

She wanted to laugh — not to mock him, but the idea seemed ridiculous. 'You have money to buy them? You can tell this man what you need when you're guarded day and night?'

'You can see him for me.'

Sunshine let out a long breath.

He spoke again. 'We can leave Gosport, get a boat across the Irish Sea. We can be together, you and me. When my countrymen invade Ireland, as I'm sure they eventually will, we can go to Germany to my parents' farm in Pulheim . . . '

Sunshine could feel and hear the excitement in his voice. His fingers were digging into her flesh as though urging her to consider his plan.

'I need to be with you for more than these stolen moments.' He paused. 'You don't know what it's like for me, knowing you're so near in this same town and I'm unable to be with you. I feel as though I'm going mad in this place.'

She could feel his tears wet against her bare breast. 'If only it was possible we could be together,' she murmured. How wonderful it

149

would be to lie in his arms every night. 'This man,' Sunshine asked, 'has he done this for other prisoners?'

'Yes.'

'I have a little money, probably not enough.'

'He will help us.' Sunshine liked it that Max had said 'us'. It meant he thought of them as a single unit. He talked long and often of how they could marry when the war was over. Of the lace his mother would use for sewing her dress. And of the local church where his family worshipped and where later their children would be baptized.

If this Gosport man could provide Max with the necessary papers there would be other, similar men in Ireland who could surely provide further necessary papers for her to continue with him to Germany after the invasion occurred . . .

'Who is this Gosport man?' she asked. 'I can go and see him.'

Max stared at her. 'Perhaps it's better you don't help. I don't want you to do anything against the law. I love you too much for that.'

'And I love you. So tell me where I can find this man. The sooner we leave together for Ireland, the sooner we can be together.'

21

Charlie Smith tapped his fingers impatiently on the Formica counter of Bert's café. Then he traced a tea stain with his thumbnail. He didn't like to be kept waiting, even though he was being paid for it.

'She shouldn't be much longer,' said Bert, wiping his greasy hands on his apron. 'Would you like another cup of tea?'

Charlie Smith shook his head and looked at Ivy and Bea, two of the three singers he was supposed to be photographing in front of the backdrops he had spent all morning preparing in one of Bert's unused rooms above the café.

'Time's money and money's short,' he grumbled. Charlie felt his time waiting for the prima donna to arrive could have been better spent helping his staff clear his shop in Stoke Road. 'I've had to discard stock damaged last night in the raid. A bomb fell near the studio. My front window shattered in the blast. Sincere thanks to you, Bert, for allowing me to use your premises.'

Bert waved away his thanks. 'These girls,' he pointed in the direction of the table where Ivy and Bea, in their air-force costumes, sat chatting, 'are going to be famous and I'm proud to be involved with them.' He gave a throaty cough into his pristine white handkerchief, then tucked it into his pocket. During the Great War he'd caught a dose of gas and every so often his chest reminded him of it. 'Jo's a stickler for time but she'll have had to wait for the bus. Bea's brother Eddie's been running them about in his van while Blackie's otherwise engaged, but he's had to do some repair work on the town hall today, courtesy of yesterday's dose of bombs. Bea stayed here last night. Tell you what,' said Bert, picking up a long-handled spoon and giving the fragrant contents of a huge pan on a low gas a stir, 'why don't you have a taste of my rabbit stew? It's very popular with my customers.'

Charlie shook his head. He wanted to start and finish the project in hand, not eat. He already knew the blonde had spent the night with her pal. Both girls had been more than willing to fetch and carry for him when he'd arrived earlier. He usually had at least one of his staff to help bring in equipment from his 1939 Singer Bantam 9 van. He was extremely proud that he'd recently had his name and profession sign-written in black on its green body. Yes, he'd come a long way since the early days when he'd accosted holiday-makers, cajoling them into buying the snaps he'd taken of them walking along the front at Southsea.

He'd had to have the gift of the gab back then to make a living. But he'd used it to good advantage and he'd progressed to a large shop in Gosport, with a darkroom at the back. Luckily the bomb blast hadn't touched that. He hoped through hard work, even with this setback, he could go on being lucky, as he was establishing a fine reputation for photography. It wasn't easy

152

and he worked long hours. Waiting around like this was getting on his nerves.

He slipped from the stool and went over to the door, peering into the busy street. The fresh smell of flowers, mingled with the processed scent of bath salts on the market stalls, assailed his senses. Gosport was busy today. He thought Bert might be getting agitated too. After all, it was market day and he had closed the café for the photo shoot. The longer they waited for the two women to arrive the more money Bert, too, was losing.

Charlie caught a reflection of himself in the window. Barely five feet five inches in his shoes, he was never despondent about his lack of height but his image still came as a shock. He cursed himself for he knew he should be getting used to the way he'd changed since Dunkirk. Like Blackie, he'd been lucky to get out alive, but a bullet to his ankle had left him with a limp and he'd been invalided out of the army.

Charlie ran his fingers through his thick grey hair, which in places was turning white. The doctors had said that shock sometimes caused it. Not that he worried about his looks: he had his shop, his van and money in the bank to buy a decent house some day. In the meantime he lived over his shop. Convenient for him: when he wasn't out and about taking images, he was usually to be found in the darkroom helping his assistants develop them.

So deeply was he thinking about his business that he started when a woman's voice said, 'Excuse me, we need to get inside and you're blocking the doorway!' He was quite affronted to think he was causing an obstruction.

Charlie's eyes narrowed at the two women before him. It was the younger one who had spoken. He caught a hint of her scent, fresh, invigorating. One look at her left him in no doubt that she was the third Bluebird.

'So, you've got here then?' he said, standing aside so they could enter.

'I don't really mind you being late. I'm getting paid by the hour so it's your money you're wasting!'

The elder of the two stifled a giggle, and as the door closed on the three of them, she said, 'Sorry about the delay. The usual bus didn't arrive, held up apparently by masonry falling in Forton Road. That raid did a lot of damage.'

Bert had elbowed his way forward. 'Come on in, Jo and Rainey. This is Charlie Smith, best photographer around these parts.'

'And possibly one of the rudest,' Rainey said.

Charlie looked straight into the girl's green eyes. In her two-inch heels she was the same height as him and he saw the glitter of amusement. He smiled at her, saw her relax and his smile turned into a laugh.

'Very quick-witted,' he said.

Bert slid the bolt across the door, saying, 'Let's get this show on the road.' Then followed his stock question to any newcomer or visitor: 'Cup of tea, Rainey, Jo?'

Both women shook their heads.

'For God's sake, Bert, don't start up all that tea drinking again. I'll never get out of here,'

154

Charlie said. 'I've a wedding to attend later today.'

'Surely not your own.' Rainey's sarcasm wasn't lost on Charlie.

'Ha-ha! I see we have a comedienne in our midst!' he said, with another grin at her.

'No. Just a singer waiting to be photographed before she joins the others and goes out again later to pay your wages!'

Charlie thought he'd probably met his match. He was still laughing as he led the way up the uncarpeted wooden stairs to the large room above the café where he'd set up a painted backcloth to resemble part of an airfield's hangar. He'd thought it apt for pictures of the girls in their uniforms.

He watched Rainey remove a gabardine raincoat and hand it to Jo, who was also clutching a large brown carrier bag with string handles. He was pleased to see Rainey was already dressed in her air-force outfit. At least that would save some time. He guessed the bag contained the second outfit he had been asked to photograph the girls in. He gasped as Rainey shook her mane of auburn hair free from the confines of a headscarf. Her loveliness stunned him. He could barely get out his next words. 'There's a full-length looking glass over in the corner for any last-minute alterations you three might want to make to your clothing.'

For the second picture he'd made up a backcloth showing a nightclub scene with customers sitting at tables watching the Blue-birds at a microphone. He'd already set up the lighting apparatus and merely needed to check with the girls in their designated places. Then he could begin.

He watched Bert, Jo and Ivy's mother, Della, move towards some chairs so they could sit and watch the proceedings. Jo had handed Rainey a small case filled with hairbrushes and various articles of make-up. Rainey brushed out her hair then shook it so it settled naturally in long waves. Charlie was spellbound. She glanced at herself in the long mirror and turned to make sure her stocking seams were straight. He wanted to say, 'I'm not photographing the backs of your legs,' but he resisted the temptation. He suddenly realized she might find it embarrassing to find him watching so he looked away.

For some reason he felt he could gladly have stood and watched Rainey all day every day. That in itself was a shock to his system. He'd had his fair share of women — his lack of height didn't seem to bother them. However, he soon became bored by the silliness of some girls who thought a man needed a woman who acquiesced to everything asked of her. He had given up on finding one who would answer him back, a woman who had a mind and will of her own and wasn't afraid to use them.

He noted that Bea and Ivy gave themselves a cursory glance in the mirror, then moved towards the upturned mock shell cases he'd set up earlier. He'd thought some prints of the girls sitting at different heights might make for a better photograph. He liked to suggest movement in his portraits as against the stock 'set-up'

156

poses some photographers favoured. The height of the boxes meant the girls would sit and show their legs to best advantage. Blackie had stipulated the photographs must advertise the girls tastefully yet inform prospective employers that they were getting their money's worth.

'Who do you want in the middle?' Jo asked.

'Blonde Bea, I think. It'll make for a good balance.'

Bea moved to the centre and sat. Ivy and Rainey perched either side of her.

'It would help if you all posed with your knees in the same direction.' Charlie pulled a face. 'I can tell you're not used to doing this,' he said. 'At present you look like a mass of stick insects, with arms and legs at all angles!' He moved in front of the girls, tucking stray clothing out of the way and spacing their caps at the proper heights so that their faces wouldn't be in shadow.

At Rainey's cap, his hand shook as he moved it back a little over her forehead and hair. As his fingers made contact with her skin he felt as though a needle had pierced him, making him sizzle. She stared into his eyes and he knew she had felt 'it', whatever 'it' was, too. He stepped away from her. His heart was beating so loudly he was sure not only Rainey but all three girls could hear it.

When at last he was satisfied he could photograph the three beauties before him and do them justice, he went to one of the cameras on the tripods he'd previously set up and began the process of taking shots of them. Smiling, grinning, thoughtful poses, pouting and laughing, his camera loved every angle of them. Eventually he said, 'All right. Now you need to change, girls, and we'll do some nightclub scenes.'

Charlie looked across at Bert. 'While they're in another room getting dressed for the next set, I could murder a cuppa, Bert.'

He was quite surprised when Bert answered, 'We'll have to wait for tea, Charlie. These girls are masters at changing their clothes. They'll be back in two ticks, you mark my words.' And all three returned to the room in no time at all.

'I want you to stand as you do when you're on a stage and I'd like to try for a shot as though you're singing.'

He thought they looked like film stars in the blue dresses they'd chosen to wear. Of course, the stills would be in monochrome but how he wished he could do justice in colour to Rainey's glorious hair and sea-green eyes.

Behind the camera Charlie began to laugh.

'What's the matter?' Jo looked perturbed.

Charlie stopped laughing long enough to say, 'Perhaps it might be better if you three girls really do sing out loud. I can't take a shot with you looking like goldfish gulping. I need synchronization.'

'Let's sing 'The Bluebird Song',' Bea said. 'We don't need music for that.'

The sound that came from their throats made Charlie want to cry with its sadness and beauty. He went on taking shots, noting that his backdrop, brilliant though it was, was simply a frame for three of the most talented and gorgeous young singers he had ever heard in his life.

Charlie felt as if he could watch Rainey for ever through a lens, but at last he clicked the final shot and said, 'Get up, Jo, Bert and Della, and stand with the girls. This one's a shot for the family album.'

Bert added, 'Then I think we're all ready for a cuppa!'

22

'I have to thank you for allowing the photographer to use these premises, Bert.'

Blackie sipped the tar-like substance he'd been given. One day, he thought, he really must let Bert know he preferred his tea a little less strong.

'Weren't no bother. Least I could do. The poor bugger's shop got caught in a bomb blast.' Bert took off his glasses and rubbed the smeared lenses on the bottom of his apron. Blackie saw he had added another piece of sticking plaster to the broken arm. The wireless high on the shelf was playing dance music. There were only a few customers sitting in the café. Blackie could smell freshly cooked bacon cutting through the fug of old tobacco smoke.

He bent down and scooped up the gift for Bert, wrapped in newspaper, and slapped it on the counter. 'I saw this and thought of you, my friend,' he said.

Bert grinned, showing his tombstone teeth. 'That's good of you, mate. What is it?'

'Open it and see.' He watched as Bert pushed his spectacles back on his nose and began to unroll the parcel. Blackie wanted to smile.

Bert couldn't conceal his joy as he tore off the paper. 'Oh!' He let out a sigh of pure happiness. 'Where the hell did you find this?'

A lacquered walking stick emerged from the newsprint. Around the handle and slithering down the stick were two entwined carved snakes. Bert stared at it as though it might disappear at any moment. 'It's a folk-art stick,' he said. 'Very old, and I bet it could tell a few stories.'

'Don't know about that,' said Blackie. 'I saw it in a secondhand shop in Birmingham and thought of you, you being a collector, a rabdophilist. I hope you haven't already got one like it.'

'No, no, this is a real find. Foreign, of course,' Bert added. 'I can't thank you enough, young feller.'

Blackie couldn't see it but he knew it was there: the German swordstick Bert kept behind the counter to ward off troublesome customers. He'd used it a few times too.

Bert was happily examining his new stick. 'You know when they opened that King Tut's tomb they found one hundred and thirty-nine walking sticks, put there to help him in the afterlife.'

If he didn't leave now, Blackie thought, it would be too late to knock on Jo's door. He badly wanted to see her and catch up on all the news. No doubt she'd ask after Little Annette. Already he was weary after the drive back south. He also knew there would be no stopping Bert once he got really into the swing of telling him about canes and sticks and King Tutankhamun. Bert's passion knew no bounds.

'I must make a move, Bert. I came to you first and I want to catch Jo before she goes to bed.'

'Of course. She coped well with the girls singing at the local pubs while you were away. The photos should be back soon from Charlie

Smith.' He cackled. 'Funny little bloke, strutting around like a demented bantam. But he knows his stuff, and when you sends out them photographs to people likely to employ the girls, they'll all jump at the chance to have 'em appear on their premises.'

Bert's voice tailed off. He stared at Blackie.

'There is one thing . . . I may be talking out of turn but I 'ad a visitor in the week.' Bert sucked his lips. 'A little blonde girly came in here asking about Jim an' his girls' place near the ferry. I saw her walking up and down outside plucking up the courage to come in.'

Blackie began to wonder where this was leading. He knew Della, Ivy's mother, had managed to get out of the clutches of a man who ran a Gosport brothel, but what had this to do with him? Of course, Bert was a mine of information about what went on in the underbelly of Gosport. Blackie was just about to insist he must go when Bert added, 'This Jim 'as a finger in every pie in Gosport, not just women an' the black-market but other stuff as well — dangerous stuff. It's said 'is boss is that London criminal feller Billy Hill, him what runs protection rackets and dishes out extreme violence.' Bert had paused for his words to have the desired effect.

'What do you mean, Bert?'

'I told her where she could find Jim. She didn't tell me what she wanted 'im for an' I didn't ask. When she'd gone, I racked my brain trying to remember where I'd seen her before. Finally, it came to me. She's the girl we met the night the Bluebird Girls first appeared at the King's Theatre. The girly young Bea's brother, Eddie, is keen on . . . '

Blackie was beginning to think Bert's neighbourliness was bordering on nosiness. He vaguely remembered the girl, a slight young thing. Then he remembered Ivy had been quite put out by the girl's presence with Eddie.

'So what are you telling me, Bert?' Blackie thought he'd ask the question but he believed he already knew the answer for Bert's concern.

Bert had had a big hand in making sure Della got out of a life of prostitution so that no scandal could fall on the Bluebird Girls. Eddie's girlfriend was asking after Jim, a notorious local hard man. Why?

Anything that affected her affected Eddie and might, only might, stop Blackie's beloved Bluebird Girls from becoming the successful trio they deserved to be.

Blackie put his hand on the older man's shoulder. 'Thanks for telling me, Bert. I'd better keep my eyes and ears open.'

*　*　*

Blackie drove along Forton Road, saddened by the sight of the bomb damage. It was the ordinary people who suffered every time, he thought, and no doubt our bombers were causing just as much destruction and heartache to the Germans. A huge crater lay opposite the Criterion Picture House but it was business as usual there.

He'd thought long and hard about Bert's news and decided he wouldn't speak about it with Jo but would keep tabs on what was happening with Bea's brother and the girl — Sunshine, yes, that was her name.

It had been his idea for Eddie to run the Bluebirds to their local venues while he himself was in Birmingham. Not only did he trust Eddie but he liked him. He was a dependable man, a hard worker, too. No wonder Ivy had set her cap at him.

He was pleased Bert didn't already have a walking stick decorated with snakes. Blackie had been crossing the road near the Birmingham hospital when he'd spotted it in the window of the second-hand shop. He liked to buy small gifts for his friends. There'd been some beautiful costume jewellery lying on a velvet cloth in the shop and he'd had to stop himself buying it for Jo — women could be funny about accepting gifts. He didn't want to offend her.

It had been hard leaving Florrie in Birmingham. She certainly had her work cut out, looking after her daughter, Annette. Annette's temper wasn't going to improve any day soon and he thought Florrie had the patience of a saint, loving her the way she did. Perhaps being together again would heal the rift between them. The pair certainly needed each other now.

As he signalled, then turned his car into Albert Street, he saw Syd Kennedy's van parked outside number fourteen. A stab of jealousy pierced his chest.

He should have telephoned Jo first to let her

know he was coming to Gosport but he'd been so excited about seeing her again he'd thought he'd surprise her. Should he turn around and go home to Portsmouth? Let Syd Kennedy and Jo enjoy what was left of their evening together? He hated to admit he was jealous of the red-haired garage owner. But Syd Kennedy had been there for Jo when she'd been at her lowest ebb after running away from her vile husband. Blackie couldn't rewrite the past. Jo would say she had a good friend in Syd Kennedy and was quite open about the phone calls she made to him and the letters they exchanged. Blackie hoped their friendship would never blossom into anything more.

He thought again of that night in Birmingham at the Rainbow Club when he'd stupidly lost his own money gambling and was tempted to start on the little accumulated by the Bluebirds' hard work. How he'd pulled back at the last moment he'd never know, but when he'd been pacing up and down in his bedroom and Jo had entered, she'd been the tower of strength that had kept him from falling to pieces.

Even now it pained him to think he'd begged her to stay and hold him through the night so he could get some measure of peace. He'd make it up to her. And so he should. Just look at the way he'd left her this past week to look after the girls, make sure they arrived at venues on time and deal with Charlie Smith.

Jo was never far from Blackie's thoughts and now he needed to see her, wanted to look at her charming smile. No, he wouldn't go home to

Portsmouth. He pulled up and parked his car behind Syd's van.

The smile he'd waited for was on her lips as she opened the door.

'Come in, come in,' she said. 'Lovely that you're back.'

'Is it too late for me to come calling?'

'Not at all. The girls are spending the night round Maud's, annoying her with Bea's gramophone.' She added, 'Syd's here. We've been to the pictures to see George Formby.'

Oh, he could see Syd was there, sitting in 'his' favourite armchair by the range!

'Hello, Syd,' Blackie said, with jollity he didn't feel. 'Good film?'

'Oh, yes,' said Syd. '*Spare a Copper*. George up to his usual tricks.'

'This is the first night me and the girls have had a minute to ourselves,' said Jo. 'Do you want a cuppa?'

'No, thanks,' said Blackie. He decided to take his coat off to let Syd know he hoped to stay awhile. 'I'm awash with tea — just come from the café. I wanted to apologize for leaving you with a heavy workload while I disappeared back to Birmingham with Florrie to reunite her with Annette.'

'I've enjoyed looking after the girls. The three-piece band turned up on time each night and we all got on well together. Eddie's been an absolute brick running us all about.'

'Does that mean you don't need me any more?'

Blackie saw her beautiful green eyes flash. 'I

166

never said that!' She laughed. He saw Syd's face darken, which made him momentarily happy. 'I've paid everyone who needed to be paid,' she went on, 'and the bars and pubs the girls sang at paid me in cash. I've kept a note for you of all money coming in and going out. The next engagement is the Coliseum in Portsmouth, then at Easter, London.' She paused. 'I'm excited about the wireless recording with Geraldo, and a bit nervous. I'm glad you'll be with us.'

He could see Syd was a little miffed that he wasn't included in the conversation.

'You had a good gossip at the photo shoot, then?' Blackie said. She looked lovely tonight, he thought. Her eyes were all sparkly — and was that a new dress she had on? Possibly not, he thought. New clothing was hard to come by but she definitely had a certain liveliness about her he hadn't noticed in a while.

'How long have you known that Charlie Smith?' Jo asked. She knelt before the range and, with the poker, riddled out the ashes.

Blackie threw his coat over the back of a chair and sat down. 'A long, long time. He's thoroughly dependable. I was thinking of asking him to come along to some of the bigger shows booked up for the girls. I'd like him to take photographs at big venues, all good publicity.'

Jo let the poker drop. 'Better watch out for him, then. He and my Rainey were catching sparks off each other. All that night she did nothing but talk about him.'

'She could do worse,' said Blackie. He thought about Charlie's tough upbringing. 'Beneath all the bluster, he's a good bloke. Has he come round with the proofs yet?'

Jo shook her head. 'Next week, he said.' Then she began to laugh. 'D'you know what Rainey said about him?' Blackie saw Syd shake his head.

'What?' asked Blackie.

'She said he reminds her of Alice Wilkes's dog, Toto, all bluster and bark! She said he's even nearly got the same colour hair!'

Blackie chuckled. Eventually he added, 'She's young — she'll meet all sorts. Actors and artists are a breed apart. And photographers.'

'Not my Rainey,' said Jo. Her face was suddenly sad, her voice quiet, as she confided, 'She never got over how her father could say he loved us but treat us so badly. That episode with Tom Marks was like another nail in a coffin for her.' She paused. 'It's my fault she doesn't trust men.'

'Don't upset yourself,' broke in Syd. 'It wasn't your fault you picked a bad 'un.'

Jo used her fingers to wipe the corners of her eyes. 'I never thought it would colour the way she sees men, though.'

'I thought you said Charlie Smith made her laugh.' Blackie didn't like to see Jo so emotional. He ferreted in his suit pocket and brought out a clean handkerchief, which he pressed into her hand. He didn't want to give it to her to use: he wanted to dry her tears for her. He watched as she wiped her eyes and composed herself. She smiled as she handed back the handkerchief. He knew he would always keep safe that piece of linen with her fresh tears on it.

Jo swallowed. 'It wasn't so much he made her laugh but that she felt she could be herself with him. She said he talked to her, not at her. In fact, much later that night she told me it was the very first time a man had made her feel necessary to him.'

★   ★   ★

As he drove back to Portsmouth, Blackie remembered Jo's words. Rainey could do a lot worse than fall for a decent bloke like Charlie. He would worship the ground she walked on.

He smiled to himself, remembering how Jo had sent him and Syd simultaneously from her warm home into the cold street and waved to them as they drove away.

23

'Two shows a night for a week would make anyone feel worn out.' Bea was sprawled over an armchair with its horsehair stuffing hanging out. Dressed in grey slacks and a green puff-sleeve jumper, her stage outfits on hangers draped across the back of the chair, she couldn't wait to get home to bed.

Rainey and Ivy were still getting dressed. The three girls weren't the only inhabitants of the large changing room. It was noisy with raucous laughter. Around them pretty girls were putting on their clothes, eager to be away from the Coliseum in Portsmouth's Queen Street. The air smelled of perfume, sweat, make-up and something more, Bea thought. Hope. Yes, that was it. All these girls packed together, like sardines in a tin, were hoping for stardom.

'Young thing like you shouldn't be tired! I'm nearly twice your age and I'm going out to dinner with that chap in the fourth row!'

'Ah, well, Maisie, I've got to protect these girls' honour,' Jo was quick to say to Maisie Redfern, the mesmerist's assistant. 'You don't need to worry about yours!'

'Cheeky,' sang out Maisie, as she threw a fox fur around her shoulders, then disappeared out of the door.

Jo laughed and said to Rainey, who was fastening her suspenders, her foot resting on a wooden stool, 'You don't mind that I take you all straight home, do you?'

Ivy answered swiftly, 'I should say not. I feel like I'm learning about the stage and the theatre all the time. But I'm shattered. It's been a lovely week and some of the acts appearing with us have been terrific. But we've still got to practise the different songs for the Savoy Hotel.'

'You did really well with 'Roses of Picardy', Bea,' interrupted Rainey. 'You were almost crying when you sang the last verse.' Now in a black skirt and black jumper, with tiny pearls sewn around the neckline, she bent down and gave Bea a hug. 'I don't think I've ever heard that Great War tune sung with so much feeling,' she said.

Bea smiled into Rainey's face. 'Thank you. It hurts my heart when I sing it.'

'You certainly do it justice,' said Jo. Bea saw she had stopped stuffing high-heeled shoes into a brown carrier bag long enough to look at the bouquets piled in the old stone sink. Their scent added to the smells in the dressing room. There was hardly a night went by that sprays of flowers weren't sent for the Bluebirds.

'Maisie didn't like it that she didn't get a bunch tonight,' said Ivy. 'Still, I suppose she'd rather go out with that soldier instead.'

'Which would you rather have, Bea? Flowers or a night out in Portsmouth with a man?' Ivy asked.

'No men for me,' snapped Bea. 'I want to sing to hundreds of them and I want them all to want me, but I'll still go home alone.'

Jo shook her head.

Bea knew she didn't like to hear her talk like that. Changing the subject, she asked, 'What shall we do with all the flowers?'

'When we get back to Gosport we could drop them off at the War Memorial Hospital,' said Ivy. 'They could cheer up the patients.'

'Good idea,' said Bea. 'My mum says we've so many flowers indoors it looks and smells like a funeral parlour!'

'It's been nice meeting you,' said one of four chorus girls, just leaving. 'I know you'll be a big success.' She held the door open for her mates.

'Thanks, Jenny,' said Ivy. 'I hope you get that part in the play.'

There were hugs and kisses, and the door banged again and again as the other girls shouted their goodbyes and left.

'Ready?' Jo asked.

Bea watched Rainey peer down through the dirty curtainless window. 'Blackie's here,' she said. 'His car's just pulled up outside on the road.'

'Give us a hand with all the flowers,' Ivy said. 'Ugh, all the stems are wet.'

Bea was the last one out, letting the door slam shut behind them. She watched Rainey and Ivy giggling as they struggled with dripping blooms and bagged costumes. Jo, her pretty face serious, was looking forward to telling Blackie all the dressing-room gossip, Bea thought. She turned and, for a single moment, looked at the scruffy closed door to the room that had witnessed fear, tears and happiness for them during the past week. The Bluebirds were on their way up now. Was that what she really wanted? Memorizing new songs, being tired most of the time, eating at odd hours, just to stand on a stage and sing her heart out?

Of course it was.

★   ★   ★

'If you're looking for Sunshine, lad, she's not here.'

Solomon coughed into his handkerchief and Eddie waited until the fit ended, the old man breathing heavily, before he dared speak. 'I can pop in to see you, can't I?' He stared around the small room, noting how comfortable and warm it was. A big family photograph taken last Christmas stood on the sideboard. Eddie couldn't see himself, then remembered he'd taken the snapshot with the old Kodak Box Brownie just before tea-time.

Solomon stuffed his hanky into his pocket, took as deep a breath as he was able and wheezed, 'You're welcome any time. But, I tell you, now that girl has the other job down St Vincent Barracks we don't see the goings of her. When was the last time you took her out?'

Eddie scratched his head. He'd expected an inquisition from his grandfather. 'I dunno,' he said. 'A while now, before Blackie asked me to ferry the girls about in my van.'

'There you are, then. A good few weeks ago. And when I've caught sight of her doing a bit of dusting hereabouts she looks as though she's gone ten rounds with that American boxer I've heard on the wireless, Sugar Ray Robinson. Dark circles round her eyes an' she's lost weight an' she didn't 'ave any to lose in the first place.'

Eddie broke in, 'I came to see you, Granddad.'

Solomon sniffed. 'Well, that's very nice of you, lad. How's your mother?'

'Fine,' said Eddie. He wasn't going to tell his granddad Maud had asked him to get out from under her feet. Since he'd finished driving the girls about in the evenings, he'd taken to staying in more and reading. Everything seemed a bit flat now that Blackie was home again from Birmingham.

'You still repairing bomb damage, making homes habitable again?' the old man asked. Eddie nodded. He wondered if he should tell Solomon his collar was hanging by one stud. Was it going on or being taken off? He decided if it hadn't fallen by the time he was ready to leave he wouldn't bring it to the old man's attention.

'Still got them damn German prisoners?'

'I have, Granddad, and they're good workers, especially that Max.'

Solomon made a noise that sounded like 'Garn!'

Eddie smiled to himself. Granddad didn't approve of the Germans being allowed to work outside the prison. He thrust a hand into his jacket pocket and brought out a couple of battered Western novels. 'I picked these up down the market for you,' he said. He knew Solomon was partial to reading about the Wild West.

He'd hardly got the words out before the door

was pushed open and Gertie swept in. She had three metal curlers ensnared in the front of her dyed-black hair. She looked cross. 'Ain't you ready yet, Solomon?' She nodded at Eddie in greeting. 'We're going down the spiritualist church, they got a good medium tonight.' Gertie tapped her red-varnished nails on the wooden sideboard and confided to Eddie, 'It takes him an age to get ready.'

Solomon sighed, looked at the wooden mantel clock and said, 'Get off with you, woman. I still got time to have a game of draughts with my grandson.'

With a loud huff Gertie swept from the room.

'She thinks she's got me twisted round her little finger,' Solomon said, reaching for the draughts board that was on the small table next to his chair. 'Black or white?'

Eddie lost one game to Solomon. Not surprising, really. You had to be very smart to get one over on his grandfather, who had taught him how to play. Solomon moved his pieces quickly and didn't like it if his opponent took a long time deciding where to go.

'You could do a lot worse than Sunshine, my lad,' the old man said shortly, adding, 'I'm going to take your piece, Eddie. You should have taken mine.' He removed one of Eddie's white draughtsmen.

Eddie puffed air out of his cheeks. 'I wish you'd leave off about Sunshine, Granddad. She wants to settle down and have a family.'

'Wouldn't you, with the awful upbringing she had?'

'Probably. But when I gets hitched I want it to last and I'm not sure she's the right girl for me.'

'Well, if I had a pretty little thing like that running around after me with her tongue hanging out, I wouldn't say no.'

Eddie saw his chance and took it. He moved his white piece to the back row of Solomon's men. 'There, make a king of that!'

'Bugger! You're getting good, lad!' Grudgingly, Solomon topped Eddie's piece. 'I think I taught you to be too clever at this game.'

A blast of warm air entered the room along with Gertie. The curlers had gone, replaced by a wave held steady with a tortoiseshell comb. This time she looked resigned and her voice came out in a strangled whine. Her heavily mascaraed lashes looked like fences round her bright eyes.

'Solomon, you promised you'd come with me. It's Helen Duncan, the famous spiritualist from Scotland, and they were very lucky to get her to come to Gosport.'

'Give me five minutes to beat this whipper-snapper, Gertie, and I'm all yours.'

Eddie watched, open-mouthed, as the old man's gnarled hands used a king of his own to jump over Eddie's remaining men.

'There,' he said. 'I've won. An' you can't get that king of yours out because I've got you blocked in.' Solomon used the arms of the chair to hoist himself upright. 'No one wins me at draughts,' he said triumphantly. 'Now clear off, Eddie, my lad. I'm taking this lovely lady out!'

In the hallway Eddie had to fumble with the blackout curtain that hadn't been pulled right across before he could open the front door. Once out in the dark he took a deep breath. The smell of gas from fractured mains hung in the air from the previous night's raid and added to the stench of burnt wood.

He loved his granddad and the old man knew it. Eddie was happy for him that Gertie had taken him under her wing. Living in Lavinia House had given him a new lease on life. Eddie was still smiling to himself when he rounded the corner of the large house and collided with a small warm body.

'Jesus! You made me jump!'

He recognized Sunshine's voice immediately. 'It's only me,' he said. He didn't like to think he had frightened her. 'What are you doing out in the dark?'

He felt her relax as she realized who she'd collided with and that he meant her no harm. 'I've just put some rubbish in the dustbin,' Sunshine said. 'I never expected to bump into anyone else out at night.'

'I've been playing draughts with Solomon.'

'And I bet you didn't win,' she said. They laughed.

'It'll be a red-letter day when I do,' he said. Now his eyes had grown accustomed to the blackout's darkness he was able to see her better. The old man was right: she had lost weight. She also looked incredibly tired. His heart went out to her. Surely she didn't need to be doing two jobs. But, then, it wasn't really any of his business, was it? She'd told him she wanted to save for her future, have a home and never be hungry again. If Sunshine thought that two jobs enabled her to put a bit of money by for her future, who was he to argue with her?

'How have you been?' he asked softly. Now he was standing near to her, inhaling her fragrance, he found he had missed her company.

'Keeping busy,' she answered. 'I saw the Bluebird Girls got a good report in the *Evening News* for singing at the Coliseum.'

'Yes,' he said. 'They're doing well. Blackie's back home now so he's ferrying them to their various venues . . . Don't mind telling you that, much as I enjoyed driving them about, working during the day and late at night fair wore me out. I don't know how you manage it, working two jobs.'

She gave him one of her beautiful smiles. 'Oh, it has its compensations,' she said. The smile was enigmatic.

For a moment he was tongue-tied. Then his words came out in a rush. 'I'm sorry I haven't seen much of you while I've been driving the girls around.' He almost paused but decided he had to finish what he'd started. 'Look,' he said, 'if you do fancy going out one night, pictures, whatever, I'd love to take you.'

Sunshine looked at him the same way she had when they'd first met. His heart did a double beat. She was only a kid, he thought, a girl who wanted to better herself, a girl who wanted, no, needed to be loved.

She pushed herself up on tiptoe and kissed his cheek. 'Thanks, Eddie,' she said. 'I'll remember that.'

Then she brushed past him. He heard the key in the front door of Lavinia House and Sunshine was gone.

24

The material was rough on Sunshine's work-worn fingertips. She stifled a yawn and used the sewing machine to finish the seam. She fastened the ends of the cotton and held up the khaki army blouson she had made. It had taken her ages to get the pockets just right and her fingers had almost bled sewing the buckles into the scratchy wool, but it was finished. She'd done a good job with the jacket and now she had only the trousers to make. They weren't going to be such a problem for she enjoyed cutting out and machining slacks. Sunshine got up and went to open the window, careful to pull the blackout curtain around her so that no chinks of light showed.

She took several deep breaths of fresh night air. Not only had the jacket been irritatingly awkward to sew but it stank of scorched material. It was probably the smell that had made her feel sick earlier. She'd been lucky to buy the yardage very cheaply off a man in the market. Warehouse fire, he'd said. Damaged stock. Max and she had discussed how she might be able to get hold of some clothing for when he escaped.

'I can hardly walk about with a huge P for 'Prisoner' decorating my trousers, can I?'

She'd managed to visit a few second-hand shops and jumble sales but men's clothing was in short supply, especially for a man of Max's size. It was make do and mend for everyone. Still, when she'd finished making the army outfit, a good disguise, she thought, perhaps the smell would go when she'd had a chance to air it thoroughly. Meanwhile she kept everything wrapped in newspaper and hidden beneath her mattress. It wouldn't do for Mrs Ford, the cook, or Mabel Manners to come into her room and discover what she was up to, would it? As far as Sunshine knew, no one had an inkling about her association with Max and that was the way she wanted it to stay.

She closed the window and put the blackout curtain in place again. She'd been gathering together stuff that Max would need so he'd not be recognized as a prisoner when he made his escape from St Vincent.

One of the elderly men in Lavinia House had recently died. He'd been tall and Sunshine had taken some of his clothing. She'd washed it, given the boots a good clean and tucked everything at the back of her wardrobe. Her aim for Max and herself was for the two of them to appear to be a soldier on leave with his girl.

Every time she thought about leaving for Ireland from Portsmouth she felt warm and fuzzy inside. She felt as though she already knew Max's family and dreamt of the warm welcome they'd eventually give her when they arrived at his home in Germany. She had a picture in her mind of Brauweiler Abbey, just outside Pulheim, where Max's family worshipped and where they would marry. She loved Max so much.

181

It hadn't felt right finding out about the man called Jim, who, Max assured her, would be able to provide fake papers for him and a false passport for her.

Max had advised her to ask in the Central Café for Jim's whereabouts, as Bert, who owned it, knew everyone in the area.

Sunshine put away the sewing machine and tidied up. When she was in bed she thought once more about her meeting with the shifty Jim.

★ ★ ★

She'd entered the open door opposite the bus station, climbed the stairs and knocked. A woman, wearing too much make-up and a silky dress that left nothing to the imagination, answered.

Jim wasn't there so she'd sat on a chair and waited for him. The dark-haired woman gave her enquiring glances as she answered a telephone and wrote on a pad at a worn desk. Several closed doors led from the room, and she could hear soft music and voices. An overpowering smell of perfume made her sneeze several times. Men occasionally appeared to speak with the dark-haired woman, then vanished down the stairs. Eventually, sitting on the chair in the room's warmth, she nodded off — and woke with a start when a foxy-looking man in a pin-striped suit gently touched her shoulder.

'Are you Jim?' she'd asked, as he smiled at her. He had very small white teeth and a gold pin in his tie that seemed to wink at her. 'I'm sorry but

I don't know your surname.'

'You don't need to,' he said, in a London accent. 'Everyone knows who Jim is.' She'd clutched her handbag closer. In it she had put all her savings.

Just then a man with a big belly that flopped over his belt came in and said to the woman, 'Is Wendy ready?' He put some banknotes on her desk, which she picked up and slid into a drawer.

Jim had stepped back, grinned at the man and answered, 'Wendy's always ready.' He'd laughed, full-throated, then banged on one of the doors and opened it so the other man could enter. Sunshine heard a woman's voice from inside and the door closed.

'Now, little lady, what can I do for you?' Jim asked. His Brylcreemed hair was slick and shiny.

She looked at the woman who was now filing her nails. 'I'd like to talk about something personal and private,' she'd said, and looked meaningfully at the woman.

Jim had stared at her, then slapped his hand on the desktop. 'Dottie, get out and buy me a packet of fags.'

Dottie had looked up from her immaculate fingertips, glared at him but nevertheless rose, taking a shiny black handbag with her, and swished down the stairs in a cloud of scent, leaving the emery board on the desk.

'Talk quickly, little one,' Jim said. He sat down beside her.

She'd taken a deep breath and then it all came out. How she'd heard he could get hold of forged papers and passports.

'I can,' he said, his eyes constantly darting towards the top of the stairs.

'But it costs money, big money,' he added. His voice had a breathy quality, like he didn't want to be overheard. 'And how do I know you're on the level with me and not some kind of a spy wanting to get me and my boss, Billy Hill, sent down?'

She'd laughed. 'Do I look like I'm out to do you harm?'

His eyes had flickered into a semblance of a smile. She carried on talking. 'My man is held in St Vincent. He wants to escape. We both need to get to his home in Germany . . . '

'So he's a German?'

'Yes. Does that make a difference?'

'Not to me. All I care about is the payment you'll have to make.'

'I've got money!' Not only was Sunshine tired but she was angry now. She had the feeling the man was playing with her. She opened the clip on her bag and upended it onto the desk. Coins and notes spilled in all directions.

'No need for that,' Jim said, in a placating voice, but he began counting the money, separating change from notes. Then he laughed. He swept some of the money into his hand and started to put it back in her handbag. 'You've got to be joking,' he said. 'This is no good. It costs real money for me to give your man a new identity. This is just chicken feed!'

'But it's all I have!' Sunshine was near to tears. Her dreams of a wedding, a family, of waking up in Max's arms were being swept away, like rainwater down a drain. When her bag once more contained all her savings, she allowed herself to cry.

'Come here.' Jim pulled her towards him, holding her as she sat next to him on her chair. She could smell his sandalwood cologne, pungent. 'There is another way.' His voice was soft. 'You could come and work here for a while. It takes time for my London contacts to do their job properly. A pretty little thing like you can earn good money. You can leave when the passports and papers come through. What do you say?' He paused, then grabbed the pad the woman had been writing on and began to ask her questions, writing down her answers. 'Tell me about this Max. Colour of hair, eyes, his height, weight? His image that my contact will use must be as like him as possible, give or take a few discrepancies. I understand there's no way we can photograph him. Anyway, passport photos always make their owners look like dead meat!' He smiled at her again.

She was beginning to see light at the end of the tunnel. Perhaps there was a way she could arrange for Max's freedom, after all. The money she had saved would be useful for ferry tickets and they would need food . . .

But if Jim wanted her to work for him, whenever would she find the time? But if she wanted Max to escape she'd have to find the time, wouldn't she?

Jim was attempting to dry her eyes with his pocket handkerchief.

'How long will it take before the forged papers arrive?' she asked.

'Good girl,' Jim said. 'So, you'll take me up on my offer for a few weeks' work as payment?'

'I don't see that I have much choice if I want to go with Max to Germany.' She sniffed. 'What will I have to do for you?'

'You'll be one of my girls servicing the punters who pay good money for favours,' he said.

Sunshine let his words sink in. Her heart began to beat so loudly against her ribs she was sure he could hear it. 'This is a brothel?'

As she asked the question she already knew the answer. Jim nodded.

'But I've only ever made love with Max. I was a virgin until then . . . '

'Don't let that worry you. That small fact will stand in your favour,' he insisted. 'You can start tonight. I can get down all the details for the forged papers. The sooner you pay me, the sooner you and Max can leave the country.'

Sunshine heard no more. She ran from him, down the steps and out into the street, colliding with the dark-haired woman, Dottie, who dropped a packet of Woodbines to the pavement.

'Oi! Mind where you're goin'!'

Sunshine ran past the station, where empty buses were parked for the night, and collapsed on a wooden seat in the ferry gardens. The clinking of metal cleats knocking masts and the lap of water swirling against the rocks and the wooden jetty broke into her jumbled thoughts. That awful man had actually expected her to go to bed with men she didn't know, to pay for the precious, expensive papers that might ensure Max's safety.

There surely had to be another way for her to raise the money.

Max was the only man who had ever touched her and in her heart and mind she would be faithful to him for ever. Even Eddie had never been allowed to lay a finger on her body.

Her tears were falling fast. There must be another way to raise the money — there had to be!

But how?

She loved to sew, but making clothes or mending other people's would raise little cash. Time was of the essence and there weren't enough hours in the day for her to take on another job. And how could she when she was so tired most of the time?

Max could be transferred from St Vincent Barracks at any time. She would lose him then. Oh, she couldn't bear to be parted from him!

That was when she decided to think about Jim's offer as a possibility.

Immediately her brain rebelled against the idea of any other man invading her body. But what if she could close her mind to them pawing her? When she was a child she'd had to shut out so many taunts and cruelties just to live through each day, hadn't she? Surely she could do this for Max, the man who loved her with all his heart.

It wouldn't be like she was being unfaithful to him. Of course not.

The men would be as nothing to her.

The more she thought about it, the more she

knew she must conquer her guilt. This was the quickest — the only — way to provide the money to be with the man she loved. Once Max and she were in Pulheim everything would be wonderful . . .

★ ★ ★

Now Sunshine turned over in her bed at Lavinia House, trying not to think of the awful men who undressed and got into bed with her in the rooms she shared with the other prostitutes Jim had working for him.

Of course, Max knew nothing of this. How could she ever tell him of the shameful other life she was living several nights a week? No, she would never tell anyone her dreadful secret. When, finally, the forged papers arrived, she would help Max escape and together they could begin a new life in Ireland then later in Germany.

25

'I was worried about coming to London.' Bea's nose was pressed against the car's window. 'Hitler's trying to hit Buckingham Palace again. I didn't fancy a stray bomb coming our way at the Savoy.'

'Oh, shut up,' said Ivy. 'If all the London people felt like that, the city would be deserted, wouldn't it?'

'Please don't start bickering now we're nearly there,' said Blackie. He looked imploringly at Jo, and she saw the concern in his beautiful odd-coloured eyes.

'Oh, my God,' said Rainey, as Blackie stuck his hand out of the window and signalled. 'Is that it?'

'Are you sure we don't have to pay to go in there?' Bea asked.

The entrance was set back from the Strand and Jo welcomed the silence as the girls, spellbound, looked with wonder at the opulent entrance to the Savoy and the uniformed lackeys standing about.

'When I first saw Tom Marks's place, the Rainbow, I thought I'd died and gone to Heaven,' said Bea. 'Has this place got a lift as well?'

'The Savoy has everything,' Blackie said. 'It was one of the first London hotels to have electricity and lifts, and its air-raid shelter is said to be the poshest in England. But never mind that now. I trusted you all to learn your words to 'When The Blackbird Says 'Bye Bye'' and 'Ridin' High'. Geraldo might also want a third song, 'I Don't Want To Set The World On Fire'.'

'Don't worry, we're all word perfect and ready to change our style to fit his orchestral settings,' Rainey said.

'Ooh! Get her talking all posh,' said Bea. Now Blackie had stopped the car, she was speaking as she got out and stood looking about her.

Jo waited until Blackie opened her door, then said, 'I'm so glad Madame sent over those new outfits.' He helped her out and she followed him towards the boot to help take in some of the luggage.

'Allow me, sir,' said a uniformed man, his peaked cap emblazoned with 'Savoy'.

'I'll take charge of the dresses,' said Jo, reaching for the bagged clothing. 'I don't want those getting lost.'

'Wait for me in the foyer,' said Blackie. 'We'll go to our rooms together but I need to establish what Geraldo wants from us.' He left her just inside the hotel and she sat down on a leather sofa that practically swallowed her. The three girls were wandering around, staring at a grand piano where a young man was playing popular music. Elderly women bedecked in furs and pearls sat nearby taking tea. Jo thought, So, this is how the other half lives. Men sat on high comfortable-looking chairs, drinks at their sides, reading newspapers. All was calm and peaceful. She took a deep breath of air spiced with perfume and polish.

After a while Blackie returned. 'Just as I thought,' he said. 'He wants to do the recording straight away. He needs the girls ready for the evening cabaret straight after the recording. He says his reputation's on the line as they haven't practised with his musicians before.'

'So what does that mean?'

'It means, my dear Jo, that we rush to our rooms, the girls get dressed and we let Geraldo do what he's best at.' He put out a hand to pull her up. Once she was on her feet she chivvied the girls to follow Blackie.

'Oh, goody, we're going in the lift,' said Bea, her face glowing with excitement. Jo held her breath as the attendant pressed buttons. Sometimes, she thought, the world was moving on too fast for her.

Their luggage was already in the suite reserved for them. Jo handed each girl her evening frock. 'Just get changed as quickly as you can, then Blackie will take you to meet Geraldo.'

Rainey stood in front of Blackie. She smiled up into his face. 'Stop worrying,' she said. 'We're word perfect and there'll be no arguments at whatever he wants us to do. We can do this. Bea,' she called, 'Ivy, tell this worrier we'll be fine.'

Jo saw the relief spread over Blackie's face and he attempted a smile. 'Get changed.' She pressed the dresses into the girls' arms and watched as they left the room. Without asking she knew Rainey and Ivy would share a room and Bea, the fidget in bed, would have the smallest. She and Blackie would have a room each.

'What do you know of Geraldo?' Jo asked.

'Not a great deal. He's more a friend of Madame's than mine. But I've heard her say he's a talented perfectionist.'

'Good-looking?'

Blackie frowned at her. 'Of course. Hair swept back and oiled, and he has a mouth — lips, actually — that most women find very attractive.'

'Don't say any more,' said Jo. 'No doubt the girls will fall for him.' Blackie laughed. 'Come on,' he said. 'You know as well as I do that the only man Ivy ever thinks about is Eddie, and it looks like your Rainey has set her sights on a certain photographer — '

'I can't listen to any more of your rubbish, Blackie,' she told him, then began wandering about the room. 'We can't make tea here like we did at the Rainbow. Have we got time for you to order some up before you and the girls leave for the ballroom?' She watched as he located the telephone and ordered tea and sandwiches to be brought to the suite. Then when he'd set down the phone he put out his hands, enquiring which of the two remaining rooms she wanted to sleep in.

'Either will do,' Jo said. 'It's a shame we're only staying for the one night. Geraldo's regular singer has another engagement, doesn't she?'

Blackie opened a bedroom door and took in her small holdall, leaving it on the carpet. Then he repeated the exercise with a small suitcase of his own in the other bedroom. 'If he likes them he'll use them more often as vocals on his records,' he said. 'That's how Dorothy Carless

192

got her big chance. She, like our girls, was young when she started singing, much younger, in fact.' He looked at the bags by the door. 'They're going to need those, aren't they?'

Jo saw he was about to knock on one of the girls' doors when it opened and Rainey and Ivy swept out. 'What do you think?' Rainey asked.

Jo let out a gasp and Blackie whistled.

The dresses were putty-coloured rayon crêpe. Jo had disliked the colour on sight. To her it wasn't glamorous, not when Madame had previously sent over gold lame and the glittery blue dresses that shimmered beneath the lights and made the girls look fairylike. She had thought Madame's latest choice of colour reflected the fact that good material was hard to come by. Now she saw how wrong she had been.

Always Madame's choices for the girls were similar yet each dress was different. The full-length draped skirt clung over Rainey's hips, nipped in at her waist, and the black lace shoulder accent lifted the pale colour. Ivy's floor-length dress had short sleeves, a deep V neckline with a black lace insert and was moulded to her figure. Its simplicity made her look exotic.

'They're a bit film-starry, aren't they?' Rainey said.

Just then Bea came out of her room. Again, the dress was long but with a side panel that hung below her hips. Her long sleeves were tipped at the wrists in black lace. The putty colour looked fantastic on all three girls and set off their very different hair colours to perfection.

'That's what I'm looking for,' said Bea, picking up her holdall. 'A bit of make-up and lipstick, I'll brush my hair, then I'm ready.' She stared at Rainey and Ivy. 'I thought I looked pretty good in this until I saw the pair of you.' She escaped back into her room. Jo noted that not only had she managed all the zips, but her figure had taken on a new sleekness.

'I can see I'm going to get some envious glances as I escort those three downstairs,' said Blackie.

The girls vanished into their rooms with their bags, and a knock at the door announced a waitress with a tray. Jo busied herself pouring tea while Blackie tidied himself in readiness for meeting Geraldo.

'Is this a sort of practice for tonight's big do in the ballroom?' called Jo.

'It is and it isn't,' he replied. 'Geraldo needs to make sure the girls' voices are compatible with his orchestra so sometimes it pays to record beforehand.'

'Does that mean a live show isn't always a live show?'

'Sometimes a live show has to be pre-recorded. It wouldn't do for a sudden fight or some loud noise to break out and spoil the wireless listeners' enjoyment. Accidents do happen, don't they?' Jo nodded even though Blackie was in his room. Then he said, 'Don't worry, Parlophone records Geraldo, and won't it be wonderful for the record cover to say Geraldo and the Bluebirds?'

Jo sipped her tea. Yes, it would be marvellous,

194

she thought, but so much better if the girls had a recording contract of their very own.

She sighed happily, knowing she needn't leave the comfortable room until a short while before Geraldo's orchestra was officially due to appear onstage. Her table and seat were reserved, so when Blackie had taken his charges down in the lift she could get herself ready with no one around to claim her attention. Then she would drift down and watch the trio live onstage, singing with one of the most famous orchestras in England and know that everyone who listened to the wireless broadcast would hear the Bluebird Girls.

26

'Twenty thousand killed, the wireless said.'

'Yes, Blackie, I heard what the announcer said about the moonlight raid over London last night.'

It wasn't that Jo didn't care about the biggest bombing so far that the capital had endured but Hitler had also had the people of Portsmouth and Gosport scurrying into shelters. Only moments before that phone call, Bert had rung to let her know that Ivy and Bea, who'd stayed over at the café last night, were safe, and tucking into a breakfast of bacon and sausages with the rest of his early regulars.

She worried that the girls spent so much of their free time in the café in North Cross Street but Rainey had assured her that sometimes there were just as many plain-clothes coppers there as paying customers, not that the customers were aware of that. Besides, since Maud had got fed up with the girls practising dance steps and singing their heads off in Bea's back bedroom, Bert had kindly donated to them the large room next to where he kept his walking-stick collection. It looked out over the privy at the bottom of the garden, but that didn't worry the girls as they were too high upstairs for anyone to gawp in at them. The customers talking downstairs and Bert's wireless meant they could make as much noise as they liked.

Della, Ivy's mum, served in the café and kept an eye on the girls, every so often providing them with food. Bert was still making delicious stews with rabbit meat. God knew where he got it from, but the customers ate it up as fast as he cooked it. Jo knew she was silly to worry as, every so often, Bert or Della would telephone to tell her what the Bluebirds were up to.

Now she said, 'Sorry, Blackie, I'm not paying attention. Rainey and I spent last night in the Anderson shelter and I feel like I've gone three rounds in the ring with Sugar Ray Robinson.'

'Never mind Sugar Ray, we've got a young British lad who's going to shake up things in boxing, Freddie Mills.'

'Did you phone me to talk about boxing?'

She heard Blackie take a deep breath. 'No, my sweet Jo, I was leading up to things gradually. I telephoned to tell you to keep the wireless on because I've just heard Parlophone's record of Geraldo's orchestra with our girls singing and it's wonderful!'

★   ★   ★

'That garden patch looks lovely. When did you plant those pretty little blue flowers?'

'Those pretty blue flowers, as you call them, are bluebells, Hans. For your information, I didn't put them in, they made their own way up through the earth, but I agree they do smell and look welcoming. It makes me wonder what else is hidden from view.'

Hans went on clipping the edge of the grass.

Everything was growing fast now. Max had dug up the crocus corms and they were drying nicely on a shelf in the shed near the creek. Because they'd made such a lovely show before the intense cold of winter was over, his request of more bulbs for the following year had been granted by the powers that be in St Vincent. Max smiled to himself. He sincerely hoped he wouldn't be here to see them flower.

Every day was a waiting game. It was a race against time for him. Could he escape before he was sent to another camp?

'Four of our friends have left us today,' Max said. 'I didn't like to see them being bundled into the back of a lorry.'

'No warning, and they certainly weren't told where they might be taken to,' answered Hans. He stopped applying the shears to the grass and stood up and rubbed his back. Max noted the boy had lost weight recently and he'd heard him coughing at night. He'd told him not to bother coming to help him today, that he could cope with gardening on his own. Hans had looked so downcast that he'd retracted his words and immediately the boy's face had glowed, like a lighted match. At least the May air was better for him than the stale stink inside the cold stone rooms of St Vincent.

'This is England, Hans.' Max smiled at him. 'Prisoners are transferred to where they can be most productive. Many go to farms. Strawberry picking starts next month and Hampshire is famous for strawberries.' The one thing Max couldn't confide to his young friend was that he lay awake at nights worrying that the false passport and other papers he needed wouldn't arrive before he, too, was sent elsewhere.

He had never worried that Sunshine wouldn't fall beneath his spell and do his bidding. After all, he always got what he wanted where women were concerned, didn't he? He just wished he could move the days along so his escape could begin.

He now had in his possession, hidden in the earth at the back of the shed, a key he had copied from an original that Sunshine had stolen from the breakfast table: a guard had carelessly left it alongside his cigarettes and matches. There had been no hue and cry when the key was found later beneath the bench in the dining room. Max had explained to Sunshine how she could take an impression of the key in candle wax, hide that in the shed, then he could file a blank key of the same size to its design. Sunshine had been able to buy a blank from a hardware store in Gosport and smuggle it into St Vincent.

His key worked well in the door lock of the Nissen hut. He'd been more worried that one of the other prisoners might wake during the hours of darkness when he was trying it out.

He longed to escape from Sunshine and her everlasting whining of weddings and babies. It wasn't as if he really enjoyed making love to her now, if he could call it making love. Coupling with her bony body was no pleasure, well, hardly any. He preferred the solidity of big German girls. He had seen starving children who looked like Sunshine. And what was she? Nothing but a malnourished woman who believed every word he said because she thought the sun shone from his backside!

But he had to go on playing the game with her because she was working for the mysterious Jim to pay off the balance for the forgeries. What she did, he neither cared nor asked. She'd merely volunteered the information that she was expected to go to one of Jim's residences near the bus station in Gosport several nights a week. He suspected it was cleaning or some other demeaning work. It was all she was fit for.

She'd told him she'd sewn a good disguise for him: the uniform of an army infantryman. He had no doubt it would fit, no doubt that it would be unrecognizable from any other infantryman's uniform. If there was one thing Sunshine could do well, it was sew. It had been one of the first things he had noticed: her own clothing was expertly made.

At the rear of the sheds on the bank of Forton Creek he had been sure that he'd not been observed filing the heavy wire that surrounded the Nissen huts. One good push and he'd be able to break out. The plan was for him to swim across the creek where Sunshine would have hidden his English clothing, and when he was dressed and decent he would saunter down to meet her. She would have collected all the forged documents and be waiting for him. They would travel to Portsmouth, then cross to Ireland. Of course she had no idea he intended to ditch her as soon as possible. Max blessed the day he had decided to tidy up the garden at the front of St

Vincent. The shed where the gardening tools and vegetables were kept had been an Aladdin's Cave of useful equipment, as well as a place where he and Sunshine could secretly meet.

It was she who had told him of Aladdin. Pantomimes! Another stupidity beloved by the English! Perhaps not as stupid as he was going to make himself look when he was next alone with Sunshine. To keep her sweet and happy he was going to sing to her! He listened to the wireless and was naturally very quick at picking up new tunes. 'You Are My Sunshine' was the ideal song for him to serenade her with. Not only would she be flattered but it would ensure she kept doing his bidding.

And now he could hear Hans coughing again. He stared at the thin-shouldered boy still cutting the grass. 'Are you well, Hans?'

Hans raised his blue eyes towards Max. He didn't look at all well. 'I'm all right,' he replied. He sounded as though he found it difficult to breathe. Max shrugged. If Hans said he was all right, who was he to argue with him?

27

'Why don't you go out? It's a lovely evening.'

Eddie's mother was staring at him, practically giving him the evil eye. He put down the detective novel *Over My Dead Body* on the arm of the chair and stared right back at her.

'I surely can't be in the way sitting here, reading. What's the matter?' The kitchen smelled of rich spices. He breathed in the aroma. His mother had a bread pudding cooking in the oven.

'You haven't been out in the evening since that night you took Sunshine to the pictures. What's the matter? I thought you liked the girl.'

Eddie sighed. Rex Stout's exciting story would have to wait.

'I do like her. But, if you must be so nosy, she hasn't got time for me. Those two jobs are sapping her strength. Have you seen her lately?'

Maud shook her head, pulled out a kitchen chair and sat down. Oh, God, he thought, she's going to want a full confession, all the ins and outs of why he hadn't seen the girl. Well, he decided, he wasn't going to tell her what had happened round the back of the Criterion Picture House the last time they'd met.

'Your business is doing well. She'd make you a lovely wife . . . '

He sighed. What did wives and business have in common? It was true, despite the war or perhaps because of it, people needed builders to repair their homes, shore up the walls of houses and shops. He was doing so well he'd had a telephone installed.

But did he want a wife? Of course he did — one day.

'You're not getting any younger . . . '

'Mum, I'm not ready for my coffin just yet!' Now Maud was tapping her fingers on the oilcloth covering the table. He stared stonily at the half-empty glass sugar bowl next to a tin of Carnation milk and the salt and pepper pots that were always left in the centre of the table.

'If you're not taking the plunge because you feel I can't manage without your money . . . ' She gripped a hairpin and stuck it further into her greying hair.

'Now Granddad's in Lavinia House and you're working again I know you can manage.'

Maud had gone back to her cleaning jobs and he knew she was happier after being stuck in the house watching over Solomon. Just as Solomon had taken a new lease on life, with Gertie making sure he got out and about. 'And now that Bea coughs up a few quid every so often, I guess you want rid of me,' he said.

'There's no talking to you, is there?' Maud rose and dusted herself down. 'I'm going to make a cup of cocoa, do you want one?'

'Yes, please, Mother dear,' he said, picking up his book again.

Eddie's eyes kept slipping from the page. He couldn't take in the words. All he could think about was Ivy and how pretty she'd looked when he was driving her, the other two girls and Jo to the Gosport pubs. She not only had a fantastic voice but she'd grown into a very desirable young woman. He'd always stood at the back, nearest the bar, watching the audience as the Bluebirds sang. Half the men in the pubs, young and old, had their tongues hanging out, slavering over them. Not that Jo allowed any hanky-panky. He smiled to himself. Jo was like an irritating terrier, the way she kept unwanted advances from her girls. Of course, he was there should there be any real bother, wasn't he?

His mind went back to that day long ago when something like a needle of fire had connected him to Ivy as he had handed her out of his van. He'd tried to tell himself she was a kid, too young for him. The truth was, as Ivy grew up the gap felt a lot smaller. She wasn't a kid any longer.

He could hear his mother clattering about in the scullery. He knew she meant well. He knew how much she loved him and only wanted to see him settled.

He turned the page down to keep his place and sat thinking and looking into the flames from the coals in the grate. But he'd blotted his copybook. He felt a sheen of sweat come out on his forehead that had nothing to do with the warmth in the room. How he wished he could turn back the clock. If he could, he'd never have suggested around Easter time taking Sunshine to the pictures, some silly film with Arthur Askey about Charley and his aunt. He'd gone to visit Solomon and felt sorry for Sunshine, whom he'd found dusting the hallway of Lavinia House. She'd looked as if she'd lost a tanner and found a farthing. He'd felt guilty at not seeing her and suggested a friendly night out at the pictures.

Anyway, in the auditorium, they'd had a bit of a cuddle in the dark. She'd felt frail and thin, but she'd let him put his hands underneath her jumper and he'd got a bit excited feeling her small breasts. She'd never let him go that far before, always telling him she was a virgin and intended to stay that way until she got a ring on her finger.

When they'd seen the film through to where they'd come in, they left and went round the back of the picture house where it was dark and quiet. She was returning his kisses with far more abandonment than she had when they'd been seeing each other regularly. He'd decided in the heat of the moment to see how far she'd let him go. His hands hadn't met any resistance when he touched above her stocking tops and he could hardly believe it when she allowed him to push himself inside her. She was so small against him but once he'd got going he couldn't seem to stop. It was all over so quickly and he hadn't pulled out or anything.

Afterwards, when she was making herself decent, he said, 'I didn't mean for that to happen. I'm sorry.'

She'd given him a funny smile. 'You're a nice man. I don't know why I made you wait so long. Will you take me back to Lavinia House? I'm on early shift tomorrow.'

He'd dropped her off outside. He didn't make

any arrangements to see her again, wouldn't have been any use: her main topic of conversation all night had been how tired she was.

He'd been up to see Solomon a few times since then, but Sunshine wasn't around. In a way he was glad because he felt bad about having his way with her when he knew he could never feel for her what he felt for Ivy.

His thoughts fled when his mother's voice cut through them: 'This bread pudding's ready. You like a bowlful when it's hot, don't you, lad?'

★　★　★

'This is nice,' said Jo, taking a sip of sweet sherry.

'What — the sherry?'

'No, Blackie. Us having a night out on our own without having to worry about the girls. Any special reason why you've brought me here?'

She looked around the restaurant, its tables decked out in white tablecloths so bright they almost hurt her eyes. Lit candles lent a romance to the room that overlooked the sea or would have done if the blackout curtains hadn't been firmly in place. Jo could hear the swish and wash of the waves as they hit the pebbles of Southsea beach. Outside, the Rose Garden was just coming into its own. She hadn't needed a coat this evening for summer was nearly here. Yes, she thought, sitting in this restaurant with Blackie was preferable to an evening indoors. They'd already ordered: cream of parsnip soup to start followed by brisket of beef. The waiter had whispered there was sultana roll and Blackie's mouth had practically watered.

Jo spoke again: 'Is this business or pleasure?'

'A bit of both.' Blackie winked at her. 'First of all, you look delicious tonight.'

Jo coughed as a large sip of sherry went down the wrong way. She put her glass on the table and gathered her thoughts. Blackie wasn't given to making extravagant gestures or saying things he didn't mean. She'd thought she deserved a new dress to go out with him tonight but there was nothing in the shops she could afford so she'd re-cut the neckline of her black dress into the latest sweetheart style and sewn a black chiffon scarf around it.

'What's the second thing?' Jo asked. 'And thank you for the compliment.'

'I don't take you out enough and thought it would be nice for us to revalue our friendship.'

'What do you mean, revalue? Either we're friends or not.'

'That isn't quite how I'd put it.' Blackie gave her his devastating smile. Then he ran his fingers through his wayward curls. He was obviously ill at ease at what he needed to say and his words came out in a rush. 'I've never forgotten the way you comforted me, the night I lost my money in Birmingham. We've not really spoken of what happened between us that night — '

Jo broke in: 'Nothing really happened, Blackie. I was a comfort to you, that's all. We didn't make love. I couldn't bear you being so unhappy.'

'Would you have done that for anyone? Say, your Mr Kennedy?'

Jo picked up her glass, drank the rest of the

sherry in one and banged the glass down on the tablecloth. 'You're jealous, aren't you?' She spat the words out at him. For a moment there was silence between them. Slowly the sounds and movements and dull chatter of other patrons in the restaurant got through to her.

Jo fumed until the sensible part of her brain took over. He was jealous because he cared about her. She'd long ago decided she was in love with him but that it was best to let things lie dormant. She'd had enough of loving a man who was wrong for her, with Alfie, so it was better for her and Blackie's friendship to go no further. Blackie was still staring at her. She spoke carefully, softly but clearly: 'No, I won't be getting into bed with Syd Kennedy. Anyway, he doesn't gamble!'

She watched his lovely lips as they tipped into a smile. 'And what else are we celebrating?' she asked.

He reached across the table and covered her fingers with his hand. 'Parlophone have had fantastic sales with Geraldo and the Bluebirds. Geraldo wants them back again at the Savoy and Parlophone want them to cut a record of their own.'

28

'What d'you want from me, mate? I can hardly give you your money back, can I?'

Jim looked the scruffy fellow in the eye. The desk was between them so if the man got ugly he'd need a pretty long reach to get at him, he thought. 'Look, you come in 'ere looking for a girl and you pays my assistant the money an' you gets a girl.'

'She's not a girl. She's a bag of bones with as much life in her as a sack of spuds.'

'You 'ad your way with her, didn't you?'

'Yes, but — '

'But nothing. There ain't nothing in the rule book what says she got to like it, talk to you, or make you a three-course meal!'

Jim saw the man was backing down. He felt braver. 'Tell you what, why don't you come back and next time you can 'ave Big Lucie? She knows what it's all about. All the men want her, but I'll make sure you have her and I'll knock ten bob off. Can't be fairer than that, can I, mate?'

'Right.' The man put out a hand to shake on it. Reluctantly Jim took it.

As the man went down the steep stairs, Jim looked at Elsie, who was taking the money that night. 'I got to get rid of her. She's more trouble than she's worth.'

Elsie set the brush back in her pot of nail varnish. 'We can't get on with her, neither. She ain't like Della. Now, she really drew the punters in.'

Jim let her chatter on. Della had been one of his best girls. No, the very best. He should never have worked her over when she said she wanted to leave, to give up the game. Automatically he rubbed his left leg where the scar still reminded him of exactly where Bert's swordstick had cut into him. Bloody mad bugger he was, Jim thought. Trouble was, Bert loved Della to distraction.

He walked over to the mirror and looked at his reflection. He tipped his Homburg hat a bit more to one side. Winston Churchill wore one just like it, he thought. But he looked more stylish than old Winnie.

'I'm going to have to get rid of her,' he said.

'There'll always be another girl ready and willin' to fill her place,' said Elsie. She began counting notes from the top drawer. Jim knew the takings were down. He'd thought she'd be fresh meat. The punters wanted a girl they could talk to, who showed a bit of interest in them. Jim had felt sure that if Sunshine wouldn't exactly embrace the new way of life she would at least have thawed out a bit by now. It wasn't the first time a bloke had likened her to a sack of potatoes. He smiled to himself. She'd lost so much weight it could only be a very light sack.

The papers had come that morning. A passport for her and one for Leonard Collins, a burly blond bloke. Jim had never seen a photo of Sunshine's fellow so had had to rely on her detailed description. Should be all right, especially if no one looked too close. All the rest of the malarkey was there, birth certificate, identity card, ration book. He smiled at his reflection. Sunshine had more than paid for the false papers in the time she'd worked for him. After all, when a bloke came up the stairs looking for a girl, unless he asked for one by name, that bloke was sent in to Sunshine. But that's what it was all about, wasn't it? Payment and creaming a bit extra off the top. He'd tell her later that she could go. Bloody useless tart but, like Elsie said, there were plenty of girls willing to step into her shoes.

⋆　⋆　⋆

When she'd been walking back from Jim's place to Lavinia House in the early hours, Sunshine thought she'd sleep easier in what was left of the night. Relieved she didn't have to prostitute herself any longer for the false papers that were now tucked in her handbag, she felt happier than she had in a long time. In the darkness she'd breathed in the sweet smell of mallow, the heady scent of the roadside honeysuckle and watched the clear skies above her with a sprinkling of stars. No raid tonight, and for that she was thankful. But now she was in bed and sleep wouldn't come.

It seemed to her that she had been working for ever to pay for the possibility of freedom for her and Max. In reality it hadn't been that long. She had another five or possibly six months to go before Max's baby was born. By then she would be in Germany, in Pulheim, with Max's family around her. She wouldn't have to feel alone any longer.

She wasn't alone when she was in the shed with him, of course not. But inside her head she was lonely even when she was in that awful room opposite the bus station and those dreadful men came to her. As soon as they were shown in, her brain and body closed down. It was as if she had died. It was the only way she could cope with what was happening to her. She'd had to do that disgusting thing: allow men to touch her. But she had had to raise the money needed for the forged papers. Of course, Max still knew nothing of this. He thought she cleaned and polished for Jim. And he must never know, even if she had debased herself to win his freedom. No, Max must never know.

Max had been her first lover. She adored him with all her heart, so why had she allowed Eddie to go all the way that night after he had treated her to the pictures?

Eddie had been kind to her. Even when they'd first met he had never touched her in any way she didn't want. She'd told him she wanted to be pure on her wedding day and he'd accepted that. But when they'd kissed and cuddled in the Criterion during the film and he'd wanted to continue in the alleyway at the back of the picture house she hadn't stopped him, had she?

So many men had invaded her privacy that one more, Eddie, didn't seem to matter. And he was so kind. Not like the men at Jim's place. Sometimes Max was rough with her. He told her she excited him so he couldn't keep his hands off her.

He wasn't so excited when she'd told him about the baby, though.

Mabel Manners had stopped her one day in the corridor of Lavinia House. 'Are you feeling all right, dear?' she'd asked. 'You're losing weight. Why don't you come in for a nice chat like you used to?'

'I'm a bit busy,' she'd replied. 'I feel fine, thank you.'

'If you ever want to talk, dear, that's what I'm here for. You can take advantage of my nursing experience any time.' Then she'd looked pointedly at Sunshine's burgeoning belly.

That same night, Sunshine had had an idea. She'd unlocked Rosa Williams's door and searched the old lady's chest of drawers until she'd found one of her peach-coloured corsets. Rosa wore the kind that fastened beneath the bust with hooks and eyes and came down past her hips. The fat old dear thought they'd make her look thinner, but on Rosa the corsets simply moved her wobbly flesh about. Rosa wouldn't discover Sunshine in her bedroom as she was at her daughter's house at Lee-on-the-Solent for the weekend.

Sunshine wasn't normally a dishonest person but she knew Rosa would never miss the garment: the elderly lady was very forgetful.

Once she had the corset back in her own room, Sunshine tried it on, wrapping it around her body and fastening the hooks and eyes. It immediately fell to the floor for it was far too big for her. An hour later, when the corset had been cut and the whalebones realigned, Sunshine stood in front of the mirror admiring her new skinny outline. Her bulging body was neatly tucked away. That she now found it difficult to breathe properly didn't matter: she vowed she'd get used to the corset. There'd be no need now for anyone to remark that her thickening body didn't match her skinny arms and legs.

At first it was difficult to work in the kitchens with the corset holding her in so tightly but she became used to it. Max remarked on it one day in the shed.

'You have different clothes beneath your skirt.'

Usually he was so quick to take her and relieve himself she could have been wearing the very sacks they piled onto the floor and he wouldn't have noticed.

'Max, I'm going to have your baby.'

There was silence and then he said one word: 'Oh!' There was more silence.

After a while she could stand the quiet no longer, so she asked, 'Aren't you pleased?'

'I am delighted, my love, and my family will be so happy. All the more reason for us to leave this place as quickly as possible.'

Sunshine was so glad he was happy. She swept away his initial silence by telling herself he was worried for her and the journey they were about to undertake.

That journey and Max's escape were upon them now. She hoped she would see him tomorrow when she went to work in the kitchens. Perhaps Hans would not be with Max as he toiled in the garden. Then they could make arrangements for Max to break out from St Vincent Barracks and to change into the set of army clothing she would have hidden behind a bush across the creek. With his new clothes, she would leave loose change in the pockets for him to catch a bus, or walk if he preferred, to the café in the town. After all the trouble she had taken to get hold of the false papers she didn't want to leave them with the clothing. It certainly wouldn't do for someone else to find them, and the night might be wet. Max had thought it better that they meet as far away from St Vincent as possible and she was to take with her only a few things she needed. They had agreed upon the busy Central Café.

From there they would take a ferry across the water to Portsmouth, then board a boat to Ireland . . .

Sunshine felt her baby move. 'Don't worry, little one,' she said, cradling her belly. 'You'll be blessed with a better life than I've had, I promise you that.'

At last she slept.

29

Bert lovingly caressed the stick with the green glass handle in which a tot of whisky could be hidden.

Blackie said, 'You really have a great affinity for those things, don't you, Bert?' He gazed at the polished sticks on one side of Bert and those yet to be carefully cleaned on the other. He took a deep breath. Even upstairs the smell of Bert's famous stew rose tantalizingly.

'Yes, I do, lad. Like I've said, each of these sticks could tell a story, if they could talk. Their journey's from when they were made to being here in this room above a café in Gosport. What an exciting book that would make!'

Blackie stretched out his long legs. 'Your favourite is the one downstairs, though, isn't it?'

'I've got two favourites down there, Blackie, my trusty swordstick and my Della.'

Blackie laughed.

Della, Ivy's mother, was looking after the customers. Blackie knew she'd been one of Jim's girls, but Bert had helped her to get away from the man's clutches. Thinking about Della and Jim reminded him of the conversation he'd had with Bert before the summer had got under way. 'You ever find out any more about that little blonde girl asking for Jim?' Blackie took a sip of his drink.

'Not really,' said Bert. 'I must have been

mistaken about her being the girl young Eddie was with at the King's Theatre. I overheard Bea talking about Sunshine and Eddie going to the pictures. So, it appears they're still together.'

'Been a while now,' said Blackie. 'Think it'll end in wedding bells?'

Bert laughed, showing all his crooked teeth. ''Ow would I know? I'm like a bloody mushroom kept in the dark!' He refilled Blackie's glass.

Blackie gestured to him to stop pouring.

'It's only a little drop,' Bert said. He put the bottle on the floor. 'Tell you what I did hear.' He began laughing almost before he got the words out. 'That Jim took on a girl who was bloody useless to him.' He snorted with laughter. 'She was so awful the blokes didn't want her!'

'Go on!'

'It's true,' said Bert. 'Serves the nasty blighter right. I can't get on with the bloke. He thinks too much of himself.'

Blackie had a sudden vision of Bert retelling him now a tale about one of his contretemps with Jim and, as he'd heard the same stories many times, decided to break in with one about the Bluebirds.

'The girls like being at the end of Southsea pier, don't they?'

'I think South Parade Pier likes having them, an' all,' said Bert. He breathed on polished wood, then rubbed frantically with his cloth. 'Two shows a day, afternoon and evening, and they still get home before the ferries stop running. It's a good revue for the day trippers

217

and the Bluebirds top the bill. What more can they ask for?'

'I'm waiting on the contract from Parlophone,' said Blackie. 'You can't rush these people.'

'S'pose not,' said Bert. 'But they all look so happy now, the girls, doing what the three of them have always dreamt of doing, appearing onstage and singing their hearts out.'

'Let's hope it stays that way, Bert. They're making money for the first time in their careers. They've paid back what's been borrowed from Madame Walker and they're serving their apprenticeship before they hit the big-time.'

Thinking about money made him remember Jo's nest egg, the couple of hundred pounds from the sale of her car. Many times she'd pressed him to borrow it. It gave him pleasure to think he'd never had to ask her for the loan of it. It pleased him even more that she trusted him.

'What are you smiling about, Blackie? What's behind them twinkling funny-coloured eyes of yours?'

'I was thinking about Jo,' he said.

Bert smiled at him. 'Maybe one day you'll see what side your bread's buttered.'

★ ★ ★

'Don't you just love this time of day?' Rainey said. 'The break between the shows when the trippers have gone back to their boarding-houses for high tea and we can laze in the sun, chat and wind down before the early-evening performance? Get off!' A seagull had swooped down

218

and whisked away a chip from the remains of Rainey's dinner left on the table in newspaper.

'They like chips, don't they?' laughed Ivy. 'Did you know seagulls are the souls of sailors drowned at sea?'

'Don't let her start on about stuff she's read in books,' said Bea. She took her sailor hat from her blonde curls and placed it over her face before she settled back in the striped deckchair positioned near the stage at the end of the pier.

Rainey was examining what was left of the fish and chips. 'I'm definitely not eating any more of those,' she said. She stood up and began twisting the baggy clown trousers she was wearing to the side. 'I really should sew up that hole,' she said, showing a tear in the material. Her foot knocked against their gas masks, left in a pile near her chair.

'Don't worry, it doesn't show — it's only a tiny tear and no one's going to notice when we're onstage,' Ivy reassured her. 'I read somewhere that if someone's finding fault with your clothing when you're acting then you're not acting the part properly.'

'These costumes are silly,' said Bea, ignoring Ivy. Her voice was muffled because of the hat. 'Half clown and half sailor — '

She didn't get any further for Ivy said, 'They're supposed to be silly. That's what having a good time in Southsea is all about. Kiss Me Quick hats, looking at the sea, going to the lake with the paddleboats and looking at the swans, coming on the pier to see the show and watching the artists . . . '

'Ooh! She's swallowed a dictionary — artists, indeed!'

'Shut up, Bea,' chorused Ivy and Rainey.

'Now, that would make a nice photo,' Charlie Smith's voice broke in.

'Didn't you take enough photographs of Rainey yesterday?' Bea said sarcastically. She threw down her sailor hat beside her.

Rainey picked up the newspaper, went to the railings and tipped the last of her food into the sea. Two clever gulls pounced and had chips in their beaks before they hit the water. She rolled up the newspaper to throw in the rubbish bin later. The laughter from the people strolling along the pavement near the pier and the noise of the waves hitting the pebbles was soothing. This was a lovely way to earn money, she thought, doing what she wanted to do.

When she looked around she saw Charlie had moved a deckchair next to hers. She smiled at him. The pictures he'd taken a while back had been sent all over London and the Home Counties to advertise the Bluebird Girls. Outside the entrance to the pier there was a huge poster of the three of them. It gave her a thrill every time she passed it. She thought how nervous she'd been that day at Bert's because she was late, and how surprised she'd been at Charlie's attitude when he was taking the photos. Now she looked at him as she lowered herself into the striped canvas of her chair.

How was it possible she'd fallen for him in such a short time? Surely, she thought, it was only in magazines that love happened so quickly.

On one of the rare evenings the Bluebirds weren't performing he'd taken her dancing at Lee Tower Ballroom. She'd surprised herself by agreeing to the date.

He wasn't a tall, handsome man but he had bucketfuls of confidence. He'd paraded her around the dance floor, the pride on his face obvious to all. And he danced with the agility of Fred Astaire. Rainey was no Ginger Rogers, but she had a natural rhythm and he held her like she was the most precious thing on earth.

After dancing he'd taken her to the Wight View Hotel for a meal. She had listened avidly to him when he spoke about his love of photography — and he hadn't talked non-stop about himself. She'd found herself telling him of her hopes and dreams and of the bad home life she and her mother had experienced with their father. This had surprised Rainey for she rarely spoke of the past. He drove her home and left her at her front door after a kiss that knocked her sideways.

Now she leaned over and ruffled his hair. 'You're really quite a sweetie, aren't you, when you're not blustering about?'

'So you've discovered my secret, have you?' Charlie asked.

'Oh, for God's sake,' moaned Bea. 'If you two are going to start talking all lovey-dovey and stupid, I'm going to be sick!'

30

July 1941

'Sunniest day for a hundred years! Fancy that!'
said Mabel Manners. 'That's what they said on
the wireless. I bet you found it hot in them
kitchens.' She was fluffing up cushions in the
leisure room. Sunshine had just emptied the
ashtrays. Why on earth some of the men
preferred to stay indoors playing cards on such a
hot day instead of sitting in the shade in the
gardens, she couldn't fathom.

'The perspiration was dripping off me,'
answered Sunshine. She didn't mention the
pains and cramps she'd been having all day at St
Vincent. She'd thought she might just get away
with not letting out the corset she wore. There
were still a few months or so to go before the
baby made an appearance but tonight was the
night of the escape, after which she could get rid
of the dratted corset. Her baby would be born in
Germany. Would that make the child German?
she wondered.

Max had told her to get out of Lavinia House
without being seen and make her way, with the
papers, to Bert's café. He didn't want to be
picked up and for the police or guards to
discover the forgeries on him. She'd told him
exactly how to get to the Central Café. He'd said
she was to treat the afternoon and evening as

usual, and when she left the kitchens it was to be like any other day she worked, even to saying things like 'See you tomorrow'.

So far she'd fulfilled Max's wishes. Sunshine felt guilty about leaving Mabel Manners, who had been so kind to her. Surely she would worry when she went into Sunshine's room and found her missing. But Max said there was no place for sentiment when they were escaping to a new life.

The Central Café often didn't close until two or three in the morning. The ferries ran between Gosport and Portsmouth until two. The railway station was but a short distance from the ferry and the trains ran early in the mornings.

'I'm going to let myself out of the Nissen hut as soon as I'm sure the other prisoners are asleep. Hopefully that will be between eleven and twelve. I can't give you an exact time — that's why it's better you should meet me.'

She had already hidden his army clothing: she'd taken it to work and he knew exactly where she had placed it beneath some bushes on the opposite side of the creek. All she had to do now was leave Bridgemary, go into Gosport town at her leisure and wait.

*   *   *

Max listened to the steady breathing around him. There were the usual grunts, groans and farts of the men in their beds, sleeping through the night. The lights were put out early, and although the summer evenings were bright,

223

blackout blinds were in place to enable the men to sleep.

Max had gone to bed in his clothes and now he stood at the bottom of Hans's bunk in the dark. He would miss the lad: he'd been a good friend to him. Over the past weeks Max had told him how he was going to prepare the garden for winter. He hoped that when Hans realized he was in sole charge, the bulbs he'd planted wouldn't be disturbed and that the boy would remember all he'd told and taught him about gardening.

The homemade key turned easily — he'd known it would. Quietly, he locked the door behind him. From building to building he ran, careful not to be discovered. He breathed a sigh of relief when he reached the shed.

Guards were patrolling the perimeter fences but mostly it was a lax affair. Of course they weren't supposed to chat and smoke but some did it anyway. During the day they held long conversations with the prisoners. Max hadn't expected to find two having a chat just yards from the shed, though.

It needed only one to lean on the wire, and the mesh that Max had painstakingly filed down would break. Then the alarm would sound and he'd be discovered hiding in the shed. They were so close he dared not breathe loudly or move. His heart was banging against his ribs. Just when he thought he couldn't possibly hold back a sneeze any longer the guards parted company, throwing down dog ends and grinding them into the earth with their boots.

How he managed to contain that sneeze he would never know but he felt luck was on his side. Surely nothing else could go wrong. It would be a little while before the guards returned and it wasn't difficult to tear through the weakened wire.

Darkness covered him as he slid silently into the brackish water and swam to the other side of the creek.

His teeth were chattering as he emerged from the smelly water and began the hunt for his dry clothing. The bag was where Sunshine had promised it would be. His heart gave an excited leap.

His cold fingers made it difficult to climb out of his wet prison clothes. He eyed the dreaded P on his trouser leg and quickly rolled all the wet things into a ball, then stuffed it into the hollow that had held the army clothing.

He felt another sneeze coming. This time he thought it was produced by the faint smell of burning that clung to the private's outfit Sunshine had made. Couldn't be helped, he thought. It would probably have disappeared by the time he reached the town.

Suddenly he threw himself onto the grass as a snuffling noise reached his ears. His blood was pounding in his veins. He lay quite still, terrified to move in case he gave away his whereabouts to whoever was hovering quite near him.

Max peered through the weeds. The creature, with a white stripe down the centre of its head, stopped walking towards him and froze. Then the badger shuffled about and scurried into the undergrowth, leaving behind its pungent animal smell, obviously just as perturbed by him as he was by it.

With a smile, Max stood up and fastened the khaki blouson. He walked across the field, keeping to the hedgerow, and out onto the road. He was free!

31

Max was exhilarated to be walking freely along an English road again. He knew he mustn't draw attention to himself. He refrained from singing or whistling — after all, a private in the British Army should be beyond reproach at all times.

Few people were out on the streets, although he passed stragglers returning home from the Criterion Picture House where he stopped to look at the stills outside advertising *Old Mother Riley's Ghosts*. Max could see in the photographs that the old woman was clearly a man. Ah, the idiosyncrasies of the English, he thought. He preferred Marika Rökk, the blonde film star who was all woman.

The day had been remarkably warm, and the night still held remnants of its heat. He wondered if Sunshine had reached the café yet. There was no definite time for them to meet because Max could not in all sincerity tell her what time he would attempt to escape from the barracks.

Stupid woman, he'd be glad to get rid of her. He congratulated himself on knowing women so well that he understood exactly what they were capable of. He'd chosen well with the little seamstress. He'd also instilled in her a trust in him. By ensuring she held on to the forged papers, it was like leaving his life in her hands.

When he met her this time he would take

charge of them and also of any money she had saved for the journey. He knew that, in England, although many women professed to hold the purse strings, when they were travelling or out for an evening the man always paid.

He would buy the boat tickets. Travelling across the water to Portsmouth from Gosport meant buying a return, the ferry company having decided that people who crossed always came back: it saved on paying wages for a ticket office on the Portsmouth side.

When they reached the station near the ferry terminals he intended to tell her to wait while he found and used the public convenience. Of course, he would not return. What good would such a scrawny specimen of womanhood be to him?

And as for the child? He was sure she was a virgin the first time he took her, but how was he to know she'd not given her body to someone else afterwards? The child could be anyone's. If she'd done it with him, she'd do it with any man, wouldn't she?

After he had disappeared and there was no reason why she should find him, he would double back to catch the ferry to Ireland. She, penniless, would not, could not follow him.

Neither would she go to the authorities. She would cry, yes, but she would tell no one she had participated in his escape. It certainly wouldn't profit her if she did. Stupid she might be, but not that stupid!

Now he passed the fire station in Clarence Road and turned down North Cross Street to where the café stood in darkness on the corner.

He pushed open the door and was met by a cloud of cigarette smoke and the smell of meaty stew. A wireless was playing dance music. He slipped inside and looked about him. Sunshine wasn't there, but he was sure she was on her way to meet him. Behind the counter a slim, dark-haired woman, her hair up in a Victory roll, smiled a welcome, showing small white teeth. There were a few customers sitting at tables. Over near the alcove two elderly men were playing dominoes, a full ashtray on the Formica table along with half-drunk mugs of tea. At another table a smartly dressed man in a suit was reading the *Evening News* while chatting to his friend, who still had his trilby hat pushed down over his dark hair. His raincoat was placed on another chair beside them. They looked up and stared at Max.

Unwilling to allow his nerves to show, Max dipped his head in acknowledgement. One returned the nod, the other smiled. Max allowed himself to relax. At another table a young woman, fettered by a pushchair and a little boy sitting beside her, was urging the child to eat. She looked harassed, tired and grubby. Max thought maybe she had lost her home in the recent bombing. Bits of food covered the table.

'What can I get you, Tommy?'

Max knew the affectionate nickname for soldiers was Tommy, so he returned the dark-haired woman's grin and, knowing he had a few shillings for just an occasion such as this, which Sunshine had provided, said clearly, 'A cup of tea, please, and a bowl of whatever is in that pot.' He motioned towards it.

'It's rabbit stew. All right?'

She put both her hands on the counter top. He noticed the lipstick she wore echoed her nail varnish. 'That's fine,' he replied.

'Tuppence for the mug of tea and threepence for the stew.'

He fumbled in the pocket of his trousers and counted out the exact money, which he put on the counter. She picked it up and put in the till, which clanged shut. 'Sit down and I'll bring it to you.'

He sat facing the door, near the two smartly dressed men. Almost at once the woman appeared at his side with a mug of strong tea and a soup spoon, which she put on the table in front of him. 'Only got one pair of hands,' she said. 'Stew's coming.'

He smiled again at her and watched her walk away in a pair of ridiculously high heels with bows on the front. He decided she wasn't young but she knew how to make the best of her assets.

'On leave, mate?'

It was the man reading the newspaper. Max had turned at his voice. 'Going back to barracks,' Max answered, and looked down at the steaming dish of vegetables and meat that had been set on the table in front of him.

'There's salt and pepper on the counter,' the woman said, but already Max had started eating. It had been six o'clock when he had had his last meal and the rabbit stew was making his mouth water.

One of the men, the one in the hat, got up and squeezed past Max's table. ''Scuse me, mate,' he said to his companion, making for the door. 'I need the privy.'

No sooner had he left the café than a big man in a grubby apron filled the doorway. 'You all right, Della?'

'Course I am,' the waitress said.

The man's gaze slid over the café's customers and back again to the hallway where he was standing. 'I'm only here if you need me.'

'All right, Bert,' she said.

Max was enjoying the stew. It was very hot and filling. He took another spoonful, relishing the meat as he bit into it.

He could hear voices in the passage outside but not what was being said. He heard a guffaw of laughter and guessed there'd been an exchange between the man in the apron and the customer, who now paused in the doorway and grinned at him before moving slowly back to his seat.

Max decided Sunshine had been astute in choosing the café for them to get together. It really hadn't mattered who had reached the meeting place first: it was a comfortable place to wait. He finished the last spoonful and licked his lips. He pushed the dish to the centre of the table and began on the tea. He was feeling full, comfortable and contented.

Suddenly there was a man on either side of him and strong hands clamped down on his shoulders. One of the men spoke.

'Right, mate. You'd better come quietly. We

don't want no trouble in here, do we?' Panic hit him. He rose from the chair but couldn't straighten up, for the men held him fast. The table moved, his tea slopped everywhere and the mug crashed to the floor.

The woman's voice was shrill when she shouted, 'Bert!'

'Get! Off!' Max managed to yell, as the heavy-set man in the apron darted from the doorway to behind the counter and grabbed what looked like a walking stick. He then moved in front of the café's exit to the street.

'Don't try nothing,' the man, Bert, warned, shaking a sheath from the stick and revealing a long, thin, extremely sharp-looking blade.

With a thump Max sat back down on the chair. It was clear he was beaten. He gasped, and his heart plummeted like a lead weight, as one of the men said, 'We're detectives. You might as well own up, mate. You're no more an English Tommy than I'm Father bloody Christmas. Let's cuff you.'

Max said, his throat dry as dust, 'How . . . ?'

The man with the swordstick said, 'Three things, mate. I ain't never had no Tommy in my café with a posh accent like yours. You sounds too upper class to be a bleedin' private.'

The man who was still wearing his hat said, 'I've been watching you eat. Your voice don't match your table manners. Posh Englishmen uses their spoons different to you. The upper class smooth their spoon away from them and you been drawing it towards you, like us common lot and the rest of the Europeans. You got to be a foreigner, a spy, to eat like that.'

Just then Max was aware of a child grizzling. He twisted his head and saw the young mother with the little boy, holding him tight, watching the proceedings, her eyes big and frightened. He looked at the two old men, who were eyeing him with great interest.

'Three things?' Max asked. 'You said three things.'

'Well, I ain't never known no private going back to barracks without his kitbag, mate.' Max closed his eyes momentarily. He couldn't stand up, he was still clamped well and truly by the men's heavy hands on his shoulders, but he could use his arms. He gave a huge sigh that seemed to well up from his soul and dropped his head into his hands. Then he felt cold metal slip around his wrists.

Max's head jerked up as the street door began to open.

Sunshine had managed to push it a little way, just enough for her to see inside and for her eyes to meet Max's. Then the man called Bert shouted, 'Can't come in, love. We just got ourselves a spy or summat. Café's closed for the night.'

Her scared face disappeared as Bert closed the door. This time he locked it and put the key into his top pocket. He called to the woman, 'Della, give the station a ring, will you? Get some coppers over here.' He stood guard again at the door. Max watched as the woman behind the counter picked up the telephone.

'Thanks, Bert,' said the detective without a hat.

'Always likes to do my duty for you, lads, you knows that,' Bert said. 'You scratch my back and I'll scratch yours. And you, mate,' he looked at Max, 'you'll be able to have a nice kip in a cell in South Street while they finds out all about you.'

32

Sunshine stood in a darkened doorway, her heart beating fast. She was a long way from the café now. The corset was digging into her and it felt like steel knitting needles thrusting through her flesh. It had begun to rain, the thin drizzle that soaked in everywhere and made the air smell sweet after the heat of the day. She let the string bag she'd been carrying fall to the ground. In it were the false papers, her purse, her wash-things, clean underwear and her gas mask. Max had told her to travel light.

She wasn't stupid. She knew exactly what had happened the moment Bert had stopped her entering the café. She'd seen the two men holding Max. She'd seen the resignation in his eyes as they'd met her own.

It was all over. Her legs buckled and she slid down the door to sit on the cold tiles in the shop's entrance. Tears were falling from her eyes. She didn't have the sensation of crying but how else could so much unhappiness be leaking away from her?

Max had been caught before they'd even crossed on the ferry. How had this come about? He would no doubt be taken to the police station, possibly kept in a cell while they decided where to send him next. She couldn't answer any of the questions that rolled around in her brain. One thing she was sure of, he'd definitely not return to St Vincent Barracks. It was highly possible that she wouldn't see him again. Max would never marry her or see his baby. Poor, poor Max, he had promised her so much and now he wouldn't be able to fulfil any of it.

He must be feeling terrible, she thought. The months she had paid for the false papers with her body had been for nothing. All his planning for a return to Germany, to the farm in Pulheim, had been for nothing. She ached to hold him, the only man she had truly loved, the only man to have wholeheartedly loved her.

She felt the child move inside her. Another sharp needle dig into her lower body. The rain was blowing right inside the doorway now. In a few hours it would be light, and she mustn't be found huddled here. There would be questions to answer. She couldn't tell anyone what had happened, of course not. That might make it worse for Max.

She had to go back to Lavinia House. Mabel Manners would assume she was in bed. She'd left no note that she'd be leaving. Max had instructed her not to. If she could get back to Bridgemary, might she be able to go into the boarding house without anyone knowing? The buses had long ago stopped running. She'd have to walk.

Sunshine put her hands on the doorstep and hoisted herself upright. She used the hem of her skirt to wipe her wet face, picked up the string bag that was fast becoming damp and set out determinedly into the rain.

A couple of days later when Sunshine was due to work in the kitchens at St Vincent, she was tempted not to go in. After all, she should have been in Ireland by now. She'd heard the gossip about a prisoner escaping and being caught and decided that if she wanted to find out more of what had happened to Max she must go to the source of the problem.

The kitchens were a hotbed of talk about other people's affairs. Some of the chatter had been embellished so much that she knew it couldn't be true. The German had been shot! He'd been apprehended by the guards. He was now in a cell at Winchester Prison. There was no talk of an accomplice, but great speculation as to how he'd managed to steal a uniform. Sunshine listened but didn't join in with the excited gossip.

It broke her heart when she was sent to the shed near the creek to bring back potatoes. She looked at the sacks on the floor and thought of the times Max had made love to her there. She thought of the dreams they'd shared.

The perimeter fence had been mended with stronger wire and there seemed to be more guards than usual patrolling inside and outside the camp. Today would be the last time she would leave through the main gate. Sunshine had decided the easiest thing to do would be to write and resign from her job instead of going to see the kitchen manager. She didn't want to answer questions while having the woman stare at what she was still trying to hide beneath the corset. There was no hope of her seeing Max again.

Leaving St Vincent for the last time, Sunshine spotted Max's young friend, Hans, pulling weeds from the garden plot. Alone, crouched on the grass, he looked forlorn. She made to walk towards him. Whatever was she thinking? Hans had no idea who she was, that she had loved Max. She turned away before she reached him, but not before she saw he had been crying.

★　★　★

'I'm off to post this letter,' Sunshine said to Mabel Manners. 'It's my notice, I'm handing it in to St Vincent.'

Mabel was sitting at the big table in the leisure room. Sunshine could see she was adding up columns of figures in a ledger, doing the accounts, she called it. The room smelled of polish. The freshly hung net curtains looked extra white because only that morning Sunshine had soaked them in Reckitt's Blue, then hung them out on the line. Mabel was alone: most of the residents were sunning themselves in the gardens or taking an afternoon nap. She looked up as Sunshine spoke.

'That's good. I didn't want them delivering your baby in the kitchen there.'

Sunshine, who was walking away, turned to face her. 'How did you know?'

Mabel sighed. 'I'm a nurse, remember?'

33

'I can't believe they've come back for another go at us in one day.' Ivy was scared. There were already too many people sheltering down in the cabin of the ferry boat so the girls had stayed up top. She was huddled against the funnel, sandwiched between Bea and Rainey. The incendiary bombs and burning shrapnel, falling from the skies into the strip of water between Portsmouth and Gosport, looked to her like golden rain.

Anyone with any sense would be in a shelter. Ivy pictured her mother Della and Bert hiding in the café's cellar. She muttered a prayer that they and the other girls' families would stay safe.

It was important that the ferries kept running. Like black beetles swimming in a puddle they certainly wouldn't stop crossing the water for a mere Luftwaffe attack, even if it was the second today. Peering through the sea mist she could see the landing stage ahead. Red sky showed something had copped a hit on the Gosport side — possibly one of the boatyards down Beach Street. The light from the flames and burning wood made the ships and boats moored in the harbour look ghostly. Ivy detested the smell of cordite and the stink of smoke that seeped in everywhere.

The whistle of another bomb made her huddle closer to Bea. She listened for the explosion but only a mighty splash followed, sending sea-spray raining on to the boat and making it rock and buck. She held her breath. Was this it? The end of everything? But there was no sharp noise, no huge explosion. Another bomb to fall silently to the sea's depths, she thought. One day perhaps the undertow would wash it, long after the war was over, into the path of an unsuspecting ship. She shuddered.

The tall outline of the Isle of Wight's Hoy Tavern on Gosport's high street loomed into view, and Ivy knew the boat would moor at any moment. The pub and the shops were dark, blacked-out windows like the dead eyes of corpses.

The squat ferry bumped against the landing stage, and as soon as the safety gates had been opened, Ivy, Bea and Rainey were among the first to jump across from the boat to the jetty and hurry through the ferry gardens.

'Are we going to make a run for the café or get to the shelter?' Bea had to shout to be heard. Ivy's gas mask was banging against the top of her leg as she ran. There were already bruises on her skin.

'We'll never get in one, now,' yelled Rainey. 'The café's not far — let's chance it. There's shop doorways for us to hide in.'

Blackie had gone to London today, hoping to finalize a contract with the BBC for a weekly wireless show for the Bluebirds. They were all excited about it. Jo was at home trying to catch up on household chores, and the girls had performed two shows at the end of South Parade

Pier while dodging Hitler's planes. All Ivy wanted to do now was reach the café, fall into bed and sleep. Bert would make sure Rainey and Bea had a safe bed, and Della would enjoy mothering them all, like a hen with chicks.

'Down Mumby Road,' shouted Ivy. 'It's quicker.'

It was clear more than one bomb had already hit the area. A tall lodging house had flames and smoke curling through its windows, and rubble spanned the pavement. Ivy didn't fancy climbing all over it but there was an alleyway ahead: they could use that. A tradesman's van stood on the road, covered with slates and bricks, its roof caved in. She hoped no one had been inside when the lodging house's roof had fallen on it.

'I wish we'd opted for the shelter,' grumbled Bea.

'I wish you'd not moan so much,' Rainey flung back at her.

'In here.' Ivy stopped, holding her side. 'I've got a stitch,' she said. The narrow alley was enclosed on both sides by tall buildings. 'Been running so much I'm puffed out.' She leaned back against the wall, panting.

All three girls ducked as a shower of incendiaries rained down.

'You can almost see the café from here,' said Bea, after a while, peering out. 'If it wasn't for the smoke . . . '

The last of her words were drowned by a gigantic crack and then the noise of sliding rubble, as slates, bricks, moss and wood fell inside the alley.

241

One minute Ivy was listening to Bea, the next she was on the cobbles, covered with dust and terracotta, and everything went black.

★ ★ ★

Bea was rubbing the grit from her eyes. 'Rainey, you all right?'

'I am, but Ivy's copped it!' Clouds of dust swirled about them, adding to the whistle of bombs falling and searchlights valiantly raking the sky.

'Copped it?' Bea's question was a scream. Rainey was kneeling beside Ivy, whose forehead was streaming blood.

'We should get someone to her,' said Rainey. Nearby flames showed her red hair was redder still with brick dust.

'You ain't supposed to move anyone.'

'Can't move her anyway — can't you see her legs are trapped?' Rainey poked in her cardigan pocket for a handkerchief and began wiping Ivy's face clear of muck, careful not to touch the freely running blood. She peered but couldn't see where Ivy's head was hurt.

Bea scrambled over and tried to heave away at a large broken chimney pot that sat atop the bricks on Ivy's legs, but without success. 'It won't move,' she wailed.

'Don't touch anything, you could do more harm than good,' snapped Rainey. She leaned close to Ivy, her face by her friend's lips, then looked up and said to Bea, 'She's breathing, but I can't tell where the blood's coming from.'

'We got to get help,' Bea said.

Rainey looked at Bea, who was trying to hold back her tears. Crying wouldn't help matters. 'Until the all-clear goes, no ambulance will come out.'

Bea's eyes were as bright as a cock sparrow's. 'I know,' she said. 'I'll run up to the café and tell Bert.'

Think! Think! Rainey was telling herself. 'Yes, that's a good idea. But when and if we can get her out, we got to get her to the hospital. Bert hasn't got a car.'

'No, but Eddie's got a van,' said Bea. 'I can phone him from Bert's. My brother'll go through fire and flood for Ivy.'

'Good thinking. Every minute counts, Bea. Go now!'

Bea didn't answer but she got up and was off like a whippet, skirting bricks in the rubble-strewn road, then out of sight as the shadows swallowed her.

Rainey sat on the cobbles hunched over Ivy, trying to shield her from bits of dislodged falling masonry. She didn't dare look up towards the roofs of the buildings in case she saw bricks or broken slates slipping out, ready to fall. All she wanted to do was keep Ivy as safe as she could until help came.

One of Ivy's hands was lying on the rubble. Rainey had never before noticed how small they were. She put her fingers around Ivy's, pleased to feel the warmth flow between her and her friend.

She thought back to when she'd first met Ivy

at St John's School. Rainey and her mother had escaped her father's clutches by running away to Gosport from Portsmouth. She, Ivy and Bea had clicked straight away in the choir Alice Wilkes had run. Thinking of Alice brought back the scent of lavender that always surrounded her.

'And Toto! What about Toto? Did you ever see such a funny little dog?'

Rainey realized she'd said those words aloud. Wait a moment, she thought. Didn't relatives talk to patients in hospital when they were unconscious?

She supposed Ivy was unconscious. Maybe if she talked to her she'd know she wasn't alone. Perhaps when you were unconscious you could still hear what was going on around you. It was worth a try, she thought. She squeezed Ivy's fingers.

'Remember how scared we were when Mrs Wilkes entered us three in that music competition at Fareham? We stood on the stage in front of everyone. I was frightened, shaking so much, and you smiled at me. That smile gave me confidence. You made me remember I wasn't alone.' Rainey gently put pressure on Ivy's hand. 'You're not alone, Ivy. Can you feel me? Wherever you are in that funny inquisitive head of yours, you aren't alone. I'm here with you and I'm not blinkin' leavin' your side until I see you tucked up in bed in hospital and the nurse is sayin' you'll be as good as new.'

Rainey was practically shouting. She took a deep breath and looked at Ivy's white face, her long dark lashes curling on her cheeks, the blood that seemed now to be congealing. Oh, God, she thought. Didn't it mean a person was dead when their cuts didn't bleed? Her own heart started pumping wildly as she bent down closer to Ivy's nose and lips and was relieved to feel a faint waft of air coming from her. Good. Brave face on things, Rainey, she told herself, taking a deep breath. 'Well, Ivy, that day we sang 'The Bluebird Song', and everyone cheered and clapped! That song always makes us cry, doesn't it? We got second place! Just imagine, all those other brilliant acts and we came second!' She paused. 'That Little Annette got first place. I don't mind telling you I didn't like her one bit, she was so full of herself . . . ' Again she paused. Perhaps she shouldn't remind Ivy about what had happened since to Annette.

'I'll never forget how you smiled at me up there on the stage, with your big dark eyes. I can tell you, now you're not answering me back, that you're the best friend I ever had.' She wiped her hand across her nose. 'You're a true friend. You and me, we've been through so much together, I feel like you're my sister. I never had a sister. You know what I mean? And Bea can be a bit dopey at times but she's like a sister, too. You're my special, special friend, though . . . '

Rainey was so deeply involved in talking to Ivy that she almost didn't hear the wail of the all-clear siren.

Then came the sound of footsteps, crunching on broken bricks, voices, vehicles.

'All right, love, I'll take over now. Let's get your mate out of there.'

Rainey could smell cigarette smoke. A big man was gently moving her aside. Her knees and legs were numb where she'd been kneeling on the cobbles. She felt herself being helped up. Big, firm hands were guiding her out of the alley and now a large man in rough overalls was standing between her and Ivy.

'Ivy!' Rainey cried, and tried to turn back to her.

'We're gonna get her out and your mate'll take her to hospital.'

The voice was gruff but kind. Again she smelled cigarette smoke. This time the smell comforted her. And then familiar arms were around her and she was glad because she was very, very cold, even though it was summer.

'Eddie?'

'Yes, Rainey, the ARPs are here. They'll soon get things sorted. You come with me. They'll look after Ivy.' He led her towards his van. She felt like an automaton, being told what to do and doing it. He opened the passenger door and helped her inside.

'Where's the ambulance?' Rainey was panicking — she couldn't see one. There was a fire engine ahead in the road, men running about, but no ambulance.

'There's a factory been hit, people in the basement. Don't worry, I can get Ivy to hospital.'

And now she could smell perfume, Californian Poppy.

Della said, 'Oh, my love,' and enfolded her in her arms. Della was warm and soft, waiting in the van for Ivy, of course she was, keeping out of the way, letting the men go about their business of releasing Ivy from the mound of rubble and that bloody chimney pot. Della was now tucking a blanket around her.

'Thank you for staying with her,' she said. Her voice was all funny, like she'd been crying and was now trying hard not to.

Rainey said, 'What else would I do?' and felt Della's arms reach around her once more and her tears wet on her cheek.

34

'You should let me take you home. You need rest, Rainey.' Eddie's face was smudged with brick dust and his blond hair was powdered orange. 'I'll come and tell you when we know something about her.'

'No, I'm staying.' Her words were clipped. She patted Ivy's mother's hands, folded loosely in her lap as she sat stiffly on a hospital chair and was rewarded with a tearful smile.

'You're a good friend,' said Della, in her husky voice. Her cheeks sported railway-like tracks where her tears had dried on her skin.

'She's been in here ages,' said Rainey. 'Here' was the War Memorial Hospital, a waiting room with sterile white walls and uncomfortable wooden seats. Posters about venereal disease adorned the walls.

'No news is good news,' Eddie said. Rainey glared at him. He was trying to be cheerful. But she knew how worried he was. They were also lucky to be in this small room, instead of the larger noisy waiting room that was full to bursting with relatives waiting for news of loved ones taken in from the wallpaper factory blast. It had received a direct hit and was still being dealt with by the fire brigade and the ambulance men.

'I hate the smell in here,' Rainey said. 'It's like disinfectant disguising death.' She'd hardly got the words out when the door opened and a pretty nurse entered with a swish of blue and white starched apron.

'Your daughter has a lovely plaster cast, Mrs Sparrow. Her X-ray shows a clean leg break and she can go home tomorrow.'

For a moment silence filled the room. Then, 'Is she awake? What about her head wound, all that blood?' Della's eyes were huge with worry.

The nurse spoke calmly. 'She's awake but very sleepy. The doctor has given her something. Head wounds sometimes bleed profusely even when there's very little wrong. There shouldn't be any lasting damage.'

'Can we see her?' Eddie was standing up now, shifting from one foot to the other with impatience.

'Yes, but don't tire her. Come with me.'

Her sensible black shoes clip-clopped out and down the corridor. It was obvious she expected the three of them to follow, so they did.

Ivy was in a ward with six other women. Rainey saw Eddie avert his eyes and gaze straight ahead, whether because of shyness or eagerness to reach Ivy's side she had no idea. Ivy had curtains drawn around her bed. She was lying on her back, her eyes closed. Over her legs there was a cagelike contraption, a pale blue blanket supposedly hiding it, to allow the cast to harden properly without being accidentally knocked.

Ivy had been washed but bits of dust clung in her dark hair. There was some brown stuff painted on her forehead that disappeared into her hairline. The skin was swollen, bruised. Rainey couldn't see any injuries — she thought perhaps Ivy's thick hair covered the wound.

Della went straight up to the bed, bent down and kissed Ivy's cheek. Ivy was unmoving.

'She's asleep now,' the nurse said. 'She's not unconscious. Tomorrow the doctor will tell you how to care for her at home. You'll probably find she'll be a little cranky at not being able to move around much. She was awake earlier, a bit out of it, talking about someone called Toto.'

Rainey smiled. So Ivy had heard her outpouring from her heart, had she? 'She's going to be all right?' she asked. It was horrible seeing her so still.

The nurse, dark-haired and smiling, said, 'Oh, yes. You can stay for a few minutes,' she added, 'but it's long past visiting hours. Please excuse me. I have to go. We're busy tonight.' Her skirts rustled as she left them at Ivy's bedside and pulled the curtain closed after her.

★　★　★

Bea was waiting at the hospital's main door for them. Despite the lateness of the hour people were milling about outside. 'I couldn't go home not knowing,' she said. She looked worried sick. 'No one would tell me anything, but I saw the van and knew you were still here.'

'Where's Mum?' Eddie asked, ignoring his sister's questions.

'She's with Jo,' said Bea. 'Tell me about Ivy.'

Della said, 'She'll be home tomorrow. Thank God it wasn't as bad as we thought.'

'She's going to be all right, then? I

250

thought . . . ' Bea's words came out in a rush.

'I know what you thought,' said Rainey, putting her arms around her. 'We all thought the same. She'll have a plaster cast on her leg but she'll be all right.'

Bea took a deep breath, then pushed it out in a big sigh of relief. 'I thought . . . I thought . . . ' she said again. Then she put both hands over her face and sobbed into them.

They had reached Eddie's van and he opened the passenger door for them to jump in and slide along the bench seat.

'Does Blackie know?' asked Rainey, remembering he had gone to London to sort out contracts.

Della shook her head. 'Jo had a phone call much earlier this evening saying he wasn't even going to try to get back to Gosport because of the bombing and that he'd find somewhere to stay and return tomorrow. He's got a contract for the Bluebirds to sign.'

'Things are messed up, now.' Bea was wiping her eyes with a grubby handkerchief. 'Ivy won't be able to sing.'

Eddie started up the engine. 'Nothing's messed up. I'll be her legs,' he said. 'I'll carry her until she can walk with a stick and I'll take her where she needs to go.' Rainey stared at him. He means it — he really means it, she thought.

'But she's lying in hospital,' wailed Bea.

'She is now,' said Eddie. 'But she won't be tomorrow.'

'You heard that nurse,' said Della. 'She'll have crutches. It'll take at least a couple of months before she can get about again.'

'I can do it,' said Eddie firmly. 'Look on the bright side. It's her bleedin' leg what's damaged, not her voice!'

35

Bert had relished the notoriety of the escaped prisoner being apprehended in his café. There had been a large spread in the *Evening News*, with a photograph of him and his premises. As a result his takings had soared for a few weeks but things were slowing down now. Ivy could hear the wireless and Bing Crosby's voice.

'If I'd known I could have all this attention from Eddie, I'd have let a chimney fall on me ages ago,' she said to Bea. She sat propped up on the bed, her left leg in a plaster cast that encased her skin from below the knee to her foot. Crutches leaned against the wall near the headboard. A long knitting needle sat to hand. It was the only thing that would satisfy the itch beneath the cast that she couldn't scratch.

'Don't say that,' snapped Bea. 'We were all worried sick. An' it was because of you I got a huge blister on my heel.'

'How come I get the blame for that?' Ivy asked, even though she'd heard it all before.

'You know I was wearing my black high heels. They look lovely but they don't half give me gyp, and I'd already had enough of them before we reached the alley that night. I was so determined to get to the café quickly to get help that I never thought to take my shoes off to run. And I ran as fast as I could. It didn't half bleed. Look!' Bea lifted her foot and, her shoe dangling off her toes, tore off the sticking plaster and showed Ivy the remains of what had been a very bad blister that was now almost healed. Her legs were evenly coated in dried gravy browning and she'd painted a black line up the back to resemble the stockings that were near impossible to get hold of in the shops now.

'Silly,' said Ivy, looking at Bea's footwear. 'Why are you still wearing those black shoes if they hurt so much?'

Bea shrugged her shoulders. 'They make my legs look nice,' she said.

Ivy shook her head. She hoped it wouldn't be ages before she could walk properly again in heels.

There was a polite knock on the bedroom door and Bert opened it. After entering he bent down and picked up the tray he'd left outside on the floor. In he came with two mugs of tea and two bowls of meat stew.

'You need building up,' he said to no one in particular, putting down the tray on the bedside table. He eyed the crutches. 'I know they're still useful to help you get about and that Eddie carries you downstairs and in and out of vehicles, but as soon as you can manage with just a stick, I'm going to lend you one you'll love to be seen with. Yes,' he said, as though agreeing with himself. 'And although I says it myself, you're much better off on this first floor than up the top of the house with your mother.'

'It was kind of you to sort out this room for me, Bert. You could be letting it.' The stew smelled delicious.

'No, it's kind of Eddie to be at your beck and call but no one could expect him to go trotting up to the top floor every time you wanted to be carried down,' said Bert. He took off his spectacles and wiped them on his grubby apron, then replaced them on his nose.

'I do feel a bit bad about it. He's got a big renovating job to see to as well now. I don't want to be the cause of him losing money,' Ivy said.

'He'll leave you when he feels you can cope,' Bea said. 'Besides, he's got blokes who get on with the work. Anyway, he likes you.'

Ivy saw Bert nod in agreement.

'I like him.' If only Eddie knew how much, thought Ivy. Of course she wouldn't say anything. She didn't want to frighten him away. Eddie had told her how Sunshine had put the fear of God into him, always harping on about marriage and kids. Not that Ivy wanted things to get that serious, not yet. After all, she had a career to explore before she thought about happy homes and the patter of little feet.

'No, not likes, *likes*. You know what I mean, likes . . . ' Bea interrupted Ivy's musing.

Bert coughed politely.

He really wasn't comfortable making small-talk with young women, thought Ivy.

'I can't make head or tail of what you girls are saying. I'll leave you to it. Just don't make Eddie go away too soon — he's agreed to paint the downstairs hall with that paint I got off that bloke what helped himself after the fire at the wallpaper factory.'

Ivy had been out cold on the night she'd been

admitted to the War Memorial Hospital, but next morning she'd heard all about the terrible bomb blast, the casualties and the high intake of patients the hospital had coped with. She'd also heard about the salvage operation of the fire-damaged wallpaper and other stock.

'What colour is the paint?' Bea asked.

'Dunno. The labels is all singed off,' Bert said, as he made for the door. 'Eat that stew while it's hot. It'll put hairs on yer chests.'

Bea set a dish in front of Ivy and handed her a spoon. 'Is it meat or rabbit?' she asked.

Ivy could do such things for herself, but she knew Bea liked to feel useful. 'Don't know, don't care,' said Ivy. 'Bert's stew is always delicious. That German runaway ate some the night he got caught.'

'He was allowed to work outside — he worked for Eddie. Did you know that?' Bea had started on her own lunch.

'Yes, Eddie told me,' said Ivy. 'He said he was a likeable chap and a good worker.'

Bea shrugged and put another spoonful of stew into her mouth. After swallowing, she said, 'You never can tell what people are likely to do.'

They ate companionably. No, thought Ivy, you never knew what people would do. Who would have thought Eddie would jump in and be such a help? It was almost worth having a plaster cast on her leg to have him sit and talk to her. He'd got hold of a wheelchair that now resided downstairs near the cellar door. It hadn't taken her long to get the hang of it. It had gone up to London, to the Savoy, when they'd been summoned to do another Geraldo recording. Eddie had put it in the back of his van, and with her in the front, and some black-market petrol from Bert, had met Blackie, Jo, Rainey and Bea at the hotel.

She'd been unable to stand for the recording, but was dressed in her finery, as were Rainey and Bea, but she didn't feel at a loose end: Rainey and Bea had hugged one microphone and a second had been set up just for her. That was brilliant, she thought as she'd listened to the playback. One of the songs was Billie Holiday's 'I Cried For You'. Ivy had made it her own.

The end-of-the-pier shows had finished now. She'd missed only a couple of performances just after her accident. When she'd returned, the audience didn't seem to mind her sitting on a bale of straw to sing while Rainey and Bea pranced about the stage. She was particularly grateful for Eddie's constant attention because she had discovered soon after her discharge from hospital that when she was in an enclosed dark place she began to panic. In bed at night she wondered if it was some kind of throwback to the buildings looming over her in the blackness of the alley. The first time it happened she'd crawled from her bed and pulled back the blackout curtain. As long as she could see bright lights, the panic lessened. She could sleep through the searchlights flashing but complete darkness scared her.

Summer was nearly over and the trippers to Southsea had trickled away. Their first record was soon to be released, not with Geraldo but with the label saying 'The Bluebirds' on it. They were all so excited about it. Again Eddie had driven her to London, wheeled her to the recording studios and, after a run-through, the three girls had gone into a soundproofed room and sung along to the music wearing head-phones.

Their first record was to be 'We'll Meet Again'. Vera Lynn had made the song fantasti-cally popular a couple of years ago but it was a well-loved tune, thought Ivy, and on the other side Parlophone had opted for 'I'll Never Smile Again', a current favourite.

They'd all, along with Blackie, signed a BBC contract for a weekly programme entitled *The Forces' Darlings* that would be broadcast in the New Year. Other female singers would also be performing to help cheer up the men serving here and abroad, as well as all the people toiling in the factories. There was such a lot to look forward to, thought Ivy, and the days and weeks went by so quickly.

'I wonder which walking stick Bert will let me use?' she said, scraping her bowl clean. 'I'm a bit worried about not using the crutches any more.'

'I think you just want Eddie to go on carrying you about,' said Bea. She took the bowl from Ivy and replaced it with a mug of tea.

Ivy laughed. But when Eddie went back to his job permanently she would miss the cosy chats they shared. When they sat together reading, Ivy had never felt such contentment. They talked about anything and everything. He had even confessed he had stolen Sunshine's virginity one night round the back of the Criterion Picture House. He'd told Ivy he'd felt bad about it ever since, especially as he knew any feelings he'd had for the girl had long since gone. He still visited his grandfather at Lavinia House but not nearly as often as he would have liked as he didn't want to risk seeing Sunshine. What they'd once had together was over and done with, Eddie had told her.

Eddie cared about Ivy.

Ivy was well aware of his feelings: they showed in every little thing he did for her. He hadn't told her how he felt, though, and he hadn't kissed her, but she wanted him very much to do just that.

36

November 1941

Eddie read the headline in the *Evening News:* '*Ark Royal* Sunk by Italian Torpedo'.

He believed the ship's aircraft had brought down more than a hundred enemy planes.

'It's a bloody shame,' he said to Maud, who was standing in front of the big mirror hanging over the fireplace, pushing in a hatpin to skewer her hat to her hair. ' 'Eighteen men lost but some believed to have been taken aboard other ships in the vicinity of Gibraltar',' he read aloud.

'I'm so fed up with this war,' his mother moaned. 'And I'm fed up with this cold November weather.' She turned to look at him. 'Why don't you come to Bridgemary with me to see Granddad? We could go up in the van instead of me having to wait around for the bus.'

'I don't want to go out, Mum,' he said. 'I've done a full day's work re-roofing a two-up two-down house in Henry Street with second-hand slates that were so cold they very nearly froze my fingers off.' He stretched both hands to prove a point. 'Then before I came home to have my tea, I took Ivy to the hospital to have her plaster cast cut off.'

'Oh, I forgot to ask,' said his mother. 'How did that go?'

'All right. Well, it will be as soon as she gets

used to walking properly again. Bert's given her a little black walking stick that's shaped like a folded umbrella and has rhinestones and glittery bits on it.'

'Oh, my!' Maud said, her voice full of wonder.

'Apparently it's one of his most prized possessions. Della bought it for him a few years ago and it means a lot to the daft ol' sod!'

'I don't think you should call him that,' Maud chided.

'Why ever not? I wouldn't say anything behind his back that I wouldn't say to his face.' He dug in his trouser pocket and pulled out a ten-bob note. 'Look, Mum, go into the Alma and see if you can get a couple of bottles of Forest Brown for Granddad. Tell him they're from me.'

'I can't go in a public house on my own. Whatever will people think?' She looked indignant.

'Go into the Bottle and Jug — you'll be all right in there. They might not have any brown ale anyway. Just get him a little something from me, please, Mum?'

She sighed but took his money and put it into her purse. She pulled on her coat, wound a scarf around her neck, careful not to dislodge her hat, which Eddie thought looked like an upside-down mushroom perched on her head, walked out of the kitchen and down the hall. She called, 'Bye,' and the door slammed behind her.

He picked up his book, *For Whom the Bell Tolls* by Ernest Hemingway, and began to read. A few minutes later he put it down on the arm of the chair. He wasn't taking in any of the words. All he could think about was Ivy and that she didn't need his help so much now that she was mobile again. He sighed.

All this time he'd felt like some soppy schoolboy with her. She filled him with happiness each time he looked at her. He was besotted with her. Yet he hadn't found the courage to tell her or even to kiss her.

A couple of years back when he'd helped her out of his van and his hand had touched hers, a spark had ignited between them. But during all the time he'd willingly carried her up- and downstairs and pushed that damned wheelchair he'd loved the feel of her skin against his, loved the smell of her, loved the tingle that went straight to his heart when he looked at her, but he hadn't dared to kiss her.

Why? Because he was frightened that the spark wouldn't still be there. Not his spark, but hers. That special something he knew she, too, had felt that day. Oh, he loved her all right. No doubt about that. He'd always loved her. She was so very young, that was the trouble. She was making a name for herself, with his sister and Rainey, and she had her whole future ahead of her. She didn't need him hanging onto her skirt while she became so famous that the name Bluebirds was on everyone's lips.

He thought about the sparkly stick Bert was lending her. He smiled. She'd be able to use the slim furled-umbrella-shaped walking stick on the stage until her leg was stronger. That stick was just as sparkly as she was.

★   ★   ★

Sunshine heaved herself up from the chair in front of her sewing machine and stretched. Her heavy belly rested on the worn sheets she'd been cutting, turning and sewing together, edge to edge, for Mabel Manners. The dull ache low down in her back hadn't gone away. Instead it had intensified over the day. She thanked God Mabel had taken away the corset.

'You'll do yourself an injury trying to squeeze yourself into that,' she had said one day, a month or so ago, when she'd come into Sunshine's room with a mug of cocoa made with condensed milk. 'Tell me you haven't been wearing it all the time.'

'I didn't want people to know about the baby because they'd gossip,' Sunshine had replied.

'It's going on the fire. Let them gossip.' She'd whisked up the offending article and carried it off with her, and Sunshine hadn't set eyes on it since. She wasn't sorry she didn't have to struggle into the hateful whalebone contraption any more but now her size caused her to hide from the residents for fear they'd notice she'd put on weight and ask questions. She took to setting her alarm clock for very early in the mornings and getting up and doing her chores while everyone was still asleep. Until Mabel found out.

'If that's the way you feel, I can find you lots of jobs where you don't have to show yourself,' she said. 'But I'm telling you now, you're not the first to have a child out of wedlock an' you certainly won't be the last. But I'll respect your wishes. Who's the father?'

Sunshine had no intention of telling anyone that Max, the German prisoner apprehended in Gosport, was her baby's father. She could imagine all the tittle-tattle and problems it would cause. The elderly people at Lavinia House were lovely but, like many aged men and women, fixed in their ideas of right and wrong.

She'd pressed her lips together and Mabel had said, 'All right, keep your secret. What's important is that I see you're eating properly and looking after yourself. You've got to eat for two, now!' She insisted Sunshine's work be kept to a minimum. The rough cleaning she now did herself, leaving Sunshine with sewing jobs and light dusting.

In bed at night Sunshine began to realize that Mabel had become the mother she'd never had. Little gifts started appearing: knitted bootees, a matinee jacket, long cotton baby's nightdresses. 'I was down the market, saw this and thought of you,' was Mabel's refrain. The woman's kindness helped ease the pain she felt at knowing she would never see Max again and that he would never see his child.

Sunshine had no control over the wetness that gushed down her legs and onto the lino. She gripped the edges of the sewing table while what felt like a sharp knife slowly gutted her. She sank back onto the chair and looked down at herself as the pain eased. At the blood staining her homemade skirt, fastened with a safety-pin.

Almost immediately the pain restarted. This

time it was like giant hands pressing down, trying to squeeze the child from her. She put her hands beneath her belly, which was as hard as iron, as if to protect the baby she was sure was going to slip away from her. Surely it was too early for the child to come, she thought. When the pain receded and she lifted her fingers she saw they were covered with fresh blood. She could smell it, sour, metallic. Sunshine screamed.

★   ★   ★

Maud Herron was on her way back from the indoor lavatory at Lavinia House and fed up with playing games of draughts that she never won with Solomon, when she heard the scream from Sunshine's room. At that precise moment Mabel Manners opened her door and came face to face with her.

'What the . . . ?' began Maud.

'Come with me,' demanded Mabel and pushed her along to Sunshine's room. Without knocking she threw open the door.

'Oh . . . my . . . God!' Maud didn't have to ask where the scream had come from or why. She took in the heavily pregnant form of Sunshine lying on the floor and said, 'She needs a doctor!'

'No time for that. She's too far gone,' hissed Mabel. 'You'll have to help me. You can start by closing the bloody door.'

Maud did as she was told, then watched Mabel tear off Sunshine's clothing until only her jumper remained on her upper body.

'Make sure no oldies come in to see what's going on. She's well on the way to having this kiddie but I don't like all this blood.' This last she whispered, and stared at Maud, knowing they and Sunshine were in for a hard time. She pulled the sheets across that Sunshine had been sewing and managed to roll them beneath the girl's body. All the time she was talking to Sunshine: 'I'm here, love. It's going to be all right. Is that another pain? That's right, go with it.' Then she said to Maud, 'Hold her hand. I need to get towels and stuff from the cupboards in the hall.' She added, 'I'll phone for the doctor. Let's hope he comes soon.'

Sweat was pouring from Sunshine. Her face was screwed up with pain and her body was writhing, trying to expel the cause of her agony.

Maud wanted to take the hurt away from her. She remembered it well. She'd gone through labour twice. She also appreciated that, however much it hurt at the time, the pain soon receded from memory.

Sunshine's nails were digging into Maud's palm. With her other hand, Maud grabbed a piece of sheeting and wiped sweat from Sunshine's forehead.

Another gush of bloody matter escaped from Sunshine just as the door opened and Mabel entered, her arms full of clean towels. Sunshine gave a grunt and a scream — enough to curdle fresh milk, thought Maud. She watched amazed as a head followed by shoulders, then little arms and legs slid into view.

'Jesus, that was quick,' said Mabel, dropping

all the stuff she was carrying onto the bed and falling to her knees in front of Sunshine. 'God, that baby's tiny. Get me the scissors,' she barked.

Maud, overwhelmed by the sight of the tiny baby nestled among the bloodied sheeting, rose to her feet and searched near the sewing machine. A thin cry suddenly got stronger. The baby was alive!

She passed the scissors to Mabel, who looked at her with tears in her eyes. 'It's always a bloody miracle,' she said.

Maud watched Mabel cut the cord and tie it with a piece of yarn from Sunshine's sewing kit. She couldn't speak: her feelings were too close to the surface. It was one thing giving birth herself but quite another watching a tiny human being enter the world.

Maud knelt down beside Sunshine. Mabel had laid the tiny, screaming infant on Sunshine's bony breast. 'It's a little girl, love. You got a beautiful little girl,' said Maud. She was entranced by the child.

Mabel was ministering to Sunshine now. She was attempting to stop the flow of blood that seemed never-ending. Mabel looked at Maud, who read her mind. The message wasn't good.

Sunshine was attempting to move her arms and hands to touch her baby. She was trying to speak. 'Hair? Colour?' Her voice was faint.

'Why, it's blonde, like yours,' Maud said. 'She's a pretty little thing.'

'Like . . . her dad.' Sunshine's voice was fading. Maud looked at Mabel, who shook her head.

Sunshine's hand gripped her crying child's body. 'Be kind . . . to her. Not . . . home like . . . me . . . ' She seemed to take a breath that turned into a gurgle. 'Get . . . Eddie . . . to be . . . kind . . . to . . . her . . . '

The silence could have been cut with a knife.

Then Mabel said, 'She's gone.' She'd hardly got the two words out when there was a fierce knocking on the door. The handle was turned and a small, tired-looking man entered. Dressed in a raincoat and trilby, he brought with him a waft of cold air from the corridor. He dumped his black bag on the table near the sewing machine and quickly took in the situation. He looked at the squirming child, oblivious to her mother's demise, and said kindly, 'Who have we got here, then?'

He knelt down and touched Sunshine, frowned, looked again at the baby, then at Mabel. 'She works for me,' said Mabel. 'She's got nobody.'

The doctor gave a long, worn sigh, stood up and said, 'I'll make arrangements.'

'Not for the baby, you won't.' Maud's voice rose. 'That's my grandchild, that is!'

37

'What's the baby like?' Rainey had listened wide-eyed to everything Bea had said.

'All right. She's small and she cries a lot,' said Bea. 'I can't believe she's our Eddie's but she's as blonde as he is . . . '

There was so much Ivy wanted to ask but she was afraid of the answers. She stirred her tea and watched it swirl in the mug. The girls were supposed to be practising above the café, but Bea's revelations had Rainey and Ivy spellbound, sitting at a table in the café. The wireless was on and Frank Sinatra was singing. As usual the air was thick with customers' cigarette smoke.

'When's Sunshine's funeral?' Ivy asked.

'Mrs Manners has managed to book it for next week. What with all the deaths from raids and everything, people have to be fitted in whenever possible . . . She said she wanted to take care of that for Sunshine.' Bea sipped her tea and swallowed.

'How's Eddie with the little one?' Ivy's voice was small.

'Oh, you know what blokes are like with babies. Mum's besotted with her. Every time the kid opens her mouth Mum sticks a bottle in it.'

'It's . . . It's . . . Hasn't anyone named her yet?' Ivy was surprised at the force behind her words.

'Grace. That's her name,' said Bea, giving Ivy

a surprised look. 'Mum said of Sunshine, 'There but for the Grace of God, go I,' so her name is Grace.'

'That's nice,' murmured Rainey. 'Her and Eddie, they're going to bring it up together?'

'I reckon so. I'm an auntie now,' Bea said, with a certain amount of pride. Her voice was thoughtful as she added quietly, 'I've been thinking a lot about Sunshine and the trouble she got herself into. And how it all ended with her losing her life. She probably thought when she went with Eddie that nothing would come of it.' She paused. 'I now know how lucky I was that night down the Fox that that sailor didn't make me pregnant. From now on I'm going to think carefully about what I do and what I want from life.' She smiled at Ivy. 'And my decisions will be my own, not anyone else's.'

Inside Ivy's head a maelstrom of thoughts was going round and round. Eddie had admitted doing it with Sunshine. Never, Ivy knew, would he have believed the result would be a child to change his and his mother's lives. And how did she, Ivy, feel about this?

Sunshine had kept the baby a secret. Perhaps she had thought there would be some way she could love and look after her without Eddie's help. After all, their romance had run its course. Eddie had told her that.

'Just before she died — that was when she told your mum it was Eddie's baby?' Ivy felt tears well up and threaten to push against her eyelids. She'd heard how the girl had suffered while she was growing up. Sunshine must have thought her

270

little girl would surely stand a better chance of being loved and cared for if she was with her daddy. Imagine, thought Ivy, knowing you were dying but you were leaving behind a helpless child. She blinked hard to stop the tears falling.

Bea was nodding. 'Mum brought the baby home that same night,' she said.

Eddie would make a good dad, once he got used to the idea, thought Ivy. She'd truly believed they had no secrets and could share anything. So why hadn't he come down to the café to talk to her about this? She could, of course, go to him. But how did she really feel about the baby? Was his silence telling her he wanted to devote all his time to the child and there was no room now in his life for her?

'Listen!' shouted Bea, suddenly. 'It's us!'

And it was: the Bluebird Girls were singing 'We'll Meet Again' on the wireless. Bea and Rainey's faces were bright with smiles, but Ivy felt like crying.

★   ★   ★

Eddie could hear the baby crying again. He pushed open the back door with his shoulder and made his way into the kitchen where he let the logs he'd been carrying fall into the fireplace. Then he went back and closed the scullery door properly to keep out the cold. His mum had said the house needed to be kept warm for the baby. He brought home as much redundant wood as he could, timber that hadn't already disappeared from the houses he was renovating.

When Maud had gone to the chemist earlier to buy national dried baby milk, the child was mercifully asleep in the back bedroom, which was warmed by the kitchen fire's chimney breast. He'd taken time off today so she could go unhindered to the shops. Not that there was much in them nowadays: the war shortages had seen to that. Christmas was fast approaching and Maud was worrying.

After the bother with Max escaping, Eddie had thought the authorities would take back the other German prisoners he had working for him. Luckily that wasn't so. Eddie was able to go on fulfilling his rebuilding obligations to the local council. He missed Max, there was no doubt about that. The German had been opinionated but he'd been a hard grafter and always ready with a laugh and a quick quip. Young Hans missed him as well. When Hans wasn't with Eddie, he was planning what to plant next year in the garden plot at the front of St Vincent that Max had loved so much.

Eddie finished sweeping up the mess he'd made riddling the grate and propped the brush and shovel against the side of the fender.

The baby was still crying.

He began to climb the stairs. What did he know about babies? One stupid, selfish act at the back of the picture house and look where it had landed him.

And just when he felt he was really getting close to Ivy. He'd well and truly blotted his copybook with her now, hadn't he? If he wasn't worthy of her before, he certainly wasn't now he had a kiddie in tow.

He should have gone and told her face to face what had happened. That he couldn't walk away from the baby and pretend it didn't exist. He couldn't expect Ivy to fall into his arms and say, 'It doesn't matter, I love you.' They'd never discussed how they felt about each other, had they? They'd talked about everything else, though, and she certainly deserved better than to hear what had happened second-hand from Bea.

The baby's cries grew louder. Is this what being a dad was all about? Listening to everlasting screams? Sitting in a roomful of damp nappies hung about the fireguard? The endless feeding at one end just for the food to run through the tiny body and out the other in a stinking mess?

Eddie pushed open the bedroom door and walked to the carry-cot on the bed.

The tiny baby's face was scarlet with fury. Her hands were grabbing at nothingness in the air. Eddie picked up the bundle and felt the dampness: she needed changing. Immediately the crying stopped. Big blue eyes stared fixedly into his own. Eddie's heart melted like an ice cream on a hot day. What's the matter, Gracie? Never mind, Daddy's here,' he whispered.

38

'Have you heard? The Japanese have bombed Pearl Harbor! They've tried to destroy the fleet so they can conquer southeast Asia without interference . . . '

Jo, woken by the telephone, had rushed downstairs, still half asleep. She recognized Blackie's voice and said, 'Don't be silly, it's nearly Christmas!' As the meaning of Blackie's words finally hit her, she added, 'Sorry! I'm half asleep! Oh, my God! That means the Americans are drawn into the war.'

'Yes, Jo. Now the girls are doing well and their name's becoming known it's time for them to do more than singing on the wireless.' He suddenly changed the subject and said, 'Did you get an invitation from Alice Wilkes?'

Jo, quite used to carrying on two conversations with Blackie at once and following his train of thought, eyed the envelope on the kitchen mantelpiece. 'For Boxing Day? Yes, it's very exciting, isn't it? Sounds like a huge affair. If they're booking the big ballroom at Thorngate, they must have invited half the town. Bit naughty of Alice and Graham to have married quietly at Fareham register office, though. I would have liked to be there to wish them luck.'

'We can do that on Boxing Day. From what

274

I've heard, the place will be packed with well-wishers . . . Anyway . . . '

Jo knew he was going to continue talking about the war and the girls.

'It will only be a matter of weeks before the Americans arrive in England. They aren't going to take this indignity sitting down. Madame feels we should do our bit to welcome our cousins from across the water.' He paused. 'She's here beside me so I'll pass her over to you.'

Jo's heart was thumping. Whenever Madame Walker needed to speak to her it was always about something huge.

'Hello, Jo. It's about time the Bluebird Girls involved themselves more with our boys serving here and abroad. They've the experience now. It's been hard won over the past year.' Jo liked the way Nellie Walker came straight to the point, no shilly-shallying about with her. 'I've been talking to Basil Dean and dear Leslie Henson. We've got the go-ahead to send out a concert party, destination still to be decided but definitely abroad. We're also going to introduce our girls to the Americans, who will set up camps all over our country.'

'Stop a moment! Let me take in all you've been saying.' Jo's head was in turmoil. She repeated back what Madame had said.

'Quite so, Jo dear,' Nellie Walker agreed. 'The girls' first record is selling near the million-copy mark, very successful, so the royalties will offset the ridiculously small amount ENSA can pay. Naturally, there'll be another record — Parlophone want to go on making money, too. The

BBC owes you for the programmes due to be broadcast in the New Year so I'd like to think cash won't be such a problem for you now. How do you feel about this?'

Jo let her words wash over her. The Bluebird Girls in a concert party going to entertain the troops? It was something Ivy, Rainey and Bea had dreamt of from the beginning. But they needed to have their say in the matter. After all, Rainey had started going out with Charlie Smith. How would she, and he for that matter, feel about putting romance on hold? Bea, Jo felt sure, would enjoy the adventure. Ivy, now her leg had healed, needed something to take her mind off Eddie and his problems — of course she could keep in touch with him. Jo sniffed. Ivy was like a wet weekend at the moment — getting back to hard work would do her nothing but good.

'I presume Blackie and I will be travelling with them.'

'Of course, dear, expenses paid, but still a ridiculously small wage,' she said. 'Ever been abroad, Jo?'

Jo automatically shook her head, then realized she couldn't be seen on the phone. 'No, never. I've only ever been to Bembridge on the Isle of Wight but that's not really abroad, is it?' She would miss Maud, she thought, but she'd hear home news from her — and Syd, of course.

Jo could hear Madame laughing. 'If you all agree, it's going to be quite an experience for the lot of you, Jo.'

Jo heard rustling noises on the telephone and

Blackie spoke again. 'Can you get the girls together, Jo? I know it's early but I'll come over to Gosport and let you see what's been planned. Everyone has to agree, of course.'

Jo knew Bea had taken to staying with Ivy at the café as the baby kept her awake at nights. Yesterday Rainey had told Jo she'd be going into Gosport today to practise some new songs Blackie had written out for them.

'Rainey and I can be at the café later this morning. Is that all right? The three girls will be there but I won't say anything to them until you arrive.'

He agreed and rang off.

Excited? Of course she was excited. The girls would be over the moon with joy, except Rainey. But Jo was sure Rainey would understand that if she and Charlie couldn't weather a few weeks apart their romance wasn't the real thing. She thought back to a conversation she'd had with Rainey when her daughter had come home from an evening out with Charlie. She'd said, 'Mum, did you know when you were first in love with Dad?' Her eyes were shining.

Jo hadn't wanted to burst Rainey's bubble of happiness so she'd said, 'I was younger than you are now and I had no experience of men . . . '

'I knew you'd say that. The terrible life we had with Dad made me wary of men. Tom Marks was like Dad.' She paused. 'If I told you Charlie was a whole different species, would you believe me?'

'I think I would,' answered Jo.

Rainey's reply to that was a hug that almost

knocked her off her feet. Her daughter was probably much more sensible than Jo gave her credit for. She pulled her flowered dressing-gown around her and went into the cold scullery. First she'd put on the kettle, then she'd get a fire started in the kitchen range. It was so cold, a cold beginning to December. By the time the tea was made it would also be time to wake Rainey.

★ ★ ★

'India? Burma? They're thousands of miles away!' Bea's eyes were like saucers.

'All the more reason to go there and cheer the lads up!' Blackie was smiling. He grinned across the tops of their heads at Bert, who, he knew, was listening while serving customers.

'Mum, did you know where we're going?'

'If you mean was I keeping it a secret, no, of course not,' said Jo.

'I think it's top hole,' said Bea, grinning widely.

Ivy looked as though she hadn't slept. 'Anywhere away from Gosport has got to be a good place to go to,' she conceded.

'That leaves you, Rainey. What d'you think?'

'It's something I've longed for but . . . '

'She's all drippy about that photographer.' Bea ducked as Rainey threw a teaspoon at her. It missed, hit the back of an empty chair and clattered to the floor.

Bea laughed. 'Being in love has made your aim all funny!'

Rainey glared at her. Bea got up from her seat,

278

picked up the spoon and waggled it in front of Rainey, who now sat stony-eyed as Bea dropped the teaspoon on the table.

'Look, there's a possibility, a small one, that I might be able to wangle a photographer onto the payroll but — ' Blackie got no further for Rainey had jumped up from her chair, thrown herself at him and was smothering him with kisses. 'Get off me!' he yelled. Not only did he have red lipstick on his cheek but embarrassment had caused his face to turn bright red. 'I only said there was a possibility.'

Jo was laughing but now she tried to get some order back into the group. 'You said they're to be part of a concert party?'

Blackie gave a cough and composed himself. Jo saw the girls were hanging on his every word. 'The others are Madame's acts, reliable people. There's Marvo the Mesmerist and his assistant. Tiny Titch is a comedian who dances in big boots. The Dancing Duo are a married couple who'll do any dance you can think of — she's got some beautiful frocks. And she's a bit jealous so make sure she doesn't catch you talking to her husband. There's Selma the Snake Woman. She doesn't have a snake but she dresses in a skin-tight snakeskin suit and she can get into all kinds of positions — her bones must be made of rubber . . . Oh, yes, there's Old Olive. She's not really old, quite young in fact, but she makes out she is so she can sing songs that'll make you laugh and cry, like 'Knees Up Mother Brown' and 'The Biggest Aspidistra In The World'.' He paused. 'And there's me. I can always play a few

279

tunes if someone's not feeling good and can't perform that night. And you, the Bluebird Girls, are top of the bill!'

For a moment the girls were silent.

Jo watched the cigarette smoke swirling around in the café. The wireless was playing band music. Bert was stirring one of his stews. Della, who had been listening avidly, was now sitting on a high stool and painting her fingernails. Customers were talking and eating and Jo was stirring her tea, round and round, scraping the spoon. The noise it made irritated her, but she needed something to do with her hands.

Blackie looked at the girls, who were staring at each other.

'Wow!' said Bea. Then the three of them were talking excitedly between themselves.

'I guess that means you all agree.' Blackie looked at Jo. 'What will Maud say?'

'Maud will go along with anything as long as we look after Bea,' said Jo. 'Same as Della and Bert.'

He smiled at her and reached for her hand. 'And you?'

'I know you'll look after us,' Jo said. She looked into his beautiful odd-coloured eyes. He gave her a slow wink and squeezed her fingers.

39

'Why have you brought the baby here?'

'And hello to you too,' said Bea. Della was fiddling with the white blanket securely wrapping the small form and making soppy cooing noises. Are all women supposed to turn to jelly when they're looking at a tiny baby? wondered Ivy. She put her book face down on the table and glared at Bea. Della's Californian Poppy scent hung on the air, vying with the café's greasy smells.

'Mum's gone shopping and Eddie's got a job to finish so I said I'd take Gracie for a walk in the pram.' Bea laughed. She was warmly wrapped up with a knitted scarf and mittens but on her feet she wore the dreaded black high heels that hurt her. She still wouldn't discard them because she was convinced they made her legs look nice. Ivy wasn't about to tell her that the gravy browning and the black line down the back of her legs didn't disguise the mottling the cold had caused. A piece of grubby sticking plaster on Bea's heel was poking above her shoe.

'We've got money now. Why don't you get some shoes that don't hurt?' Ivy grumbled, eyeing the bundle that had been passed to Della.

'Two-inch clumpy heels aren't my idea of nice,' said Bea. 'And that's all you can buy in the shops, supposing you can get them. I've left the pram outside the café. Will it be all right?'

'Course it will. Who on earth would steal a baby's pram?'

Ivy was at a loss as to what to say to Bea.

'Get that down you,' said Bert, putting a mug of tea on the table. 'It'll warm you up.'

'Thanks, Bert,' called Bea, as he retreated, picking up a couple of overflowing ashtrays from tables on his way back behind the counter.

'What's in that?' Ivy nodded towards a string-handled carrier bag Bea had put on the Formica table. Now she'd taken off her coat Ivy saw she was wearing a fluffy green jumper and a black skirt.

'A bottle for the baby, nappies, cream and a change of clothes, in case she messes.'

'All right, all right, I get the idea.'

It seemed to Ivy that you always needed to carry around such a lot of stuff when you had a baby. She really didn't want to think about babies. 'Alice Wilkes has printed on the invitation card that she doesn't want wedding gifts. Why d'you think that is?'

Bea stared at her. Sometimes a sudden change in a conversation's direction could be a bit much for Bea, Ivy thought.

'Well, they're both quite old,' said Bea, 'and they both have homes. Shouldn't think they've got room for any more stuff. Besides, what can you get for them when there's nothing to buy because of the war?'

'Makes sense, I suppose,' said Ivy, grudgingly. 'What are you going to wear?'

'Rainey said it wouldn't be right to wear any stage outfits because it's a celebration for Alice and Graham, not a performance.'

'She's right,' admitted Ivy. 'Anyway, we don't need to be dressed the same, do we?' She had a sudden thought. 'You should go out and bring that pram inside and put it by the cellar door in the passage. Leaving it out in the cold, it'll be freezing when you put the baby back in it.'

'I suppose you're right,' said Bea, and slung her coat across her shoulders.

Ivy knew why Bea had called in today. It had nothing to do with questions and answers about presents and dresses: it was because Ivy was the only one who hadn't met the baby yet.

She looked around for her mother. Della was still in some fairytale world of her own talking utter nonsense to the bundle. She had unwound the white shawl to reveal a pink blanket now swaddling the child. Her mother had also thought about the effect of heat and cold on the baby.

Through the window, which was running with condensation, Ivy could see Bea wrestling with the pram. A young man had joined her. He was laughing and pointing to the wheels. Ivy recognized him from St John's School — he'd been in the same class as Bea. Now Bea was flicking back her blonde hair in that suggestive way she had. Ivy groaned. That was Bea all over: she couldn't resist flirting with any lad she knew.

Della's voice cut into her thoughts. 'Take her, will you? I need to pop out the back. Bert says we're out of bacon.'

Ivy's heart plummeted but she accepted the child. In her arms now lay Gracie, whose mother

283

was dead. The warmth of the child against her jumper was amazing. Long blonde lashes curled against soft cheeks. Her nose was like a tiny pink button. Della had also taken off the little hat. Gracie's hair was as white as snow but long enough for Maud to have wetted and fingered it into a curl on top of her head.

This was Eddie's little girl. Eddie, the man Ivy loved, the man she hoped one day to marry. Kind, generous, gentle Eddie . . .

The coat landed on the back of the chair and slid almost to the floor.

'Brrr! It's freezing outside,' said Bea. 'Silly me couldn't move the pram because I'd forgotten about the brake — ' She broke off. 'Oh. Good. You've got Gracie away from your mother.' She fumbled in the carrier bag and took out the bottle of baby milk. 'It's her feeding time. I'll ask Bert if he can warm this up.'

Ivy said, 'Can I feed her?'

★　★　★

Mabel Manners could see the taxi waiting outside Ann's Hill cemetery gates. She tucked her arm through Maud's and began walking across the frosted grass. Her bunions were giving her gyp today. When she got back to Lavinia House she'd have a go at soaping the leather inside her shoes to see if she could stretch it a bit. Anything was worth a try.

The doctor raised his hand to acknowledge her. Nice of him to be here, she thought. He had a surgery full of people to attend to, so he wouldn't be coming back for a cuppa and a sandwich.

Maud unthreaded her arm and moved towards Solomon and Gertie. He had on his best suit and no overcoat. Silly man, she thought. He'll catch his death . . .

Gertie was done up like a dog's dinner, with a hat that had an enormous veil.

Ah, well, Mabel thought, we're a small mourning party but we cared about Sunshine. She looked back to the grave. The vicar was talking to two gravediggers. Tiny flakes of snow were now falling. Mabel headed towards the taxi and, with satisfaction, noted that Maud, Gertie and Solomon were walking carefully in the same direction. Solomon's appearance had cheered Mabel, though he'd not uttered a word on the journey in the taxi from Lavinia House to the cemetery.

There had been no flowers. They were hard to get hold of now everyone was digging for victory. Maud had made a tiny bouquet of evergreens and holly with berries and tied on a label that said, 'Goodnight, Mummy, from Gracie.'

Eddie hadn't shown his face. Just as well, really, for Solomon was disappointed in his grandson. Eddie was the old man's favourite and to think he was responsible for the young girl's death had hit him hard.

Mabel had had words with Solomon. 'It was that damned corset that was the cause of the trouble. Eddie didn't know anything about the baby. Look how he's come up trumps with young Gracie. Sunshine didn't want that kiddie to have the life she'd had and Eddie'll make sure she's loved and looked after.'

Eventually Solomon would forgive Eddie. That was what families were all about: fighting and forgiveness.

Last night, to stop herself feeling maudlin, Mabel had made a start on clearing Sunshine's room. Sooner or later she'd need to advertise for another cleaner, wouldn't she? Poor little bugger didn't own much apart from her sewing machine. There was quite a lot of assorted material, so Mabel had folded it small and put it into a carrier bag. Sunshine's clothing went into another — she'd put all that out later for the jumble sale at the church. In her dressing-table drawer there were odd bits of make-up, some toiletries, a hairbrush and comb. At the back she'd pulled out some papers that looked as if they'd been left out in the wet at some time. Mabel smoothed out the ink-stained pages. She hadn't known Sunshine had a passport.

But, then, there was a lot she didn't know about the girl. The name Leonard Collins was a mystery too. There was a birth certificate, identity card, ration book and a passport for the same man. Mabel had peeled open the passport. The photograph wasn't clear but it showed a brawny-shouldered man wearing spectacles. He had a mass of blond hair. Mabel sighed. Perhaps he was some relation of Sunshine's. Yes, that had to be it. She peered at the dates. Everything was current. If this man was a relative and he'd died or been killed in the war that would account for Sunshine having all his details, wouldn't it? She poked around at the back of the drawer to see if there was a condolence letter. Nothing. There was some paper money, which she would put in with the passports.

Mabel had folded the papers as small as she could, then opened the little drawer in the sewing machine where the spare bobbins, needles and thread were stored and pushed it all inside, closing the drawer afterwards.

The sewing machine she'd move into her own rooms. Perhaps one day when Gracie was older she might inherit her mother's gift for sewing. Then Mabel would present her with the sewing machine that had belonged to her talented mother.

'Hurry up, missus, it's cold keeping the door open!'

The taxi driver's voice cut into Mabel's thoughts. Gertie, Solomon and Maud were all inside the black cab. Mabel, careful that she didn't slip on the icy pavement, climbed in beside them.

40

'My dear, you'll have to go to Drury Lane. That's where the headquarters of ENSA are and I expect you'll travel by troopship.' Jo couldn't wait to escape from the boring woman who seemed to know everything but was telling her nothing she didn't already know.

'Mrs Barraclough, how wonderful to see you again. You look divine in that colour.'

'Do I, young man? Well, thank you.' The woman simpered.

'No, thank you for keeping Jo entertained. I really must introduce her to an associate of mine, after the dance she promised me.'

Jo felt herself being propelled across the floor, then clamped to Blackie's chest in a bear-hug shuffling dance that was supposed to resemble a waltz.

'Thank you,' she said. 'I thought I'd never get away from her. Who was she?' Jo took a deep breath of Blackie's sandalwood cologne, pulled away from him and stared into his beautiful eyes.

'She was once a teacher, one of Alice's oldest friends,' he said. 'There's a fair few people here I don't know. What do you think of the band? And Madame's gifts to the girls?' There he goes again, thought Jo, asking me two questions at once.

She glanced at the stage. The band, dressed in dark suits, played well and looked extremely happy to be showing off their talents at Alice and Graham's gathering at Thorngate Hall. She felt they would accompany the girls well when it was time for them to sing.

Near the stage Rainey was dancing with Charlie. The red dress clinging to her every curve also brought out the auburn highlights in her hair. Earlier that evening, at home in the kitchen, Rainey had wanted to wear flat shoes because her very high heels made her tower above him.

'I'm so proud to be seen with you, my love,' Charlie had said. 'Don't you realize how thrilling it is for me to have other men of my height see that size doesn't matter when a beautiful girl cares for you? I want you to wear the highest heels you have.'

Rainey and Charlie had picked up Bea to drive to the hall. Jo looked around for Bea. Maud had been invited but preferred to stay at home, listen to the wireless and look after Gracie. Alice's choir had received invitations but not their families. Bea was laughing with Ivy. Both were sitting at a table with Bert and Della, who wore her fox fur, its malevolent eyes glaring at everyone. Bea was wearing a full-length yellow dress. Not a colour Jo would have expected to look so good on a blonde.

Blackie's eyes had followed Jo's. 'She looks as lush and wholesome as a pat of freshly made butter, doesn't she?'

'I don't think I would have put it quite that way.' Jo saw the sparkling gold dance shoes and wondered who had persuaded Bea not to wear her favourite black ones. She laughed as she felt Blackie's hand tighten against the small of her back.

Ivy, like Jo, was in black. Both wore floor-length gowns, but Ivy's flared out from the waist and hung in folds whereas Jo's clung to her slight frame. Madame had made sure the dresses matched exactly the girls' hair. They looked sensational.

'Madame always knows how to treat the girls,' Jo said, remembering her words: 'They aren't on show, they're individuals, and these are a gift from me as a thank-you for their hard work.' Even during clothes rationing Madame could work wonders.

The hall was decked out in green, white and red crêpe-paper garlands, as befitting Christmas, and on a small dais near the stage two chairs were reserved for Alice and Graham. Graham was happily listening to the music, waving his hands as though he was conducting. Despite the noise, chatter and laughter in the hall, a small white dog hung across his lap, paws dangling, fast asleep. By Graham's side, eyes closed, her head leaning against his knee, was his own faithful Labrador.

Alice, Jo saw, was talking to a woman with a faded blonde bun, pinned high on her head and from which wisps of hair escaped. Her hands were resting on the back of a wheelchair. Every so often the woman in the wheelchair joined in the conversation. A blue blanket covered her lower body. Jo thought she had seen the wheelchair-bound woman somewhere before.

Blackie must have noticed her staring for he stopped dancing and said, 'Come on, I want you to meet someone.' He guided her through the dancers until they stood next to the three people. 'Lovely party, Alice,' he said, picking up her hand and kissing it.

She giggled girlishly. 'I'm a married woman now,' she said. 'Behave yourself, you young whippersnapper.'

'Blackie, darling, how lovely to see you,' said the woman in the wheelchair. 'And who is this?'

Jo was amazed to see the fresh-faced woman in the chair looked barely older than her own Rainey, which was ridiculous as her lined neck and heavily veined hands showed she was much older than Jo had at first thought.

'Jo,' said Blackie, giving a sort of theatrical bow towards her. 'She's my right-hand woman and mother of one of the Bluebird Girls. Jo, I don't believe you've met Florrie and her very talented daughter, Annette?'

'I believe it was your daughter who came to find me at Priddy's munitions factory when my daughter here was taken to hospital after a raid.' Florrie smiled warmly at Jo. 'I can't thank her enough.'

'Yes,' said Annette. 'If it hadn't been for her, I wouldn't be here now.' She reached forward and Jo put out her hand and felt the warm grip of Annette's fingers.

'You'd have got through it somehow, Annette. I know your indomitable spirit,' Alice told her.

Annette shook her head at Alice's words. 'I might not have been reunited with my mother.'

She looked up at Florrie and smiled. There was a small silence between them and then Blackie spoke.

'I hear you're going to be fitted with a prosthesis.'

Annette said, 'They can't keep a good act off the stage. I may never dance again but I can sing and recite. Madame's promised to help me restart my career.'

Jo saw Blackie frown and Annette give a sudden giggle. 'Oh, I'm not going back to childish songs and ringlets.' She touched her long fair hair, which had been curled around a ribbon and framed her face in a roll.

Suddenly Jo remembered the woman's extraordinarily clear diction as she'd recited poetry at the Burns Night supper in Stratford-upon-Avon. She also remembered how her face had been plastered with make-up. She saw how much softer and prettier Annette looked now, without it.

'I'd be happy to help in any way I can,' Blackie said to her. 'Now if you'll excuse us . . . ' He grabbed Jo's hand and pulled her towards the French windows that led to the gardens. She looked towards the table where Bea and Ivy were and caught Bea grinning at her.

Outside Blackie took off his jacket and put it around Jo's shoulders. 'If I don't get you on your own for five minutes I shall go mad,' he said, his lips close to her ear. He rummaged in his trouser pocket and brought out a flat, square box. 'I know we all promised not to spend money on gifts this year. Because of the war there's nothing decent to buy.' He looked into her face. 'But I saw this and knew I had to buy it for you.' He pressed the box into her hands.

'I didn't get you anything,' Jo began. She looked up at the dark sky, at the stars that shone like diamonds on black velvet, and then at his eager face.

'Open it,' he urged.

Jo clicked the box and its lid sprang back, revealing a gold chain bracelet. Jo let out one word. 'Oh!'

Blackie took out the heavy piece of jewellery and fastened it around her wrist. She saw a small charm hanging from a link. She raised her arm and peered at the nugget of gold. 'It's a tiny tiger,' she said, looking up at him. Wonder filled her heart.

'There are tigers in India,' he said. 'I'm going to buy you a gold charm for every place we visit.'

Jo felt so overwhelmed she had to stop herself crying. Her eyes met his. 'You really do care for me?'

Blackie put his arms around her. Jo felt safe, and so very happy. Blackie pulled her close and put his fingers beneath her chin, raising her face to kiss her . . .

'Mum! Blackie!' The yelling voice was Rainey's. Blackie dropped his hand as Jo turned towards the French windows. Two of the three Bluebird Girls were hanging out of them into the cold night air.

'Get that blackout curtain back in place,' cried Jo.

'Alice is making a speech about everything

'— and us!' yelled Bea, before Rainey pulled her inside again.

Jo let out a deep sigh. She saw Bea had pushed the blackout curtain to the back of her and was gesticulating at them wildly through the glass.

With the bracelet resting on her wrist, she allowed Blackie to lead her back to the hall. He pushed open the door just as the girls were climbing the steps at the side of the stage.

Alice Wilkes hugged the microphone as Toto, eager to be the centre of attention, chased his tail excitedly at her feet, his claws scratching the wood. Jo heard Blackie close the door and the blackout curtain fell back into place.

'There's a new life ahead for me and my darling husband.' Alice smiled at everyone and continued. 'Nineteen forty-one has been a year of surprises for everyone. One of my happiest has been to see the meteoric rise to recognition of three of my most talented girls from St John's Choir. A long time ago they promised they would sing at my wedding reception and that time has now arrived. This folk song was sung to me by my father and now I want you all to share with me the wonderful voices of this trio, Rainey, Bea and Ivy, who have made 'The Bluebird Song' their own. Ladies and gentlemen, I know you'll wish them further success for nineteen forty-two.' Alice stood aside, careful not to tread on Toto as the girls moved to centre stage.

As their soulful voices filled the hushed room, Jo thought her heart would break with the sadness of the song's words. The emotion was draining her.

Just when she thought she couldn't stop her tears spilling over, she felt Blackie's fingers enclose her hand.

'They're good, aren't they?' she whispered.

'Damned good,' he replied.

Acknowledgements

Thanks go to Juliet Burton, my agent. Also to Therese Keating, my editor, and all her fantastic colleagues at Quercus. A huge thank you to Hazel Orme. Thank you to my readers for your continuing loyalty and a big thank you to Toby — I'm so glad we found each other.

We do hope that you have enjoyed reading this large print book.

Did you know that all of our titles are available for purchase?

We publish a wide range of high quality large print books including:
Romances, Mysteries, Classics
General Fiction
Non Fiction and Westerns

Special interest titles available in large print are:
The Little Oxford Dictionary
Music Book
Song Book
Hymn Book
Service Book

Also available from us courtesy of Oxford University Press:
Young Readers' Dictionary
(large print edition)
Young Readers' Thesaurus
(large print edition)

For further information or a free brochure, please contact us at:
Ulverscroft Large Print Books Ltd.,
The Green, Bradgate Road, Anstey,
Leicester, LE7 7FU, England.
Tel: (00 44) 0116 236 4325
Fax: (00 44) 0116 234 0205